DEATH COMES
TO PERIGORD

DEATH COMES TO PERIGORD

John Ferguson

Dover Publications, Inc.
NEW YORK

This Dover edition, first published in 1983, is an unabridged republication of the work as published by Dodd, Mead and Company, N.Y., 1931. (First British publication: William Collins Sons & Co., Ltd., London & Glasgow, 1931.)

Manufactured in the United States of America
Dover Publications, Inc., 180 Varick Street, New York, N.Y. 10014

Library of Congress Cataloging in Publication Data

Ferguson, John Alexander, 1873-
    Death comes to Perigord.

    I. Title.
PR6011.E64D4   1983   823'.912   82-17820
ISBN 0-486-24434-2

Contents

DEATH COMES
TO PERIGORD

WITH a screech of rusty hinges the green door in the high blank wall opened and the avocat Le Marinel, for whose house I was then looking, stepped into sight. He was a neatly dressed, dapper little man, and there was something bird-like in the succession of eager, snappy little nods he made when he saw me. As he advanced with outstretched hand it now struck me that he looked more like an Oriental than a European. And it was probably those almond-shaped eyes of his, and the swart complexion, which prompted my first remark.

"You know," I said as we shook hands, "it's deuced hard to believe this island of yours is real."

Le Marinel, as if to consider this, cocked his head to one side, like a thoughtful bird this time. I had been but one week on the island, having come to look after the practice of a doctor friend, an old fellow student, who needed a change. The duty so far had been almost a sinecure, although I was, in fact, then meeting the avocat to report on a patient about whose condition he was anxious.

"You mean," he said at length, "that it looks the sort of place where nothing happens."

This time the side-long glance he gave me was more than ever bird-like.

"That's true; it does look like that; but it's not what

I

I meant. What I meant was that for an island in the Channel less than ninety miles from England it has too many incredible differences; it looks in fact almost Oriental."

The avocat seemed mystified.

"Oriental?" he repeated, with a rising inflection.

"More like a bit of Tunis or Algiers," I affirmed. "Why look, for instance, at this very road, so long and narrow, stretching between those high blank walls, with invisible houses and hidden people behind them, I suppose. And look at those tall palm trees which seem to be peering over the walls as if stretching their necks, watching for something to happen in this deserted alley. Look at those shadows too, sharply cut as if by a knife in this brilliant white, un-English sunlight; and look at the colour, is that not Eastern?"

I indicated the end of the tunnel-like Rue Galette along which we were now walking, for at the far end, framed like a picture by the tall shadowed walls, one caught a glimpse of an incredibly blue sea, on the horizon of which another island was just discernible, pale as an opal, and ethereal as a mirage of the desert.

Le Marinel smiled indulgently as he followed my pointing finger. He was, I fancy, not quite sure whether my suggestion about the Oriental quality in his island pleased him or not. He stopped as if to re-examine, in his lawyer-like way, the evidence I had adduced. But before his deliberate mind found any comment to make, and while I too pulled up, another of those doors in the wall opened noiselessly, almost at Le Marinel's ear. It was not, however, the unexpectedness of the thing that took me aback; it was the appearance of the man and the woman seen in the doorway. The woman seemed to be showing the man out; and that, from the look of him, was what any decent person would want to do with him. Familiar as my East London hospital experience had made me with so many types of humanity, there was something about this fellow that took my eye so that I scarcely glanced at the woman. He was tall and almost incredibly thin, but did not suggest any delicacy of constitution. On the contrary he seemed wiry and active, rather, as regards physical strength, like an Arab in that his strength was that of tendon and sinew rather than muscle. Yet though he somehow had the air of being unused to his present clothes, he was certainly a European. His face was rather long, with sharp features that showed no trace of hair. Even the eyebrows above the shifty, pale blue eyes were hairless. Lipless too, he was; but long in the nose like a rat.

So much, with the swift eye which a medical practitioner inevitably develops, I took in before we passed on, and Le Marinel spoke.

"I see what you mean," he said; "the Eastern effect is undoubtedly there in those palms and in our architecture."

But when I touched his arm he turned in surprise.

"Who are those two?" I inquired.

"Those two?" he echoed vaguely.

"The two we passed just now."

"Oh, yes. The woman is Cæsar Brisson's housekeeper; the other I have never before seen."

Le Marinel had his eye on me as he said this. He was, I thought, mildly surprised at my rapid shift of interest from the island to the pair I had seen.

"Now," he went on, "if it had been Cæsar himself who attracted your interest, that I could have understood."

"And who is this Cæsar Brisson?" I inquired.

"He is a wine seller, and keeps his shop on the quay. A man with a personality nowadays, and of very striking appearance; big as a bullock and broad as a house, you would say. French, of course, Cæsar never wears a hat on his blue-black thatch of hair, and has bold eyes that take in everything, not like that fellow who caught your interest just now."

"Well, you know," I explained half apologetically, "I've a curious feeling about that man: I fancy I have seen him before."

"Ah," Le Marinel nodded, "and you cannot recall where or when?"

"No; and that is odd too, for he is of a type one would not readily forget. Besides, I have a notion, from the swift, furtive glance he shot at me that he remembered me."

Le Marinel smiled.

"Which suggests his memory of you is something less than pleasant. No doubt he can remember the where and the when of your meeting. Of course," he went on in the tone of one dismissing a trifle, "we get a fair number of undesirables here, mostly men who seek refuge from justice."

"French or English justice?" I inquired.

"Chiefly French; but they are not all criminal, you understand. As often as not they are here simply to evade their term of military service."

By this time we had reached the end of the narrow Rue Galette, and the avocat paused at the top of the hundred or so of steps which ultimately led down, and round, to the small square in which the Court House stood. The view opened out by the high point at the top of those steps was what a guide book would call panoramic. Far below lay the harbour, its smooth waters fretted by the rigging of ships, and out beyond stood the dark mass of Castle Cornet, keeping guard, like a great battleship, at the harbour's mouth. The English mail boat was just clearing the breakwater, her red funnel topped by a whirling column of black smoke. And, far away beyond that heavy line of smoke, on the horizon of the crystalline sea, dream-like in the faintness and delicacy of its outlines, one saw the French coast. On either side of me all the quaint old houses of the terraced town seemed to be rising one above another, in a wild endeavour to miss nothing of the spectacle.

Indeed, so enchanted was I by the sudden vista of vivid colour and wide space that opened out after we emerged from that dark alley that, for the moment, I forgot the rat-faced man, forgot even the purpose for which I had come to see the avocat. Le Marinel's soft voice recalled me.

"And de Quettville, you have seen him?"

The question was one I had been waiting to hear. And for a reason that will be obvious presently.

"Yes, I went last night. You need have no immediate apprehension. He has certainly got a heart; but for a man of his advanced years the beat was wonderfully strong." The recollection of certain details connected with the visit Le Marinel had requested me to make came back, and I added dryly, "Age seems to have made havoc with his temper rather than his heart."

Le Marinel smiled and shook his head deprecatingly.

"He never was an amiable character. Your friend, Dr. Wright, he did tolerate occasionally. I'm sorry if he was rude, but I tried by a telephone message to break the ice for your visit."

"Leave the ice unbroken next time; if I have to walk on ice at all I prefer it unbroken," I remarked laughingly, for he seemed concerned.

We were then, I remember, descending the flight of steps towards the passage which ultimately led into the Court House square. The avocat pulled out his watch.

"I have still a spare half hour before my case comes on," he said. "Would you care to have a look round the Court? We have some documents there dating from Edward the First."

Well, I wasn't as interested in documents as the lawyer might be. My interest was in human beings.

"I'd rather hear about Hilaire de Quettville," I said.

He stared at me.

"You are interested in him?"

Before I could reply Le Marinel was met and stopped by a straight, soldierly man, who, with an apologetic nod to me, took his arm for some private word in his ear. I passed a few paces on out of range and waited.

Interested in de Quettville? Certainly I was interested. To come to such an island out of the sedate, humdrum respectability of a middle-class London suburb was like stepping suddenly into the Middle Ages. English by possession this island in the Channel might be, yet in the streets of St. Peter Port one heard as much French spoken as English; exactly, I reflected, as one might have heard French spoken in England in the years immediately following the Norman Conquest. But above all I was interested in de Quettville. No medical man is without his queer experiences, and in some way hard to define, this visit of mine to de Quettville ranks among my eeriest. Possibly the long drive on the deserted roads, and then my arrival at that great, lonely house affected my imagination.

Le Marinel's message had been merely a request that I should go out to Perigord in the parish of St. Pierre du Bois and make a report to him next morning about the condition of de Quettville. For all I knew the report might have been desired in connection with a life insurance. This duty I took as a matter of routine, assuming that de Quettville had at least agreed to the examination. Indeed, the one thing to which I gave a thought was the name of the house, for I remembered that Perigord happened to be the name of the estate owned by the great Seigneur de Montaigne; and I wondered whether the man I was going to see were old too, and wise, like the great French philosopher, and if I should find surviving in him the noble dignity, the courtly manners, of a long dead régime.

Well, the house when I reached it seemed stately enough, and the grounds spacious, but the old woman who, at last, got the door open and peered at me while shading a guttering candle from the night breeze, about her there was little indeed of courtliness. And, as I was presently to discover, there was still less in her master. But once she knew my errand she was glad enough to see me. And the strange atmosphere and flavour of a bygone age was still there. For as the old crone, candle in hand, muttering satisfaction in a French *patois,* led me across a spacious hall and up a wide oak staircase, so old that it seemed to be made of stone—well, I *was* in another world from that of the familiar spruce and natty little villas of Ealing to which I was accustomed. I felt, indeed, that I had stepped into another century when I was ushered into that bedroom. And probably there was nothing in it, except the occupant and the candle the woman pushed into my hand as I entered, less than two hundred years old.

The bed was an immense, towering affair with four thick carved columns, black with age, supporting a canopy as big as the ceiling of a small room. And in the centre of that hearse-like bed there lay, motionless as any corpse, Hilaire de Quettville. I might have thought him dead but for his eyes, which, catching points of light from the candle I held, glittered wickedly at me beneath the big white nightcap he wore. That nightcap was for me the best touch in the grotesque, and fixed the impression that I had somehow stepped back into a world of the past. For I had never before seen a nightcap except in woodcuts of eighteenth century life.

Abruptly he raised himself, his long grey beard moving like a flag as he did so, and, withdrawing one arm from beneath the sheet, with pointing forefinger indicated the door.

"*Va t'en.*"

The command was hissed rather than spoken. But I had no intention of going before I had done my job, and as soothingly as possible told him so. For now I felt sure that Le Marinel must have good reason for sending me the urgent message I had received, though to me it looked as if I might have been more usefully employed in examining into his mental rather than his physical condition. And examine him I did, in spite of all his expostulations. His heart was certainly in a flutter; but that might be set down to his anger just as much as to any cardiac weakness, for in other respects he was, for his age, in surprisingly sound condition. He seemed, in fact, to be, with ordinary care, good enough for many years to come, and I could not see why I had been so urgently pressed by Le Marinel to go out that night. That thought had puzzled me even before I left Perigord.

Once I had done with the man I took up the candle from the bed side table with that little flurry of irritation a doctor is apt to experience in such cases. Short of accident, many a much younger man would go before de Quettville. The flutter at his heart was nothing. He probably smoked too much. All these Channel Islanders smoked too much: tobacco was so cheap for them. Even the taxi man who drove me there had kept a cigar going all the time. And my irritation over the needless call was certainly not lessened by contact with such an ill-mannered patient. He had sunk back the moment I finished, and now reclined with closed eyes, his sharp nose and white nightcap silhouetted grotesquely in black against the bed curtain, the long beard showing like a waterfall. But he was not asleep. As I watched him with disfavour an eyelid fluttered and he waved a hand towards the door.

"*Va t'en*," he repeated crossly.

This time I went, leaving the crusty old fellow alone in his stately chamber, and thinking it was no wonder he should be left to himself in it.

But scarcely had I descended the wide staircase before I was made aware that de Quettville was not so much alone as I had supposed. At the foot of the stairs I was met by the same old woman as had admitted me to the house, and she taking the candlestick out of my hand was leading the way across the hall when I was startled by a sudden sharp sound that seemed to come from overhead. The solitary candle which the woman carried could not, of course, really illuminate more than a yard or two around us, but as I glanced up I dimly discerned a figure in white on a gallery that ran across the end of the hall. It seemed to be a woman or girl with her hair in two long plaits, and she was leaning over the balcony to watch us. But the next moment there came a crash of metal and total darkness, for the old woman stumbled over some object or other and let the candle fall. It took some time to find the candlestick and relight it, and when I looked up again as I pocketed my matches, the gallery was empty.

Interested? Certainly I was interested. Not least in Le Marinel himself, who had sent me out to Perigord and who was so incurious as to what happened there. Then just when I was beginning to fear that the half-hour would expire before my curiosity could be satisfied, I saw the avocat detach himself from the other and hurry after me.

"Sorry Carey collared me," he said, "but there's enough time still left to let you see of the documentary treasures in our archives."

This took me aback. Did the avocat not want to tell me about de Quettville? Or had he forgotten? That could hardly be, for I had indicated my interest bluntly enough. After a moment's thought I said:

"These documents have been here a long time?"

"Yes; some of them from the twelfth century."

"Then they'll keep a little longer. I'd rather hear about that old fellow de Quettville." But as he seemed a trifle disappointed, or disconcerted, I added, "You see, as a medical man my interest lies not in dusty documents but in living flesh and blood."

Le Marinel smiled a little grimly.

"As to that, my friend," he said, "there are many

here in Guernsey who would tell you there's just as little flesh and blood in Hilaire de Quettville as in my documents."

"That of course increases my interest in the man."

For the first time the avocat seemed—well, annoyed would be too strong a word, but *ruffled,* like a small and very neat pussy cat when one has begun to stroke it the wrong way.

"There really isn't anything to tell that isn't ancient history," he declared.

"Well, as to that," I said, using his own favourite phrase, "my curiosity begins with the history of last night."

"Last night?" he echoed, stopping dead.

"Last night," I reiterated, having decided to press him on a point where my curiosity was certainly legitimate. "Why was it necessary for me to see at such a late hour and at such a distance a man who is in perfectly sound health?"

Le Marinel laughed, resuming his walk.

"Ah. So that's the trouble, is it? I'm sorry, but it couldn't be helped. Yes, it's easily explained. You see, Mrs. Bichard—that's the housekeeper—sent me word in the evening that she was frightened about him. He'd taken to his bed, and refused to have any one near him. Once when she stole up and listened at the door she heard him talking to himself."

"Talking to himself?"

"Raving was the word she used. Well, I couldn't go myself last night as I had a conference on the case I am appearing in just now; and, after all, it was a doctor's affair, you know. I'm sure Wright would not have minded," he added, a tincture of reproach in his tones, "even if he had found nothing wrong when he got there."

This stung me.

"He would have found nothing wrong beyond a slight palpitation. The man probably smoked too much."

"That's wrong anyhow. He does not smoke at all."

Le Marinel seemed pleased over my mistake. He spoke in the tone of a man who was getting his own back on one who had bothered him. But his assertion surprised me.

"You are quite sure?" I asked.

"I know: de Quettville has none of the minor vices."

By this time we had come out on the small square in front of the Court House, and were making for the row of offices tenanted by the avocats of the Royal Court which forms one side of the square. It is queer how small a thing, if it be connected with his work, will irritate a professional man; and to be corrected by a layman in a matter of diagnosis—the doctor who is not hyper-sensitive about that would indeed be a man superior to human weaknesses. So as we walked on in silence I was striving to recollect whether my inference that de Quettville was a heavy smoker had been supported by any other observed facts than the condition of his heart. But we had reached the door of Le Marinel's office before I found any additional support for my inference.

"Then," I declared, "he must have had a lot of

trouble lately to have a heart like that after a day spent in bed."

"As to that," the lawyer replied, "he's had a lot of trouble all his life; most of it of his own making."

"This must have been very recent mental trouble."

As I looked up at Le Marinel standing on the upper step of his office door I saw his eyes wandering over the square behind my back. There was alertness in those eyes, as if he were scanning the sunlit square for something or some one, and it was noticeable that when he spoke again he did not look at me.

"Yes, he's had some worry lately. Most of it is confidential, you understand; not for me to talk about though I've only been his agent for the last six months, and he'll probably have another in the next six weeks. But some of his trouble is public property: you might hear it from any one on the island. The trouble connected with Mère Trouteaud and the Neptune probably is what sent him to his bed."

"Mère Trouteaud and the Neptune?" I echoed.

Le Marinel nodded. He seemed disposed to talk while he watched the square behind me. Indeed he had the air of one filling in a time of waiting.

"Mère Trouteaud is an old woman who lives in a cottage bordering on the Perigord estate. One day while cutting vraic—that is our word for seaweed you know—she fished out of the water what she took to be the statue of one of the saints. Really it was a life sized effigy of the sea-god Neptune which had been the figure-head of some wrecked ship; but as he was represented kneeling, Mère Trouteaud insisted he was a holy man, in spite of the three pronged fork in his hand, and set the figure up in her garden. I suppose, as a sort of presiding deity, and no doubt with some vague idea of bringing her good luck. And there Neptune might have stayed, looking out to his sea till he rotted; and no one have known anything about his existence but for what—"

"Yes," I encouraged the avocat as he paused to watch something.

"But for what happened some days ago," he went on. "For last Friday some malicious person or persons—probably two, for the feat needed two at least—removed the figure from Mère Trouteaud's garden and placed it right on the top of the arch of the main Perigord gateway. Before setting it there, though, they decked out the figure with a night cap and shirt and beard to suggest an image of de Quettville himself. That was bad enough, but it wasn't all. It was the last touch that got home on de Quettville. For on the three prongs of the extended trident they stuck three gilded balls."

"Three gilded balls—why?"

"Oh, well, it's an open secret that de Quettville has money at heavy interest all over the island. And it was the sight of that effigy, kneeling in his shirt over the gateway, and holding out the pawnbroker's sign that sent the island into a roar."

But as I myself laughed at the ludicrous vision thus conjured up, Le Marinel shook his head.

"If only the incident could have ended there," he said with a sigh, "but it's not likely to end there: it has made bad blood among too many for that."

A sudden dark flush came over the avocat's face on which my eyes were fixed, and seeing that flush, I knew he had at last seen that for which he had been watching. I wheeled round to the square. Over at the entrance I saw a compact body of people making for the Court House. Towards this crowd many individuals were hurriedly converging from all directions, and it was clear from the purposeful way in which all were moving that they had a common aim in view. Then I observed that the mob was headed by a woman, an old woman, roughly clad, and evidently of the peasant class. Wondering what they were up to I looked back at Le Marinel. The flush had gone from his face. He replied to my unspoken question.

"That is Mère Trouteaud herself. She is going to raise the *clameur*."

"The *clameur*—what is that?" I asked, bewildered.

"The *clameur de Haro*, doctor, is the cry that a Channel Islander has the right to raise whenever he suffers a wrong. It is an appeal for help, elsewhere denied him, to the long dead Duke of Normandy who was the lord of his ancestors. This will not end here." He looked at me with troubled eyes and added, "You thought this was the sort of place where nothing happened, didn't you? Well, go over and see for yourself, if you are curious."

He had certainly made me mighty curious.

"Won't you come and explain?" I begged.

But he refused with a wave of his hand.

"No, indeed. I'll be dragged into it soon enough."

Well, I wasn't likely to be dragged into the affair. So it was in the spirit of a detached observer that I strolled towards the mob now gathered round Mère Trouteaud by the Court House steps. Mère Trouteaud, for all her years, was a tall, well-built woman, whose dark sun-tanned features reminded one of an Indian squaw, not only in their clear-cut outlines but also by the determination stamped on every line of her face. But, as she broke into speech, standing before the steps that led up to the big door of the Court House, speech that hushed the eagerly jabbering crowd of men and women around her, she looked in the black knitted shawl tightly crossed over her breast and tucked into the waistband of the short and rough dark blue skirt, more like a witch, a sibyl or a prophetess.

What she said I could not tell. Most Channel Islanders are bilingual, but while the townsmen's choice is English first and French afterwards, it is the other way round with the country folk, and Mère Trouteaud spoke in the French *patois*, far too strange in itself and far too rapid in her utterance for my comprehension. Yet her very vehemence as well as the bare brown uplifted arm crowned by the tensely extended claw-like fingers were eloquent enough: it was protest, appeal and denunciation in full blast.

They left a clear space round her, now whispering comment to each other, now excitedly translating a particular word or obscure phrase to a friend less familiar with the *patois*. As for myself, about the one word I easily detected was the name de Quettville, and it occurred too often to be mistaken. Finally a stout policeman in a white helmet began to move the crowd back, and though he dared not interfere with Mère Trouteaud's purpose, he apparently told the old woman, in the correct French equivalent, to get on with it. At any rate the climax to the strange scene followed. Separated now by yards of open space from the nearest spectators, down the old woman went on her knees before the old grey Court House. Then with bowed head and arms extended high, Mère Trouteaud made her appeal for help to the semi-mythical hero who, in a long vanished past, had been the protector of her race. In the hush of silence that fell on the crowd I could distinguish every word.

"*Haro! Haro! Haro! à l'aide, mon Prince; on me fait tort!*"

After this loud cry the silence lasted a moment or two. Then a woman near me, probably a stranger like myself, spoke in a hushed whisper.

"What happens next?"

The question sounded banal enough. But it was the question I had been putting to myself. And I had not long to wait for the answer.

LIKE every one else I suppose, my own eyes were on
Mère Trouteaud as she rose to her feet. The moment
she did so two men moved towards her. As I have
since learned, those two were the formal witnesses
which the procedure required, and she and the two
ought now to have said the Paternoster in French.
Indeed, one of the men, a stout little black-bearded
fellow in his Sunday clothes of rusty black did start
off *"Notre Père qui est au ciel"* in a high-pitched,
nervous tremolo. But he got no further than that, for
the old woman, after swaying momentarily as if in a
vertigo, fell forward against the stone steps. It was
a heavy fall, and as she half-turned in her collapse her
head struck the edge of the step with a quite audible
thud.

After that I was no longer a detached observer of a
curious incident, and I can remember how as I knelt
down beside Mère Trouteaud the thought came that
what the avocat had so dreaded for himself had, after
all, happened to me: I had been dragged into the affair
—even before Le Marinel himself.

The beefy policeman in the white helmet did his
best to keep the rush of sympathetic helpers at bay.
But he could not stop the torrent of advice they
shouted at me; and when it became evident that something more was needed than the air he had secured
by driving back the crowd, we carried her over to Le

Marinel's office. We carried her there simply because it was not only the nearest but the one place I knew of, and I had to find a place, since by this time the perspiring officer was too flustered and excited to think of anything beyond the opprobrious epithets he was hurling at the noisy, swaying crowd.

The avocat was then, no doubt, deep in his case before the Court, but his clerk, who must have seen me earlier talking to his chief on the doorstep, admitted us without demur. Mère Trouteaud we laid out on an extemporized couch in the avocat's private room behind the office. Then I turned every one out except Daniel Sarchet, the little bearded man in his Sunday clothes, who, it appeared, had walked all the way into town with her to act as witness.

"Is it that she is dead?" he whispered as soon as we were alone, the bowler hat trembling in his hand.

"Oh, no, far from that," I reassured him. "Just a slight concussion."

He placed his hat carefully underneath his chair, and then sat forward to watch me while I examined Mère Trouteaud's head for the point where it had made contact with the step.

"It is ill-luck she has had ever since it happened," Daniel Sarchet remarked.

"Ever since?" I repeated almost absently. There was no scalp wound. Her hair, though grizzled, was still thick and plentiful, and had softened the blow. Mère Trouteaud was certainly lucky there. So nothing remained to do except wait for her to come round. I took the other chair.

"What was all this about?" I asked Sarchet.

The little man, sitting forward on the extreme edge of his chair, and resting the palm of each hand on his knees, regarded me blankly.

"The *clameur*," I explained, "why did she raise the *clameur?*"

A light broke on Sarchet's face.

"Ah, you do not know the Guernsey French, is it? You did not understand! Why, sir, naturally, it was because Mr. de Quettville has the holy figure taken from her garden. For what was it but to mock him, putting the holy image up there in a shirt, for all the people to laugh at?"

The heat of indignation with which Daniel Sarchet spoke seemed to prove that de Quettville was, at least, not unpopular among his own neighbours, who, after all, would know him best. This was interesting.

"So you do not like to see Mr. de Quettville made a mock of," I said.

He stared blankly back.

"That was what you said, was it not?"

"No, sir. I said that it is not good to mock a holy image the way they have done. No good can come of it. The Mère Trouteaud there, she could tell you that, for it is the ill-fortune she has had ever since she lost him."

"But has not the figure been taken down and returned?"

"It has been taken down—yes; but not returned. Mr. de Quettville says it belongs to him, as it came ashore on his land. He is going to set it up in his own garden, and says that any good luck it has belongs to him. But Mère Trouteaud, she pulled the grand saint out of the deep water, and so she has raised the *clameur* to get him back."

It is curious to reflect, now, that I listened to Sarchet, interested indeed by coming across such an example of insular ignorance and superstition, but with one eye all the time on the old woman's condition. Certainly it would have astonished me to know how much was afterwards to result from my gossip with Daniel. For a moment I wondered whether it would be possible to disabuse him of the ludicrous conviction that this figure of Neptune was the figure of what he called a sacred saint. Not aware of the tenacity with which a peasant in his state of isolation holds on to the superstitions abandoned centuries earlier in places less remote, I did think I could bring him round to see the real truth about that old ship's figure-head. But at first I did not think it worth while. Then, however, I perceived that all this, and probably future, trouble might be avoided, if only he and Mère Trouteaud had received some instruction in elementary mythology. And, foolishly, that is what I now began to give—to Daniel Sarchet at least, for Mère Trouteaud still showed no symptoms of a return to consciousness.

"Look here," I began, "you know you're quite, quite wrong about that figure. It isn't a sacred figure at all, it's a heathen image."

Sarchet blinked at me.

"Heathen?" he echoed blankly, his mouth agape.

"Yes, heathen. In fact it's nothing but a representation of Neptune, the god of the sea."

He pondered this news for a moment, squirming meanwhile uncomfortably inside the Sunday suit that was much too big for him. Then he shook his head with decision.

"That cannot be," he said. "You have not seen him, sir, or you would not say it. Oh, in St. Pierre du Bois we do not make a mistake like that. No! See you, he must be a holy man, for he has a golden crown on his head, and he kneels. A heathen he cannot be, nor a god, for he kneels, you see. Wait till you see him, sir."

"I have seen many carved figures like that on ships. They make him kneeling merely because he takes up less space, and that allows the figure to be larger. Besides, I understand Mère Trouteaud's figure has the trident in his hand, and that alone proves he is Neptune."

"The trident?"

"The three-pronged fork. That is Neptune's symbol. You can always tell Neptune by that. And as for bringing good luck—well, he doesn't seem to have brought much of that to the ship he once adorned, does he?"

But Daniel Sarchet was not to be rushed like that!

"The three-pronged fork," he said musingly.

"Well, you can make nothing sacred of that fork at least."

"Oh, sir," he protested in a shocked voice, "but it is a spear he holds, not a fork. A fork belongs to the

Evil One. Many of the saints hold spears. One has seen them so in the windows of the Church. And the crown as well as the three-pronged spear of Mère Trouteaud's saint shows that he has fought the good fight and conquered by the power of the ever Blessed Three. In the parish of St. Pierre du Bois even the children know these things."

After that I gave it up. Possibly if the old woman had not then begun to show signs of recovery I might have gone on to the question of the ill-luck which had befallen the ship of which the supposed saint had once been the figure-head. I recall that as I attended to Mère Trouteaud I thought that on that point Daniel would have been hard put to find an explanation that squared with his illusion. But the old woman had shifted herself round and we saw that her eyes were open.

"Feeling better?" I asked.

She regarded me steadily, without so much as dropping her eyelids by way of assent. The next thing she did was to sit up, which proved that the concussion had been much less severe than it seemed. When she spoke this became certain.

"I heard some of your talk," she said slowly, disjointedly. "You are a young man still, I see." Passing a hand over her face she then asked, "What day is this?"

"Friday," I replied. "You've had a slight accident, but you're all right now."

She shook her head.

"It was last Friday they took the good man from

me, and it is the ill fortune that began that night, and has not stopped since."

Coming on top of my futile efforts with Sarchet this was too much for me.

"Now look here, Mère Trouteaud," I began.

But she cut me short.

"Oh, I heard what you were saying to Daniel. That makes no difference to me. I know what I know."

"You'd better not talk much yet," I advised.

It was advice she disregarded.

"On Friday night they took him, sir. Well then, see what happens next. On the Saturday my goat went dry, with nothing to account for it. On Sunday my clock falls off the wall and was broken. On Monday the chimney of my lamp burst itself. On Tuesday my baking would not rise; on Wednesday night my dog Mimi, she is taken ill and died; and on Thursday morning I go out to find that I can draw no water for my garden from the well, for the rope is gone; and the sheets I had drying on the line were lying trampled on the earth as if evil spirits had been there in the night." Mère Trouteaud, her colour heightened, paused for breath. Daniel Sarchet, looking at me, nodded wisely.

"See that now! What did I tell you?" he demanded.

"But that is not all," the old woman resumed. "You say there is no good in having a sacred image kneeling outside a house? Well then, it was on Monday they took him down from the gates, and the same day people said that he had been put up in the Perigord garden. On the Tuesday I went into the garden of Mr. de Quettville to see. I waited till it was dark before going, but I took my dog Mimi with me. Oh, yes, we found that what people said was true. We found my holy figure set up on a high stone beyond reach. I showed him to Mimi, and Mimi *barked* so at him that I had to run in fear that they would come from the house and catch me. Now tell me this, sir: unless Mimi *knew* the holy figure should not be there why should she bark like that?"

But it was Daniel Sarchet who, jumping in his excitement, replied.

"Dogs bark at those who have no right to be there —is it not so?" he demanded.

"But yes," Mère Trouteaud affirmed, "that is what all dogs do. It is indeed what they are for. And Mimi, mark you, had never once barked at him while he was in my garden."

The bad logic of all this was obvious, but chiefly it was the credulity displayed by this pair of old simpletons that amazed me. I had not thought it possible that such *naïveté* could anywhere survive the age at which children cease to believe in Santa Claus. But though a few days later I was to be glad enough to have listened to the Mère Trouteaud and Daniel Sarchet, at that moment I had had enough.

They were not difficult to get rid of. As the vigour with which she spoke was by itself enough to show that the old woman had recovered, my hint that the office would now be required by its owner was accepted, and they departed, Mère Trouteaud over her shoulder prophesying for those responsible worse misfortunes yet to come.

But all the same I determined to do what I could with Le Marinel to get the Neptune returned to the poor old woman. Of course this resolve of mine was not taken through any belief that there was virtue in Neptune. I simply acted as I would have acted towards any child whose doll had been stolen. And when Mère Trouteaud's prophecy came true—as it did that very same night—I, as any one else would have done, treated the fulfilment as no more than a coincidence.

So after lunch I rang up Le Marinel. When I got him
at the other end of the wire I began with an apology
for commandeering his office earlier in the day. This
I did by way of form, for it did not seem to me that
in the circumstances there was need for any apology.
From the tone of voice, however, in which the avocat
replied that it could not be helped, I gathered he did
not share my view.

"Yes," his voice came, "yes, it was unfortunate."

"Unfortunate? Why?" I demanded brusquely.

"Oh, well, as to that, Mère Trouteaud came to raise
the *clameur* against de Quettville, and I happen to be
his agent." After giving me time to let this sink in he
added, less lugubriously, "But, as you say, it could not
be helped."

Without more ado I plunged into the real reason I
had for ringing him up.

"Look here," I said bluntly, "it strikes me as unfortunate that your client has not returned the figure-
head taken from her garden. It is over that she raised
the *clameur,* and that at least is something that can be
helped. Can you not advise de Quettville to restore
the old woman's property?"

It was quite a time before he replied. Was it because I had spoken rather hotly? Was the silence
meant for a rebuke? But Le Marinel's voice came
through at last, a calm, controlled, lawyer-like voice.

"In the first place, doctor, my advice on this matter has not been asked. In the next place if my advice had been asked I should have said that in law the figure-head belonged to my client, since it was washed ashore on his land."

"But it wasn't washed ashore. She got it among the rocks while cutting seaweed," I protested.

"That cannot be the case. By an ordinance of the Royal Court the cutting of vraic is limited to specified seasons, and this is not one."

Then I saw the cleft stick in which Mère Trouteaud· found herself!

"So she can only claim the thing by admitting a contravention of the ordinance?"

"Precisely."

"And de Quettville believes she could not be guilty of such a crime, eh?"

"He—ah—*prefers* to believe that."

"Precisely," I echoed his tone; "because that enables him to retain possession of the figure-head."

Something that sounded like a chuckle followed. When, however, I remembered the poor old woman's anxiety to regain possession of her figure-head I stifled my anger and began to plead.

"Look here, this figure can't be a thing of any value; don't you think de Quettville could be induced to—"

"Sorry," he cut me short, "but the telephone isn't suitable for this sort of discussion. Better come and see me about it."

"Right. I'll come now," I said hopefully.

"No; I meant to-night. There's—there's a good

deal to be said, you know." He paused as if in thought. "Look here, come and dine with me if you have nothing better to do."

It was an invitation I accepted gladly, not only in the hope that over the dinner table I could the more easily move the avocat to do something for Mère Trouteaud, but also because I had become very bored with my solitary dinners.

So at the hour appointed I found myself at Le Marinel's door. The house in the Rue Galette which I saw only when I stepped inside the green door in the wall was one of those square Guernsey houses, built of the native granite. But for the smooth lawn, gay with bordering flower beds, it might have looked grim in its stark solidity. As it was, the old grey granite building made a contrast on that summer evening to the brilliant fresh green of the small lawn pleasing to the eye. On the lawn, as I entered, I saw Le Marinel stooping over a flower bed. He had evidently dressed early and come out to wait for me. At the click of the gate behind me he stood up, his black clothes and wide expanse of shirt front suddenly introducing another bit of effective colour contrast to the scene. But when he began his jerky little bird-like nods of welcome I was reminded of a magpie hastily swallowing a worm he has just pulled out of the turf.

We had not, however, been long at dinner before I perceived that the avocat was an epicure in the matter of food. His soup was a miracle to one accustomed to the horrible concoctions English people, knowing no better, are content to accept. And for the first time

I knew what red mullet could be in itself when so cooked as not to taste like a substitute for salmon. It was, in fact, the sort of dinner to which one has to give oneself and in the process of the appreciation which I felt was due to such cooking, Mère Trouteaud, whose troubles had brought me there, dropped altogether out of my mind. Indeed it was not till the end of the dinner that I recollected the old woman and the three-pronged spear of her "saint"; and then it was in an almost grotesque way that the affair was brought back into my mind.

The maid, who moved like a shadow and had the hands of a magician—I could not help observing her hand as she filled my glass—replaced the decanter on the shining mahogany, and set a match to the little candles on the alabaster cigar-lighter. She then melted, as it were, from the room. My eyes remained on the little candles she had lighted. There were three candles. Idly I poised my glass in front of them, and through the glass saw the three small golden globes of flame. The deep ruby of the wine made those golden globes look as if they were afloat in blood!

But that sight raised no premonition in my mind of the tragedy hovering over us that night. And just as little did Le Marinel appear to be affected by any sense of impending calamity. On the contrary, as the dinner progressed he became almost jovial, the lawyer-like stiffness and formality oozing out of him, till, under the influence of his own excellent wine, he began to address me familiarly by my surname alone. The first time he did so was after a considerable pause in our talk. I had sunk into a reverie in which Mère Trouteaud and Neptune and his three-pronged spear figured when he thus broke the silence:

"I say, Dunn."

This woke me up.

"Yes?"

"You were very curious about de Quettville this morning."

"I still am. But I remember you carefully refrained from telling me anything that wasn't public property."

He laughed.

"I could tell you much more inside those limits which might interest you pathologically."

He looked inquiringly at me across the table.

"Then go ahead, Le Marinel."

But when he left his place, and came round to seat himself at the corner of the table nearest me, so close indeed that he could whisper in my ear, I wondered if, after all, he meant to tell me more than was public property about de Quettville. Anyhow I observed that he forgot to bring his glass with him. This indication of his eagerness to speak so struck me that, mechanically, I laid down the cigar I had just cut. He in his turn noted this act.

"Better smoke," he nodded; "the story, though a comedy, will take time to tell."

Smilingly he held out the lighter for me. When the cigar was fairly going he sat up again, elbows on the table.

"On the face of it," he began, "one would have

thought that the inhabitants of an isolated island would tend to be all very much like one another, with few peculiarities and little variation in character. Yet it does not work out like that. The island does look the kind of place in which, as you observed, nothing happens; and yet it is a place in which anything may happen. It may be reaction; I don't know. It may be a flaring up of the old wild Norman blood that has slept in our veins for centuries." He laughed shortly. "Interesting to the psychologist, but awkward often for the lawyer. For it is among our old families that the odd things happen. Now for the de Quettville comedy.

"First of all I must tell you that the de Quettvilles are one of the oldest families in the Channel Islands. And that, remember, is saying much. Originally they were Normans, as most of our ancient families are, Normans who did not go over with the riff-raff who accompanied the Conqueror. But that is enough about their extraction. The story opens with Hilaire de Quettville, the father of the Hilaire you saw last night. When Hilaire died he left two sons, Hilaire and Peter, and one daughter, Judith. Soon after the father's death Hilaire considered it his duty for the sake of the estate to marry, and accordingly got engaged to a friend of his sister's, Mary Collet, a daughter of David Collet of Vazon. Although the disparity in age was great, Hilaire being over forty, yet as she belonged to an impoverished family the match was considered a good one for a penniless girl. However, three days before the wedding Mary Collet eloped with the younger brother, Peter. Neither was ever seen on the island again, and it was understood they had gone to America.

"Hilaire took the blow badly, though it was a blow to his pride more than his heart. Never an amiable character, he became more morose than ever, and gradually getting dropped by all his acquaintances, he devoted himself entirely to Perigord. The next blow came from his sister Judith. Life at Perigord with such a man as Hilaire, and with no one coming near the place, must have been a joyless affair, a mere existence for a young girl. She endured it for two years, though, and then ran away—ran away with Brisson."

"Brisson? Not the man you told me of yesterday?" I said.

Le Marinel nodded a rapid assent.

"With Cæsar Brisson, at that time a dashing type of commercial traveller, selling cheap Bordeaux on commission. No one knew how he contrived to scrape up an acquaintance with the girl. But I've heard that in those days Cæsar's impudence was matchless. Always well-dressed, and with what an inexperienced girl might take for fine manners, he could remove his hat with a flourish, place it on his heart with an exaggerated bow, show his nice teeth, or make his black eyes languish with devastating effect. But this second elopement was of course the direct consequence of the first, or rather of the way Hilaire took it; for by cutting himself and his young sister off from all social intercourse—and I've calculated she was only seven-

teen when her brother Peter went—he deprived her
of the experience which would have saved her from the
cheap gallantry of the Brisson type.

"Well, they say that Hilaire felt the flight of Judith
more keenly than the flight of Mary Collet. That is
likely, I think. For, after all, it was with another de
Quettville Mary Collet fled. But that his sister should
go off with Cæsar Brisson—that gave the measure of
what she found life with Hilaire to be."

Le Marinel extended his hand for the wine, and then
finding himself without a glass went to his former place
to recover the one he had left there.

"Does this bore you?" he asked as I passed the
decanter.

"I was just wondering where the comedy came in,"
I prevaricated. And in fact my thought had been that
if these islanders considered all this to be comedy they
must have a queer notion of tragedy. Le Marinel,
sipping his wine delicately, set down the glass, nodding
reassurance.

"Ah, my friend, now we arrive at the comedy.
Attend! Hilaire, he is left alone in Perigord. He
hates every one now, a surly, sulky man. No one
calls at Perigord now. But does Hilaire then sit down
and twiddle his thumbs in the chimney corner? Oh,
no!"

In Le Marinel it was noticeable that under excitement the French idiom was apt to come out in his
speech. This peculiarity was probably due to the fact
that, like all the avocats, he had to address the Royal

Court in French, and was not due at all, as I then thought, to the amount of wine he had consumed.

"Ah, no!" he repeated, as if the word spelled *non*. "The ladies are no longer at Perigord in the afternoon. No, but the men, they come in the evening. Not to drink tea, you understand, but to borrow money. Oh, many came for that; and there was always money to be had—if you had good security. Yes, I think it was so that Hilaire recovered the sense of power he had lost when his bride and his brother, and his sister, escaped from him. So he just sat there in Perigord, yes, like an old spider in the centre of his web; and now it is quite evident to the world how wealthy he is."

As the avocat paused to refill his glass I felt constrained to question this.

"Is it? I saw no evidence of wealth at Perigord."

He pointed his finger at me.

"You saw no evidence of spending: a different thing, my friend. The good Hilaire's popularity as a godfather by itself proves that he is wealthy."

"His what?" I asked, bewildered.

"Ah, you do not understand? It is a little custom we have here. To cheer a lonely old lady or gentleman who has money but no relatives, what can one do but make such a one godfather to one's own child? And our Hilaire, who has a sense of humour of a sour sort, has quite a family of godchildren. Oh, I do not say he went to the church and took the vows for them. They excused him that. Even Drury said it was unessential, and Drury was a thoughtful St. Peter Port clergyman, whose son George was one of Hilaire's earliest godchildren, though Mrs. Blampied's Claire was not long behind. Oh, but they have been useful to Hilaire, these godchildren."

"Useful to him?" I said. "Surely the intention of the thoughtful clergyman, and the rest, was that he should be useful to his godchildren."

Le Marinel gazed at me with almost comical sadness.

"My friend, it is clear you do not yet sufficiently appreciate our old Hilaire. Just consider how useful were these little ones when our old acquaintance Cæsar Brisson returned!"

The mention of Brisson reawakened my interest which would certainly have died long ago but for one fact that gradually grew more apparent to me as the night wore on, and that was the antipathy Le Marinel felt for this old man, de Quettville. That did interest me, though I was careful not to allow the avocat to perceive the extent to which he was revealing his distaste. It was in this dislike I now found an explanation as to why he was so ready to talk. Love may keep us silent: hatred, like murder to which it is akin, will out.

"And why did Brisson return?" I asked.

Le Marinel shrugged.

"Who knows? Maybe he heard of the growing family of godchildren. Maybe he remembered Hilaire was now old. After all, they were brothers-in-law, and he had provided Hilaire with a niece, which is better than a godchild, or so Cæsar, who was all for reconciliation, thought. The story goes that it took six men to kick Cæsar out of Perigord when he called there, and two of them spent a month in hospital afterwards. I do not know. And I should not care to ask Cæsar. *Ma foi,* no! But his wine is good, is it not?"

He held up his glass, a little unsteadily.

"Is this his wine? It is excellent."

"Ah, Cæsar knows good wine. But, yes!"

"And after he was kicked out of Perigord?"

Le Marinel needed prompting now.

"Oh, yes. He stayed on here and opened his wine shop on the Quay, calling it Perigord in honour of Hilaire. Hilaire didn't like that! But he couldn't do anything. Neither could he prevent the next blow to his family pride. As soon as Brisson learned what his brother-in-law looked like, and said, when he first saw the word *Perigord* in gilt letters above the wine shop door he thought of another stroke at Hilaire's pride. And he got it home by putting his daughter to serve in the public bar. The girl was named Judith, after her mother who had died in France."

"And wasn't she de Quettville's heir?"

"Assuredly. And Cæsar pointed this out to him. Cæsar is very proud of his daughter. But Hilaire got one back on Cæsar there, for though the girl stands to inherit Perigord, Hilaire can leave his money—which could buy half a dozen Perigords—where he likes. And *that* is where the godchildren are useful to Hilaire. He flourishes them, as it were, over Cæsar's head. And there of course Cæsar is helpless. Moreover, Hilaire can let Perigord become a ruin, and that is what he has done. Was I not right in calling it a comedy?" He laughed. "And you thought this island looked the sort of place where nothing happened! Instead of which," he laughed again boisterously this time, "instead of which it is the kind of place where the queerest things happen."

Mingling with his laughter I heard from somewhere in the house the rapid ringing of a bell. Le Marinel did not at first hear it. The ringing went on. I drew his attention to the bell. He cocked his head on one side, bending an ear to the sound. He got to his feet.

"The telephone," he said. "Excuse me a moment."

While he passed through the door I stole a glance at my watch. It was twelve minutes past eleven. I remember thinking that though Le Marinel, the man, liked good wine, Le Marinel the avocat had, after all, not told me one single fact about de Quettville that was not public property. And how much more he must know! He, if any, would know how de Quettville had left his money. Yet not a hint had fallen. Dislike the man as he obviously did, he had yet in essentials respected the client. At least so it seemed to me then. And I had ample time for other reflections before the avocat returned. Speculation on the outcome of the conflict between de Quettville and this Brisson chiefly interested me. So far the honours lay with the bitter old Norman aristocrat, with his sardonic humour, rather than with the younger plebeian Frenchman. Brisson was proud of his girl, was he? Well, that gave one the measure of his hatred for de Quettville. For with a truly Gallic hardness he did violence to his own

personal pride in her so that he might mock de Quettville by the knowledge that his niece was serving liquor
in a bar—serving liquor to drunken sailors and the riff-
raff of the port.

As Le Marinel returned I got on my feet to take my
leave.   At first, with this in my mind, I did not take
any particular note of the fact that he seemed more
quiet and restrained than when he left the room.   Then
I saw his eyes as I offered my hand, and perceived he
had had a shock.   He stood still, not observing my
hand.

"Anything wrong?" I felt constrained to ask.

He nodded.

"The call was from Carey, the Chief Constable.   He
tells me de Quettville has disappeared."

"Disappeared?"

"Disappeared.   This morning Mrs. Bichard found
his room empty and the study upset.   She thought he
had come into town on business.   She is a foolish old
woman.   It was only when night came, and he had not
returned that she became uneasy.   Carey is to be at
the end of the road in ten minutes; we are going out
to investigate."

Again I offered my hand.

"In that case I'd better clear out."

Le Marinel, alert enough now, shook his head in a
vigorous negative.

"No, you'd better come with us.   If he is my client
he is your patient.   Carey was glad to know you were
here.   For it seems you were the last person who is
known to have seen de Quettville."

THE Rue Galette was as dark and silent as the grave, and seemed almost as narrow, when we hurried towards the corner at which the car was to pick us up. Le Marinel had rapidly changed into clothes more suitable for our journey, but I had necessarily to go as I had risen from the table except for my overcoat.

Rounding a corner we saw the tunnel-like entrance to our alley all lit up by the radiance from a car's headlights; and a second or two later Le Marinel was introducing me to Colonel Carey who sat at the wheel of the big four seater. A sergeant of police stood on the pavement like a statue, holding the open door. The Chief Constable motioned me in beside him; Le Marinel, followed by the sergeant, jumped in behind, and the car glided quickly up the street, accelerating rapidly to take the hill out of the town. In the light of a passing street lamp I noticed the time on the dashboard clock—11.35. But soon the lamp-posts ceased to flash past us, and we were out on the country roads, running between high hedges. It was a mild, windless night but very dark.

Not, however, till we topped the last ascent and entered on a long level stretch did Carey speak; and by that time the rush of cool air in the open car had restored my head to something like normal clarity.

"You saw Mr. de Quettville last night?" the Colonel began.

"At ten-thirty, for about half an hour."

"Did you form any opinion as to his mental condition?"

"Not at the time. He was certainly very taciturn. But that I did not trouble about, since, for all I knew, it might be a natural trait, and my concern was with his general health. So my examination was confined to his physical condition."

The Chief Constable digested this in silence as we sped on.

"Doctor, you were, I understand, sent for by the housekeeper in consequence of certain peculiarities which Mr. de Quettville had developed. He had taken to his bed, refused to see the housekeeper, kept her outside the door when she tried to enter his room with food, and when she went up from time to time she heard him, as she says, raving wild talk to himself."

"These are facts I heard only to-day from Le Marinel."

"Very well; but taking them into account now, do you think it likely that they point to a mental breakdown?" As I was about to speak he continued: "This may have very serious consequences, you know. You have heard of the trick played on him by some malicious persons who set an effigy over the Perigord gateway. If any ill has happened to him in consequence it will be my business to discover who these malicious persons are. On the other hand, as de Quettville is advanced in years, and has had many troubles in his life, may this not be merely a case of senile decay?"

The Colonel took his eyes off the glaring road ahead

to look at me. He was, I imagine, anxious that the case would turn out to be one of senile decay. That would make no scandal, nor involve any one in serious consequences. For in that case the explanation would be that de Quettville, suffering from cerebral arteriosclerosis, had wandered off like a child and got lost. I thought it out, and the Colonel had to get his eyes back on the road long before I reached a definite conclusion. In fact he became impatient.

"Well," he queried crisply, "what do you think?"

This time I was ready for him.

"I'd rather wait to see and hear what they have to say at Perigord, if you don't mind."

Whether he minded or not he had to accept it. The rest of the journey I used for a close consideration of such of the facts as were already known. But I did spare a moment or two to ask myself why the police were taking the disappearance so seriously. That Channel Island law was not the same as English law, and followed a different code, I knew by this time; but even so I could hardly see why they should be on the road at this hour unless—yes, unless they suspected de Quettville of some form of delusional mania with homicidal tendencies.

The car slowing down to swing through the Perigord gates roused me from my meditations. This time the open car and the brilliant head-lights permitted me a full view of the gateway, and I observed the structure with curiosity. Two massive pillars supported a sort of sham Gothic arch with a straight top, fronted by a parapet of imitation battlements, and at each end of the parapet there stood an ornamental stone vase, to finish off, as it were, the loopholed parapet. The whole erection was, in fact, an example of eighteenth century taste at its worst; and seen in the white glare of our headlights, standing against the great chestnut trees overtopping it from behind, it looked as if it had been cut out of cardboard. Ridiculous indeed it must have been when Mère Trouteaud's Neptune in a nightcap and a white shirt knelt on its battlemented top, holding out his trident with the three golden balls!

There was nothing pinchbeck about the house, however. A great, square, massive block it looked as we emerged from the avenue, its dark frontage unbroken by a single lighted window. But when we swung up to the steps a woman advanced from the portico, and before we could get out she was excitedly, and with much gesticulation, addressing Colonel Carey in the Guernsey French. The others gathered round her, and as they, I suppose, naturally followed her example in using the *patois,* I had to play the part of a mere spectator, to glean what I could from their faces. And, as their faces were almost as invisible as their speech was unintelligible, I soon got impatient. But a new voice sounded behind me.

"Ah, there you are at last!" The voice came peevishly.

"Mrs. Blampied," Le Marinel breathed, and the jabber ceased.

Carey gave a little groan.

"I was just thinking you would never come," the lady went on. "Hadn't you better come inside?"

It was at once evident that Mrs. Blampied intended to take control of the situation. And she might have but for Carey. For though we followed like sheep as she led the way across the big hall and into a room beyond the staircase, we were not three minutes there before the Chief Constable took command. Mrs. Blampied, whom I now saw to be a large woman in black rustling silk, began by seating herself in a large easy chair, and from there indicated to each of us the seat she desired us to occupy.

"Now what I would like to know—" she began imperiously.

But Carey, who had ignored the pointing forefinger of her bejewelled hand and taken up his position on the hearthrug, cut her short.

"To-morrow, Mrs. Blampied, to-morrow, if you please," he said softly; "to-night we are here to ask questions, not to answer them."

Mrs. Blampied, her hard mouth still harder, eyed him as if she could not credit her hearing. But the tall, lean man with the blue eyes had the advantage: she had to look up at him while he stood there looking down at her, one hand holding the other idly behind his back. When her eyes fell to the carpet he pushed home his advantage.

"And as you, Mrs. Blampied, were not here when Mr. de Quettville disappeared, I am afraid we have not even questions for you."

"But my daughter was here," she retorted, "and I am a mother with her child's interests to look after.

Every one knows Claire was his favourite godchild, and the poor girl is so dreadfully upset."

So even then the lady proposed to sit on and listen, in her child's interests, to all that passed! But here the colonel was more decided than suave, and at his nod the sergeant opened the door for her. She sailed off, head in air, the colonel standing as if to attention until she passed through the door.

Then crisply the command came: "Call the housekeeper."

Here I became afraid I would again miss all the old woman had to say if they started off in their barbaric insular French. But I had reason to thank Mrs. Blampied. She had led off in English, because, as I now know, she considered the island *patois* to be vulgar and unbecoming. Still, consciously or not, when Mrs. Bichard came in Carey continued in English; and in the course of her examination I was able to gather much of what I had missed on the doorstep.

No trace, I now learned, of Mr. de Quettville had been found, although the whole male population of the parish, organized by the parish constable, Peter Vaudin, had been searching over a wide area for many hours. Nor had any one been got who had seen him. She herself had last seen him when she opened his bedroom door to show the doctor in on the Thursday night. That was last night. He had been in bed all Thursday. No, it was not the case that he had eaten nothing all day. Thursday morning when she entered his room about nine to ask if she was to bring his breakfast he almost screamed at her, telling her to leave him alone.

But at one-thirty she and the parlour-maid, Alice Mauger, went up together with some lunch on a tray. He was then asleep. She put the tray on a table where he was bound to see it when he awoke. Later she went again, and found him asleep; but he had eaten some of the food. That eased her mind.

She first became uneasy when she went up once more about seven and heard him talking to himself. She opened the door softly, and looked in. She could see him lying there. He was waving his arms about; it was as if he were preaching in a church. No, she could not catch much of what he said; but he was always repeating one word: *l'épouvantail*—that meant *the scarecrow*. She then went down and sent Alice to telephone to Monsieur Le Marinel. Yes, Alice was the only maid in the house, the kitchen-maid, Suzanne Dory, having been sent away last Saturday, because the master saw her come in laughing about the nasty figure in the shirt set over the gate. Yes, she herself did think Mr. de Quettville was referring to that figure when he used the word *l'épouvantail*. But she went to bed more easy in her mind after the doctor had gone.

Even this morning when she found his room empty she was not alarmed, at least not after she had been to his study, and found the drawers of his desk open, and many papers lying about. She knew he had been having a lot of business with Mr. Le Marinel, and thought that he had risen early after his long rest, and gone to town to see him. He was certainly upset by the effigy on the gate. It had been put up on Friday night, exactly a week ago, and it was several days before they got it down, for the big ladder belonging to them had got broken. The men could not get any one to loan another, as the people didn't like Mr. de Quettville, and lots of them came to laugh.

Here Colonel Carey who had been making rapid notes of the woman's statement, looked up and was quick to notice that the housekeeper had had enough. She in fact was not far from collapse.

"Thank you, Mrs. Bichard, that's all just now," he said gently.

The old woman started precipitately for the door, and then remembering her manners turned round to drop a curtsey just as Le Marinel was saying he wanted to see the study. His words arrested Mrs. Bichard.

"Well, sir," she said apologetically, "we have not yet finished tidying up."

The avocat stared at her aghast.

"Tidying up!" he cried. "Tidying up what?"

"The mess of papers in the study, sir. We had to see if—"

"Who are *we?*" Le Marinel almost thundered.

"Mrs. Blampied and myself, sir, Mrs. Blampied being very anxious to see if he had left any message to say where he had gone, or when he'd be back. I was so upset myself that I hadn't thought of that till Mrs. Blampied came here."

I heard the avocat's groan and saw Carey's wry smile.

"It probably doesn't matter," he murmured. "The case seems clear enough."

Le Marinel nodded a thoughtful assent, and turning to me said, "Would you mind, Dunn, if I had a word with Carey?"

Of course I did not mind, but the avocat did not wait for my assent; drawing Carey into a corner where they talked together for a minute or two. I removed myself out of earshot. Presently Carey called me over.

"Dunn," he said, "we both consider that in view of the circumstances you might like to have the benefit of consultation with—er—another medical man."

His hesitancy, as well as the formality with which he spoke, suggested that he was not at all sure how the proposal would be received.

"By all means," I said heartily.

His face brightened. Le Marinel too seemed happier. And it was the avocat who hurried off, saying he would send some one to telephone for Dr. Sullivant. Whom he got or where he went I do not know, but he rejoined Carey and myself in the study after a few minutes.

But at first I had no eyes for the condition of the study. I was busy wondering why Le Marinel wanted to call in another doctor. It was something new, something that had come out of Mrs. Bichard's statement. I tried to think what it could be.

WE found the study did certainly stand in need of an hour or two's work. Indeed it looked much more likely that Mrs. Blampied and the housekeeper had been disarranging rather than re-arranging its documentary contents. For it was difficult to believe that any but an insane owner or a burglar could have made such a complete mess of the study. The methodical lawyer stood rigid, and open mouthed, appalled at the litter. But Carey, after one swift glance around, promptly crossed to the fire and dropped on his knees on the hearthrug. From the way his head went down, and he poked about, he was looking to see if there was any trace that anything had been burnt in the fire. When he stood up a look passed between Le Marinel and himself.

"It is my duty," the lawyer said, "to demand that this room be locked and sealed before we leave."

Le Marinel with a wave of his hand at the scattered papers, said, "I think we ought to have Mrs. Blampied in to tell us just how much of all this is his work and how much hers."

Carey assented.

"Yes, that must be settled at once. What the deuce did they want a fire for on a night like this? That bothers me. Better have her in and ask that too."

When Le Marinel went off to find the lady the colonel glanced at me.

"Ever had any experience in this sort of thing?" he enquired.

"I don't quite know what to make of it," I replied. "If the room was left like this by de Quettville it does look like insanity."

"Ah, that's what we must talk about later. When Sullivant gets here. That fire is odd, though. He certainly never lit it before he left so early, unless he was insane. There is simply no sense in it. But I doubt if he lighted it. Come and look at this. See, the indications are that it has recently and hastily been lit; for there's small pieces of fresh coal still on the hearth, which would otherwise have been swept up. And yet this fire has certainly not been used to destroy any large amount of papers; if it had, some of the carbonized fragments must have been left, while the fresh coal lying there proves that the hearth has *not* been swept. Yet unless a large amount of paper had to be god rid of a fire was needless; a candle, or a match, would serve for a few documents." He shook his head. "No, I'm hanged if I can make anything of it."

I followed his eyes as he began to gaze about the room from where he stood. The study was a small room as nearly as possible square, filled with heterogeneous pieces of furniture. Under the one window stood a bright yellow varnished American roll top desk, flanked by an ancient Breton armoire of black carved oak, about seven feet high, the interior of which had been fitted with drawers alphabetically labelled, and apparently, like the two large drawers forming the base, these had been used to store books and papers. Most, but not all, of these drawers stood open, and undoubtedly gave the impression of a hasty and incompleted search for some document, the exact position of which was unknown to the searcher. The fact that some of the drawers remained shut showed that the search had not been completed, but whether that was because the searcher had found what he sought or had been disturbed before he could finish was more than I could determine.

The room would be more accurately described as an office than a study, for books there were none; and from the incongruity of its contents it might have been taken for a storeroom in which a dealer in antiques kept the odds and ends of his trade. On my right as I stood inside the door a four-fold Chinese screen in red lacquer hid all but the upper half of a large oblong of silk French tapestry, depicting a hunting scene, with equestrian figures in costumes of the seventeenth century. Except for this tapestry all the walls were bare till the eye reached the fireplace, over which hung a large steel engraving of two retriever dogs by Landseer.

The fireplace itself had chairs on each side, one a dainty, flimsy Louis Quatorze brocade-seated chair in dull gilt, and its *vis-à-vis* was a so-called easy chair in brown pegamoid that at once revived in me the memory of Tottenham Court Road. Over the top of the gilded French chair which stood on the side of the fireplace furthest from the door I saw a green safe, the massive doors of which stood open, a bunch of keys hanging from the one key inserted in the lock.

Swiftly as the eye can take in the major contents of a room I had not begun to look at its less conspicuous furnishings before the avocat and Mrs. Blampied came in.

It was clear from her face that the lady had been left unaware as to why she had been summoned. Carey greeted her pleasantly.

"Ah, Mrs. Blampied, sorry to trouble you, but we have, after all, a question or two for you to answer."

He lifted the Louis Quatorze chair and set it down for her use. With tight lips and in silence, stiff with dignity, she seated herself.

"I find," he repeated, "we have one or two questions for you after all, Mrs. Blampied."

The lady bowed coldly. Carey began his questions. But not with the question I expected.

"Miss Blampied has been staying here?"

"Yes, for the last week."

"She was here, then, when that—that figure-head was put up over the gate?"

"Oh, yes. She came on Friday, the day Mr. Drury left."

"Mr. Drury is another of Mr. de Quettville's god-children, I believe?"

"Yes, but he had been invited for a couple of days only."

"And Miss Blampied had been invited for a week?"

Mrs. Blampied shifted in her seat.

"For two weeks, one of which has gone, Colonel.

My daughter is his favourite god-child. She is a very intelligent girl, and frequently helps him with his correspondence, and so on."

"Quite. And Mr. Drury when here also, I take it, helps in the same way?"

After a moment's hesitation the reply came with sneering deliberation.

"Mr. Drury, I fear, is more prone to seek help than to give it."

Carey smiled.

"Thank you, Mrs. Blampied. We may hope, then, that your daughter will help us now. Will you call her, please?"

"Call her? The poor child has been in bed for hours. She is terribly upset."

"I'm sorry I must insist, but you see, her knowledge and intelligence may be of the greatest use at this very moment."

There were further protests from the lady; Carey, however, remained adamant. Yet he stopped her just as she reached the door.

"Oh, by the way, Mrs. Blampied," he said casually, "was this fire lit when you got here to-night?"

"It was not. It was lit by my orders."

"You felt cold, I suppose, with all the anxiety. Wouldn't it have been better in your bedroom?"

"Dear me, no. It was lit here because I had enough foresight to perceive that a fire might be very necessary if Mr. de Quettville returned, or were brought home in an exhausted condition." ·

"Quite," Carey nodded, rather crestfallen.

"Besides," the lady added, "some one had to sit up on the chance of his return."

"Quite."

Le Marinel avoided my eye. He was amused, I fancy, at the Chief Constable's discomfiture. Carey turned with renewed briskness to us as soon as Mrs. Blampied had gone.

"Well," he remarked, "I take it that each of us is making deductions along our own line of business from the facts as they emerge. You, doctor, can I rely on it that you are noting all the facts from the medical aspect?"

"You can," I replied confidently. "I've quite a lot to say already."

"And you, Le Marinel? Yours is easier, eh? Of course the lady has been vainly searching here for his will, prompted by curiosity to see what he had bequeathed to his favourite god-child."

"Why vainly?"

"Well, his will would be in your charge, in one of those japanned boxes in your office."

"That it isn't. If he has executed a will at all I've never seen it."

Carey's eyebrows went up; he indicated the scattered papers.

"Oho!" he said. "So there *was* a motive for the methods employed!"

The lawyer shook his head.

"Don't be so sure, Carey, don't be so sure. In the first place, would even feminine curiosity have pushed her to make such a mess of this room? In the next, if

Miss Blampied were only a half-witted assistant secretary there would have been no need for the search: she would have known where to look. Again, Mrs. Blampied had no need of a fire except for the purpose she mentioned. Cæsar Brisson might have been glad to have a fire at his hand had *he* discovered de Quettville's will; but a fire was no use to Mrs. Blampied since her daughter can only benefit through his testamentary dispositions, and *that* she would not wish to burn."

Carey sighed.

"Hanged if I know what to make of it," he said. "Here we are talking of de Quettville's testamentary dispositions as if he were dead. And for all we know the man himself might walk in on us at any moment, eh, doctor?"

"I do not think he will," I said.

Le Marinel turned his head swiftly.

"How can you know that?" he asked, watching me.

"I merely said I do not think he will."

The Chief Constable lifted his hand, cutting in:

"All right. That means you, doctor, have got *something* out of this investigation, something positive, while our results are so far only negative."

There came then the sergeant's tap on the door. Mrs. Blampied and her daughter were shown in.

Claire Blampied was a slim, fair girl of medium height, and appeared to be in the early twenties. A pretty picture she made in the Tottenham chair, her shy, delicate face still flushed with sleep, the dressing gown hastily wrapped round her, the two long fair plaits framing her white throat, her feet in bedroom slippers that seemed comfortably large. Sitting so upright in the chair, a hand gripping each of its arms, she seemed, with her apprehensive eyes, rather like a child steeling itself for a scolding.

"We won't keep you long, Miss Blampied," Carey said gently, almost nervously. "But we are sure you can help us in our investigation."

Mrs. Blampied sniffed.

"Investigation indeed!" she muttered. "Inquisition I would call it."

Carey fired his questions now.

"When did you last see Mr. de Quettville?"

"Yesterday."

"You mean Thursday? It's Saturday morning now, you know."

"Oh, yes."

"Where was he?"

"In bed."

"Tell us about it."

She took a long breath, thinking hard for a minute.

"I wanted to tell him about the ship's figure-head. Alice said Mrs. Bichard said he was hiding himself in bed because people had mocked him."

"What did you want to tell him about the ship's figure-head? He already knew about that."

"Oh, yes."

"Well?"

"Well, when the figure-head was taken down from the gate on Monday night Mr. de Quettville got the men to put it up on the old pillar by the summerhouse in the garden so that nobody could get at it again. But early yesterday—I mean on Thursday—when I looked out of my window I saw the figure had fallen, and was lying on the grass at the foot of the pillar. Then while I was dressing I saw some of Mr. de Quettville's men come and carry it away. Alice told me they had locked it up in the stable because they were sure some one had been trying to get at it so as to put it over the gate again."

"Yes," Carey encouraged her.

"I thought Mr. de Quettville might have looked out of his window after the figure had been carried off and think the people who hated him had got it again. I thought that that might be why he was staying in bed. So I went up to tell him about it."

"Do you remember when that was?"

"Just after lunch, about two perhaps. I pushed open the door so as not to awake him if he were asleep."

"And he was?"

"Oh, no! He was sitting up in bed eating his lunch, and he saw me at once."

"Did you tell him?"

"No, I had no time. He waved his hand at me, telling me to go away as he was ill."

"Did he look ill?"

"I thought he looked dreadfully ill." The girl threw an apprehensive glance at her mother. "He was quite rude too."

"Do you remember his exact words?"

"He almost screamed at me, *'Va t'en, je suis malade,'*

and waved me off, as if it were something infectious."

Carey spared time for a meaning glance at me. He did not think there was any need for further investigation at Perigord. It seemed conclusive that Hilaire de Quettville's mind, strained already as we knew, had given way under the dread of a repetition of the derision to which he had been publicly subjected. Carey nodded, half to himself, half to the girl, abstractedly. Mrs. Blampied rose.

"May I ask if my daughter's ordeal is over?" she inquired coldly.

"Thank you, Miss Blampied, you have been of great help," Carey said.

But the girl hesitated on her way to the door.

"I—I found this in godfather's room to-day," she said. Thrusting a hand into the big pocket of her dressing-gown she held out a round object that shone in the lamplight. "It had rolled into a corner. I looked for the other two but couldn't find them," she explained.

What I saw, as Carey extended his hand, was a gilded tennis ball. And we knew where it had come from when he turned it over and exhibited the puncture into which one spike of Neptune's trident had penetrated.

"So he kept this in his room," Carey said when we were alone. "That tells us how it had stung him." He held up the shining ball delicately on three finger-tips as if he might himself be stung. Then going over to the desk he extracted a large envelope from one of the pigeon holes and into the envelope he placed the ball, carefully as if it were as breakable as an egg. He looked up as we watched. "The only question now is: where is de Quettville? And for the answer," he added, addressing me while sealing the envelope, "we must wait to hear what conclusion you and Dr. Sullivant come to."

Le Marinel, yawning, took out his watch.

"Another half hour at least," he remarked.

Carey, however, filled in the time by having the study door sealed and then going to inspect the bedroom with the housekeeper, with whom he ultimately arrived at a decision as to what clothes de Quettville must have been wearing when he left the house. It took indeed considerably over half an hour and much head-scratching on Mrs. Bichard's part while the missing man's wardrobe was ransacked and the various garments inspected, before a description was obtained. Then we went back to the more comfortable morning room to wait.

I thought I knew why Le Marinel had got the Chief Constable to call in this other doctor. If de Quettville had become insane a second medical signature would be required. But what I did not see was why his presence should be necessary then in de Quettville's absence. I fancied Dr. Sullivant would not be over pleased at the summons. And if I was wrong in my surmise as to why the doctor had been called in, I was not wrong in that.

The doctor when he arrived was not in his best humour. He was a plump man of about sixty, with a good carriage; rather fleshy in the face, but with keen eyes and a pugnacious mouth. He listened without comment while Colonel Carey detailed the situation, the interlaced fingers of his fat, white hands locked round one rotund knee.

"Therefore," Carey wound up, "it seems to me that my next step must be decided by the conclusion you and Dr. Dunn arrive at as to Mr. de Quettville's precise mental condition when he left the house."

On this Dr. Sullivant turned to eye me over, not so much appraisingly as belligerently. I had heard of his high local repute with elderly female patients, and I felt he was looking at me much as a bishop might have looked had his lordship been requested to take council with a choir boy.

"Well, sir, and what conclusion have you arrived at?" he inquired. The tone was not supercilious; but it certainly had a touch of kindly condescension that reminded me of a pompous examiner who had put me through it when I was a nervous youth undergoing the first professional at Edinburgh.

"Homicidal melancholia," I said, and not at all as I would have said it to an examiner.

His eyebrows went up.

"Really—as bad as that? Why not ephemeral mania?"

"Because, for one thing, ephemeral mania does not begin with sleep, as his did."

"Is that certain? At all events it ends in deep sleep, and he may be sleeping somewhere now. Still"—he waved a hand—"I'll have to consider that possibility. By the way, have you—er—envisaged the probability of its being a case of senile dementia? He was an old man, you know."

"There was no evidence of childish degeneration when I saw him. His will-power was strong and his physical condition good."

"And you do not consider that points to some other form of mania?"

"No, he slept for hours on end."

"He certainly did," Carey intervened. "All the testimony we've had confirms that; but is it important? You've twice mentioned sleep."

Whether or no this intrusion was meant for remonstrance by the weary Chief Constable I cannot tell, but Sullivant turned on him.

"It is of decisive importance—a maniac is entirely sleepless," he almost snapped back.

This mollified me, for if Sullivant addressed me as if I were still a student, he spoke to Carey as if Carey were a schoolboy. But he hadn't done with me yet. He had seen me going about St. Peter Port bare headed and in flannels, while he himself was upholding the dignity of the profession in frock coat and topper. And thus for a time this so-called consultation went on, each apparent symptom of mental derangement cited and debated. Finally it was agreed that de Quettville was suffering from a form of melancholia, but Sullivant dismissed bluntly my notion, as he called it, that the disease had advanced to the stage of homicide.

"The man," he declared, "started brooding over the insult offered him by that practical joke with the figure-head. He became self-absorbed and unhappy, exhibiting all the symptoms of melancholia in its simple form. The acute form began when he took to his bed and refused to see any one. The transition from one stage to the other is well marked. There is even the element of delusion present, for he told Mrs. Blampied to go away as he was ill, an indication that his delusion was of some infectious disease. After that the next, and final, stage might have been anticipated even by a medical practitioner with no experience in mental diseases, and it came when he began to talk to himself. When Mrs. Bichard and the parlour-maid overheard him, as they put it, talking to himself, he was of course replying to imaginary voices."

That hit me hard. The implication, hinted at, was that I, who had seen de Quettville later still that night, ought to have diagnosed his condition. The worst of it was, I then thought he was right—more right than he knew. And when I felt the eyes of both Carey and Le Marinel fixed on me, waiting for my reply, while Sullivant twiddled his fat thumbs and complacently regarded the carpet, it made one of the bitterest moments in my life.

"I think you are wrong," I blurted out.

"Eh?"

The ejaculation suggested Sullivant could hardly believe his ears.

"I think it is worse than that."

"What is worse than what?"

"The man's condition is worse than you have presented it."

Sullivant passed his tongue over his lips and then smiled oddly.

"Well, let us hear why you so conclude," he said encouragingly.

"The talking to himself overheard by the housekeeper is the determining feature. I agree with you that he was in reality replying to imaginary voices."

"Good." Sullivant nodded in pretended delight. "Well?"

"Your inference was that those voices were prompting him to take his own life; I have to disagree there. In my opinion those voices were urging him to take the life of some one else. That is the secret of his disappearance: he has gone away to kill."

Carey rather jumped when he heard that.

"By George," he breathed, "that would be worse indeed!"

He stared apprehensively at Sullivant. We were all rather on edge now, except the cool little lawyer, who, lying back in his easy chair, exhibited no sign of tension. But Sullivant reassured the Chief Constable with a wave of the hand.

"My considered conclusion is that this is a clear case of suicidal melancholia."

"And mine that it is a case of homicidal melancholia," I doggedly rejoined.

Dr. Sullivant rose to his feet as if the consultation were over.

"Ah, Youth, Youth," he sighed, looking round for his hat, "always jumping to extremes. Here is Dr. Dunn, my young *confrère,* as an example. First, when he sees his patient he is certain there is nothing the matter with him, and now he winds up by being equally certain he is a homicidal lunatic."

Carey, however, did not smile. He looked perturbed. He had his responsibilities perhaps in mind.

"But Dr. Dunn hasn't told us why he is certain of that," he said.

"Chiefly," I said, replying to his look, "it is because he had a sense of being persecuted. That feeling was roused by the practical joke with the ship's figurehead. In persons of weak will, that might, and often has, led to suicide. But de Quettville was not weak willed; therefore his madness has followed the line of character, and led him to seek revenge, a revenge out of all proportion to the offence, since he is insane. If the prompting had been to suicide, I should have expected him to have acted much sooner than he did."

"Because of his strength of will?" Carey asked.

"Yes."

"But, don't strong-willed people sometimes collapse?" he persisted.

"He did not. All the evidence we have goes to show that. His reason collapsed, not his will. His will in the end overcame the last shreds of the moral sense, and as in all such cases, his disordered brain became convinced that to kill was a duty entrusted to him."

Carey nodded gravely.

"I see," he said. "The position, then, is that you both agree as to all the earlier symptoms, but disagree as to how far the insanity developed."

Sullivant, hat in hand, turned.

"Precisely. I say, for the reasons given, it developed from simple to suicidal melancholia. As for the point made about his will-power, if de Quettville had been weak willed, he would have continued to wring his hands, as the girl saw him, like a person preaching, she said, and to the end of his life complain to every one who would listen, and do nothing."

"Instead of which," I amended, "he sought revenge and, after a day's brooding alone, sublimated it into an act of justice."

Colonel Carey rose.

"Well," he said moodily, "if only you could have agreed, we might have known where to find him."

Sullivant nodded from the door.

"Well, Chief Constable, where do your suicides usually go?" he asked lightly.

"Oh, as you ought to know, Sullivant, it's a healthy-minded little island, this; but when a Guernsey-man does go off his head he usually proves the fact by trying to throw himself off the island."

"Precisely. That's what de Quettville has done. You will find him in the sea."

With that he was gone. Carey produced a cigarette case, turning to the lawyer.

"What do you think, Le Marinel?"

But Le Marinel refused to arbitrate.

"When doctors differ—" he said, with a shrug, as he picked out a cigarette. Carey extended his case to me.

"Sullivant's a clever chap, you know," he remarked.

"But in spite of that, I dare not disregard what you say if there's the slightest chance you are right. And," he added, "if he is out for murder, the question remains: who is his man?"

The tension seemed to have relaxed scarcely at all with Dr. Sullivant's departure.

"You have no clue, of course," Le Marinel said.

"Oh, yes, we have—that gilded tennis ball."

The avocat seemed surprised. "What can that tell you?"

"A lot, perhaps. Tennis balls often are marked by their owners. We may find something of the sort under the gilding. The gilding itself is so well done, it is possibly the work of a professional gilder. If not, we may ascertain who sold the gold leaf, for which the demand on the island must be limited. Then there's the finger prints on the ball."

"The other two will have been handled less," I suggested.

"Yes. They won't have been touched since they were placed there. I'm going for them now."

The Neptune had been stowed away in an outhouse, and the sergeant was sent off to get the key. Weariness and reaction were heavy on us as we loitered in the hall waiting for Torode. I saw that Colonel Carey's idea was to establish the identity of the person responsible for sending de Quettville out of his mind. It would be lucky for the man if the Chief Constable succeeded; yet though I doubted not of his success, I doubted whether he would be in time.

The dawn was at hand when we left the house and

walked round the garden towards the outbuildings. In the west the sky still hung leaden and dead, but in the east it seemed to be stirring into life, for there the dead patches of cloud were edged with a tremulous, rosy fire. But down in the garden it was still dark, so dark that the stable lantern carried by the sergeant threw a pool of moving light about his feet.

I was not sure Carey wasn't wasting far too valuable time in going to inspect the Neptune. For myself I was too weary to have any curiosity left. But I recall, as the sergeant put the lamp on the ground at the out-house door and produced the key, being very sorry for Carey: he would not be able to tumble into bed when we got back to St. Peter Port. I wondered whether my own face looked as haggard, white, and drawn as Le Marinel's when Torode, throwing open the door, held up the lamp to show us inside.

The place must have been a stable, long disused, for it smelt dank and musty. The Neptune was not hard to find. They had, in fact, set it on a large round corn-bin standing up against the further wall. The sight woke me up. To tell the truth, the figure was a trifle startling. Seen in the dim light of the lantern, amid all the enveloping shadows, it looked at the first glance so life-like. But that was only at the first glance. A nearer approach dispelled the illusion, and one saw that the workmanship wasn't very good. Indeed, my thought was that if the ship which had carried this particular figure-head had not better work put into it, it was no wonder she had gone to the bottom.

Just then a queer strangled cry sounded behind me.

Turning, I saw Carey standing with the tennis ball held up in his hand.

"Look," he cried, "look—look at the trident!"

We did look. Spiked on the trident we saw the golden balls which had been put there to deride Hilaire de Quettville. But Carey had found more than he sought. For all three balls were still on the trident. And Carey had a fourth in his hand!

WHILE he stared at the ball in his hand Colonel Carey's face took on an expression which stayed there a long time. It was a look compounded of bewilderment, wonder and irritation, and reminded me of a small boy scratching his head over a hopeless problem in higher mathematics. And the look was still on his face while Sergeant Torode began to crank up the car in the grey light of dawn. He was taking the sergeant in front, beside him, on the return journey, for they had to consider the most likely methods by which de Quettville might be run to earth before he found his victim. At the moment, however, it was the fourth tennis ball that worried Carey, as was made plain when he turned to us just before Torode got the engine to fire.

"It's unaccountable, you know. No sense in it," he growled.

Le Marinel leant forward.

"That fourth ball, you mean?"

"I do," Carey responded emphatically; "the thing has no sense in it now. I feel as if I were being mocked like de Quettville himself. They put the three balls on the trident to mock him with the pawnbroker's sign; and then just when I imagine I've got the hang of the affair this fourth one turns up to make a fool of me. Yes, exactly at the moment when we think we know all about it, a darn, silly, extra tennis ball which has no right to be there, which has no right to exist, rolls up, and over goes my apple cart. No," he concluded with a shake of the head as Torode settled down beside him, "no, there's more behind this than meets my eye."

But I wasn't worrying about that just then, my own eyes being almost glued up with sleep. In fact I have a notion I went to sleep on Le Marinel's shoulder before the car passed under the Perigord gate.

Later that morning, however, my interest rekindled. By that time I had slept for four hours, had a bath and begun a leisurely breakfast, after receiving the welcome news that in my absence no professional calls had come for me. It was Saturday morning, a fine bright morning too, with the air coming in sweet and cool through the open windows, bringing with it the murmur of voices, the voices of people passing down the Grange on their way to market. But there was no excitement in those voices. None that I could detect, even when I went over to the window to listen. And excitement there must have been if in the night Hilaire de Quettville had found his enemy. Such news would go round an island like wildfire.

At the corner of Uplands road, just under the Grange club windows, a horsey-looking man in gaiters with a bored looking, brindle bulldog squatting at his feet, stood idly watching the passing people. But he looked as bored as the dog. And as he seemed the type who would know whatever there was to know, it was safe to infer one of two things: either de Quettville had not yet got his man, or Carey had got de

Quettville. So far so good. I went back to finish my breakfast with an easy mind.

The forenoon I had to spend on a round of visits to patients. More or less perfunctory these visits were, for patients, unless very ill indeed, do not take kindly :o a *locum,* especially a young one. Still, though not one of those dear old ladies I saw was really ill, it became a matter of more than duty to look after them, simply because they were another man's patients. Getting back about one, I did not sit down to lunch till I had rung up the Chief Constable's office for news. Carey, I learned, was not at the office, and the man who took my call was pretty short when I asked if they had found de Quettville. That made me peremptory; and I reminded him that de Quettville was my patient. Le Marinel had stressed that fact the previous night, and though I had relieved myself of any responsibility for what de Quettville might do by giving my opinion as to his mental condition, I was, all the same, mighty curious to know how Carey had got on in his efforts to trace him, and the persons he judged to be responsible for the man's mental collapse.

Ultimately, after much hesitation, the official at the office said he would call the sergeant. Luckily the sergeant proved to be Torode, and he did not haggle in his replies to my questions. Not that there was much news for him to give. They had not got their man yet; but he was very confident they would. Every available officer was out on the hunt. In fact it was rather surprising they had not already laid him by the heels.

"But you see, sir," Torode added, "we're bound to get him, for our men are passing the island through a sieve, as you might say."

"And Colonel Carey, is he on the job now?"

"The Chief hasn't been off it since last night, not for more than his meals, that is." The question seemed to astonish Torode.

"Where is he?" I inquired, thinking I could guess something if I knew.

"Oh, here one minute and anywhere the next."

"Do you happen to know where Mr. Le Marinel may be?"

Torode responded to this question with bright alacrity.

"Yes, sir, I can tell you that. Mr. Le Marinel is at Perigord going through those papers in the study."

And that was about all I could learn. But the sergeant promised to ring me up as soon as anything definite came in. He was quite aware, he said, that I should have to see de Quettville professionally as soon as they got him.

That kept me quiet for an hour or two. But, getting no call by five o'clock I rang up again, only to be told that the sergeant was out on urgent duty. The worst of it was I felt tied up to the house, being certain, in the way one is on such occasions, that the call from the office would come the moment I left. About six, when I was mooning restlessly around my room I chanced to look out of the window and saw two men with their heads together, reading something in a newspaper, and seeing other men emerge from the club to catch the shouting newsboy as he passed, I dashed downstairs to collar the lad as he came away. There was, it seemed, something in that paper of unusual interest. And when I unfolded the sheet this is what I found:

STRANGE DISAPPEARANCE

Considerable anxiety is being felt over the reported disappearance of Mr. Hilaire de Quettville of Perigord. It is learned that Mr. de Quettville left his residence Thursday night or Friday morning without notice to his household, and under peculiar circumstances. Although it is known Mr. de Quettville did not leave the island, he has not been seen. Prior to his disappearance Mr. de Quettville was confined to bed, and under medical treatment. It is thought that he may possibly be suffering from a temporary loss of memory.

I read the paragraph through more than once before starting to think it over. The suggestion as to a temporary loss of memory was nonsense. Had that been the fact, de Quettville would have been found wandering aimlessly, long ago, especially on such a circumscribed area. The island had been sifted to catch him, and since he had not been found it was clear he must be concealing himself, concealing himself till he had achieved his purpose, with all the astuteness and craft peculiar to the delusional homicidal lunatic.

It would be idle to pretend that this knowledge left me untouched. As the paragraph stated, the man had been under medical treatment. That might make things awkward for me later on. Ought I to have recognized his condition, or at any rate to have foreseen it that night? With the thought of my responsibility to Dr. Wright, whose patient de Quettville was, my qualms increased to such a degree that about eight I put on a hat and went down to the Chief Constable's office.

Sergeant Torode was back again at the counter, alone. He looked up, almost, as I thought, guiltily, to tell me the Chief was still out.

"Any news?" I asked.

"No, sir, none."

"Ah!" I breathed in a way he did not like.

"Our view now is that it may be a case of accident, or—or suicide," he ventured.

"Nonsense."

"Well, sir," he protested plaintively, "what else can we think? We've practically combed the island for him, and even if he'd been in bits we'd ought to have got some of the pieces, somewhere, by now."

"That disposes of the accident theory, doesn't it?"

"More or less," he was compelled to agree. "I think it must be suicide myself; but whatever it is we're quite certain he is dead."

Dead? Standing there at the counter I examined the possibilities. If only I could be quite certain of that!

Dead and harmless. That was what Sullivant maintained—dead by his own hand. Mrs. Blampied, too, I remembered, seemed to have made up her mind last night he was dead. She had spoken of being there to protect her daughter's interests. But what did she know? With her the wish was father to the thought. She had the man's death in her mind as far back as the day on which she made him a godfather in her daughter's interests. And with the local police was the position not the same? They wanted the man to be dead. For from my experience I knew that nothing gives the police graver anxiety than the reported escape of a homicidal lunatic. In a murder case the crime is committed before the police know; but when a homicidal maniac gets loose it is equivalent to a notice that murder is about to take place. And when I recalled de Quettville as I had seen him in bed, his truculent rudeness with me, and his really, for his years, excellent physical condition, I remained convinced his could not be a case of melancholia with suicidal tendencies. Having reached this unwelcome conclusion I looked up to find Torode watching me.

"Sergeant," I said, "you know the man; does he seem the sort to commit suicide?"

Torode rubbed his chin with slow thoughtfulness.

"I know about him," he began. "All the island does. I wouldn't have said he was that sort. No, I wouldn't have said that. Tough stuff he is. Has been all his life, as I've heard. Not the soft, spongy sort that takes to the water, not him. Still, there it is."

But my own theory had strengthened. By this time it had strengthened into a conviction. I was certain that de Quettville, finding his victim away from home, possibly absent from the island, had gone into hiding to await his return. If this were right, then it became immensely important that the interval thus made available should be used for identifying the person or persons responsible for his mental collapse, so that they might be saved from the insane fury their practical joke had set loose.

"Has anything been done about those tennis balls?" I enquired.

"Why, yes, of course, sir, everything possible."

"For instance?" I insisted.

Torode's eyelids lifted ever so slightly, while he hesitated.

"Well, we've ascertained the gilding wasn't done locally, nor the gold leaf sold here neither. We stripped two of the balls after taking the finger prints, that is, and underneath we found just the usual marking, nothing more."

"Nothing else?"

"No, sir, nothing else; just what's stamped on most balls of the kind, the maker's name and the date of manufacture."

"And what about the finger prints?"

"Oh, we got them all right. But it'll take time before they come in. You see, we've got no finger print register here, and if we had it would be no good, for the parties responsible couldn't be of the criminal classes, could they?"

To me it seemed that no real progress had been made. But the sergeant did not appear to share my disappointment.

"And Mr. Le Marinel," I asked, "has he made anything of those papers?"

Torode, leaning against the counter, shook his head.

"Not that I've heard. But there were so many papers, I daresay it'll take time to go through them all,
won't it, sir?"

Just then the shadow of a suspicion crossed my mind
that Torode knew more than he was telling me. The
suspicion, I fancy, had its origin in his easy attitude,
and confident manner, which were certainly not justified
by anything he had told me. What was he keeping up
his sleeve? An odd feeling that I was being shoul-
dered out of the case came to me. As I tried to read
confirmation on the sergeant's face he smiled back at
me.

"I wouldn't worry, sir, if I was you," he said confidentially. "Leave that to us. Nearly every case begins with a mussy little lot of odds and ends we collect.
At first you can't tell what's important from what isn't.
But you find afterwards that the bits that matter fit in
together, and what is junk just drops away. Yes," he
nodded thoughtfully, "and as often as not you discover
that what at first you took to be a find is junk really,
and what you took to be junk is actually glittering
gold."

Then just as I was getting bored with Sergeant
Torode's philosophic dissertation on the difference between appearance and reality, the door softly opened
and Le Marinel stepped inside. From where he
paused, with the door knob in his hand, he took us both
in.

"Evening, doctor," he greeted me, nodding in his
snappy fashion. His eyes went to Torode. "Ah, sergeant, Chief still out, is he?"

"He is, sir. Can I take down any message?" The sergeant spoke briskly, getting a hand to the pencil behind his ear. Le Marinel hesitated, his dark eyes wandering to me. The feeling of being an intruder leapt up in me.

"No-o," the avocat replied. "No, it will keep. I'll see him later."

Already I was on the way to the exit. But the little lawyer for some reason did not accept the chance I was so hurriedly offering, and came out with me. He walked in silence through the courtyard towards the arched entrance into the street.

"Those papers are in an infernal mess," he said with a sigh.

"Isn't it a lovely night, even for the time of the year?" I remarked.

He half stopped to stare at me.

"I was remarking on the state of the Perigord documents," he said.

"And I was remarking about the state of the weather," I returned.

He whistled.

"Ah! Something got you on the raw, eh? I'm sorry. What is it?"

"Well, to be frank," I said, "you gave me the impression just now that you would have said more if you had not found me in the office."

"Surely not," he protested, taken aback by this directness.

"More than that, I have a suspicion the sergeant knew more than he told me."

"Very likely. He probably knows more than I do, since he is Carey's confidential man."

He was moving on again, but I laid a firm hand on his arm.

"Look here," I said, "you are seeing Colonel Carey later; will you remind him from me that as this man's medical attendant I have more concern with him than the Chief Constable, at least till a crime is committed."

"You mean that?" Le Marinel cried.

"I mean more. As de Quettville's doctor my responsibility is graver than your own, since my concern is with the man himself while yours is only with his property."

That got Le Marinel himself on the raw. He was so upset his eyes fairly goggled in their sockets. I was walking away, leaving him stationary under the archway and looking very like an astonished little goldfish; but he stepped after me, grabbing my arm.

"Stop," he whispered. "Stop, I beg you. You are under a misapprehension—so far as concerns myself at least, for there is nothing I need conceal from you."

The rapid, eager fashion in which he whispered this gave his words a confidential kind of air, and it was natural that I should draw back under the arch, away from the crowded street. Dusk was then deepening, windows were getting lit, and under the low, deep arch with the house above fronting the street, was one long shadow.

"Go ahead then," I said shortly.

The little lawyer gave a sigh of self-pity.

"More trouble for me. And more to follow, now

that Brisson is back, and Mrs. Blampied and the others out for the pickings."

"Brisson?"

"Ah, yes, I remember Cæsar did interest you. Well, the good Cæsar, it appears, has been away, for I saw him coming from the St. Malo boat. I fancy when he hears the news I'll see him soon at Perigord. And who am I to keep the peace between Madame Blampied and Cæsar Brisson? And Cæsar is no gentleman, mark you."

"Never mind about them," I said, "it's the search for de Quettville I want."

"Oh, well, what exactly did Torode tell you?"

He nodded away as I recounted the substance of what the sergeant had said.

"Well," he began when I had finished, "this is the position at the moment. Torode told you the Chief had got finger prints on the tennis balls; what he did not tell you is that the Chief, acting on information I obtained at Perigord from the papers, is busy collecting the finger prints of various people to whom de Quettville had made large financial advances. Carey is very adroit and is getting prints from people who don't know they are giving them, as for instance with George Drury whose glass he stole while having a drink with him. But the women aren't so easy to get."

"The women," I interjected. "Does he think there's women in it?"

"He doesn't think it, he knows there *is* a woman in it. Deep in it, too. It is obvious that those three balls could not be stuck on the trident without handling. At any rate the people who fixed them wouldn't bother about removing their finger prints afterwards.   They would not think of finger prints at all. Well, on two of the balls found on the trident, the only prints discovered were those of a woman."

"And the third?"

"The same woman, but also on this third ball a man's. Undoubtedly a man's. I've seen them. No woman ever had fingers so broad in the tips. But notice this: the two bearing the woman's imprints had no other prints, while the third ball with the man's had *also* the woman's."

"But there was a fourth ball," I reminded him.

"Yes, and the Chief has established a connection between it and the others, for the fourth ball has the imprints of two different women on it."

"One Miss Blampied's, of course."

"Exactly, and the other set are those of the same imprints which appear on all four. But here comes the snag. I have supplied Carey with the names of all those I could get who owed de Quettville money; and not one is a woman. Therefore the woman is in some way connected with one of the men who are his debtors, and whose names I supplied—but whether as wife, mother, sister, aunt, grandmother or what not—" Le Marinel shrugged, "who is to say?"

"It was probably this woman who did the gilding."

"Probably, since we know now the job wasn't done by any local firm. And that woman fixed on two of the balls while he was fumbling over one. Oh, yes, the indications of fumbling are plain enough. She clearly helped the man with the third."

"Has Carey formed any theory as to why there was a fourth ball?" I asked, remembering the Chief's perturbation when he discovered there was a fourth ball.

"No. He guesses they may have had a fourth in case one got lost. The jest would of course have no point had there been only two balls on the trident. It would not have suggested the pawnbroker. So they may have got one ready as reserve. Another line of investigation lay through the shops in the town which sell tennis balls, especially those which deal in this make of tennis ball. We know from their condition the balls were new, have indeed never once been used for the game, and so were probably bought for this one purpose by people who do not play tennis, since if they did they would surely have put old used balls on the thing. How easy to find out who has recently bought, say, half a dozen, and then if we found that that person's name figured among de Quettville's debtors, why, our search is virtually over. But as a matter of fact we found no dealer who had recently sold any of this particular make and date. The conclusion then was that the balls had come from England. Carey tried the post office. Half a dozen balls would come in a special box with the dealer's label attached, and a box might well take the postman's eye. But here again he drew a blank. Most of the postmen agreed they would notice such a box, but unfortunately not one remembered having carried such a box on his rounds."

All this did interest me. It was not what I expected to hear, but at the moment I was taken with the fascination which the solution of a difficult problem provides.

"Has the Neptune itself been examined?" I asked.

"Of course. But Carey got little there. The figure, you know, was decked out in a shirt, and even had there been a hundred imprints they would have got rubbed out by that garment. Besides, it had been handled several times by de Quettville's own men."

"Does Carey do this finger print business himself? That's unusual for a Chief Constable, surely?" I said.

"Carey spent most of his life in India, in the police, and what he doesn't know about finger prints isn't knowledge. In India the police use people's finger prints as a substitute for their signatures, in preference to it, in fact, since you cannot forge a finger print. But I forgot to tell you one thing he learnt from the Neptune. You remember the beard had first been painted white the better to suggest de Quettville? Well, Carey found out that the white paint used came from an artist's colour tube; it was, in fact, what is called Chinese white. That suggests some one who at least dabbles in painting."

"Exactly, when taken with the gilding."

This looked hopeful.

"Oh, Carey will find them," he added with conviction.

In this I was glad to concur.

"Yes, it looks as if he may save them yet."

The avocat showed surprise.

"Save them—save who?" he inquired, staring.

"Why, the person or people responsible for sending the man off his head."

The bewilderment in the avocat's eyes passed away, being replaced by a look of extreme discomfort.

"Well," he said hesitatingly, "Carey, of course, wants to know who they are; but he no longer regards them as standing in any danger from de Quettville."

I could hardly believe my ears.

"Is that really true?" I heard myself asking. "Why does he now think that?"

"Because he is now sure de Quettville is dead."

"He is sure of that on what grounds?"

"Because he has not been found. And that being the fact he is now convinced Sullivant's theory of suicide was right. No other theory fits the facts."

"He will find he is mistaken. But I have said what I think, and hold myself free of responsibility for the consequences."

"Well, as to that," Le Marinel said slowly, "Carey has seen Sullivant again, and I'm afraid they both consider you in some degree responsible. It is thought that when you saw de Quettville on Thursday night you might have diagnosed his mental condition. Sullivant considers the melancholia must have developed from the simple to the acute form by then. But he was most sympathetic about it, and of course does not blame you in the least."

Le Marinel must have misread my face as he said this, for he hastened to add in an off-hand fashion,

"After all, my dear fellow, what does your mistake matter? The man is better dead on all accounts, his own not least."

He was startled when I threw off the hand he had laid consolingly on my arm.

"Le Marinel," I cried, "the man I saw that night is alive. He left his house bent not on self-destruction but murder."

Le Marinel, mortified, I suppose, by my fierce rejection of his unwanted sympathy, looked at me with a sudden flush on his face, anger in his eyes.

"Very well," he said, "if he is alive, why don't you find him? After all, it was you who let him loose."

He can hardly have meant what he said. But in the heat of the moment I took up his challenge.

"All right," I said. "I'll find him—somehow."

The avocat laughed.

As I turned away, with Le Marinel's subdued laughter behind me, it is the bare truth to say I had not the slightest notion as to how de Quettville could be found. Yet on the spur of the moment, being hot and sore with the treatment I had received, I had pledged myself to find him. And the avocat's laughter, not so much the amusement as the mockery and pity I seemed to detect in it, simply strengthened my resolution. So I turned my back on him and marched off down the Pollet, much as if I already knew where to put my hand on de Quettville within the next half hour.

I did not, however, walk far along the narrow street before the rashness of my self-appointed task began to strike me, and pulling up beside a shop window gay with cigar boxes and bottles of local perfumery, I perceived that Le Marinel's amusement was not unjustified. For where the local police, with all their resources, authority and knowledge of the island, had failed, how should I, alone and a stranger, hope to succeed? Yet I remained unshaken in my conviction that the man had not taken his own life. Nothing I had seen, and nothing I had heard about him, lent the least support to Sullivant's opinion. A man mentally unhinged, possessing similar virility of will-power as I had witnessed, seeks refuge not in self-destruction but in revenge. Apart from that, it seemed absurd to suppose a man of such a hard, cold nature could be driven to suicide by any insult, much less by a ridiculous trick played with a derelict ship's figure-head.

Emerging from the Pollet I crossed the road, behind a tram-car with an open trailer that went clanking past, and took the upper promenade of the breakwater which stretches out to sea like a gigantic finger. And though, while I walked on, I kept calling myself an ass, it was not because I became shaken in my belief about de Quettville but simply because I had so rashly undertaken to find him.

I reached the end of that far-flung breakwater before the least glimmer came as to how he could be found. So I jumped on to the parapet, and sat there to think it out. It was a good place for thought.

Far below me in the dark the flood tide rippled in whispers against the base of the granite breakwater. Fronting me, across the inner harbour, rose the terraced town, its host of lighted windows reflected like stars arranged in rows on the smooth velvet blackness of the water. From somewhere alongside some quay the fussy rattle of a ship's derrick, loading or unloading cargo, came, and an occasional cry from a directing stevedore, but too distantly to disturb my thoughts. And to sit perched out there at the extremity of the sea wall gave me, too, the sensation of detachment, so that I felt able to view the island, as it were, objectively, at a helpful distance.

At first, however, this helped me little. To be quite satisfied that the man was *somewhere* on what, from where I sat swinging my feet, seemed a small enough island, was one thing; to find him on it was quite another. I started however with the knowledge that he had not left the island. Sergeant Torode had satisfied himself on that point. It was impossible, he asserted, that a man so well-known, so distinctive in appearance, could have left by either of the English mail boats without being recognized a dozen times over. And he brushed aside the suggestion that de Quettville might have left in a fishing boat from one of the places round the coast. None of those boats needed to go far, none of them remained out for long; and while Torode admitted the man might in his insanity have gone off by himself in a rowboat, the fact that no rowboat had been reported missing, as it very quickly would have been by its owner, disposed of any such theory. It was, indeed, the impossibility of leaving the island unrecognized, coupled with the fact that he could nowhere be found upon it, that had in the interval forced the police to accept Dr. Sullivant's theory of suicide. But this theory I rejected. And if I were right, de Quettville was still somewhere on that island. But where?

My eyes wandered along the stretch of coast, visible merely as a great hump of black shadow, from where the square tower of S. Barnabas cut an elongated wedge in the skyline, right along and beyond the range of lighted houses and hotels to the fretted coast near St. Sampson's harbour. Far away in the north, where lights were few, I noticed what looked like a small, but brilliantly lit window moving rapidly along the shore. The next moment I knew it for what it was: a tram on the St. Sampson-St. Peter Port line. Almost idly I watched the little blob of light twisting and turning as it followed the swerving coast-line, seeing it grow larger the nearer it came. But not till its speed slackened, and it began to mix itself with the lighted windows of the town did the hint I needed come.

Slowly the tram crawled along the Quay like some luminous beetle, and in its very slowness there was a suggestion of an advance that must be stealthy because of some enemy lurking ahead. When some irregularity of the cobbled street, or a worn joint in the rail, sent the lights jumping from the concussion, it looked so like a succession of frightened shivers that the fancy made me smile. But a quick thought struck the smile away. I sat up.

Cæsar Brisson! Was it not on that same quay that Brisson had his wine shop? A flurry of hitherto unassociated facts jumped into my mind. Cæsar Brisson had called his shop Perigord, and Le Marinel had told me how that insult angered de Quettville. Could Brisson be the author of this latest insult with the Neptune which, unlike the other, was supposed to have driven de Quettville to suicide? There was certainly a Gallic flavour in its mockery. And had not Le Marinel just told me he had seen Brisson coming from the boat?

I jumped from the parapet, startled by perceiving that if the insane de Quettville was out to murder any one the most likely of all must be his detested brother-in-law. And from this it followed that Perigord was the most likely place to find de Quettville, the Perigord on the Quay, that is. Indeed, when I recalled, as I then did with hasty apprehension, the almost devilish cunning with which a homicidal maniac can bide his time and make his chance, I thought it quite probable that de Quettville was even at that moment hanging around among the shadows of the ill-lit quay, watching the wine shop.

I ran the whole length of the deserted promenade, slackening down only when I reached the end near the foot of St. Julian's Avenue. Then I turned to the left by the careening hard at a more sober pace.

The exact position of the wine shop I did not know, but I remembered Le Marinel saying it was on the quay, and as the quay had but a single line of houses fronting the inner harbour I knew the shop would be easy to find. And so it proved. Indeed, to miss it one would need to have been both deaf and blind, for the voices of its clientèle were audible long before one reached its well lit front with the word "Perigord" displayed in large shining letters above the door.

Before entering I sauntered past to have a look at the surroundings. The houses facing the quay were chiefly used as marine stores, offices and ship's chandleries, but behind these there appeared to be a perfect rookery of tenements with flights of steps and foot passages rising to the High Street above. Few people were about in that quarter, but among the twists and turns of those labyrinthine passages one might pass perhaps a dozen men, and never see one, had they cared to remain in the shadowed corners.

Most of the men who went to the wine shop seemed to use the steps that led down from the High Street; and twice hearing footsteps I stood aside in an angle of the passage wall, to find not only that I remained unobserved myself, but that it was barely possible to tell whether the dim figure which slipped past me were man or woman. The place was just made for murder. One forward thrust, and a knife would go between a man's ribs and he be unaware that there was more than a knife or a hand there in the darkness.

With this perception came a quick distaste for the place. So easily could I imagine the maniacal old man lurking there to get Brisson on his way home that, to be quite frank, I turned and ran helter-skelter for the wine shop.

My horror, however, passed as soon as I emerged on to the quay, and after a breath or two I was able to enter the Perigord with a fair imitation of being at my ease. The shop held a large number of customers that night; but it was a large place, and divided up as they were, some in groups standing about the bar, and others seated at the small round tables placed in front of benches which backed the walls, it did not seem crowded.

Following my unobtrusive entrance I was left standing at the bar unnoticed for some time. The wine shop had a length perhaps four or five times greater than its breadth, and at the far end the shirt-sleeved proprietor himself stood behind the bar, conversing to a group of his patrons. The only other attendant, also in shirt sleeves, but with an apron tied round his slim waist, had his back towards me, while drawing some liquor from a bin against the wall.

A pleasant place the Perigord certainly was, as unlike anything in England as could be imagined, with nothing about it that was meretricious or gaudy, not even a mirror. Behind the bar, on a low shelf, resting on their sides, and showing their round varnished ends, there was a long range of over twenty great wine casks, each with a shining brass tap, and each with a white china plate on the shelf underneath to catch any drip.

Above these great barrels several tiers of bottles rose to the roof. Some racks were filled with bottles in straw, lying on their sides, so that their corks showed like rows of coins. The highest racks were filled with wire-topped bottles standing upright, their parti-coloured labels suggesting rows of soldiers toeing a line.

But it was the serried ends of those mighty barrels that gave the wine shop its atmosphere of dignity and solidity. That they were permanent fixtures was obvious, not only from the fact that they were in a highly polished condition, but also because they projected through the wall from some apartment behind, from which, it seemed, they would have to be replenished. Then just as I was speculating on this operation a call came:

"Catulle!"

It was a big, pervading voice that sounded through all the lesser chatter of the wine shop. Turning, I saw the call came from Brisson, and from the nod in my direction that followed, I perceived it was meant to draw the other man's attention to the fact that I had stood there too long neglected. The fellow, who must have already seen me while I was glancing about, turned, as I thought, with some hesitation, to look at me. At once I recognized him. He was the same rat-nosed man I had seen with Brisson's housekeeper in the Rue Galette on Thursday morning. Instead, however, of coming to serve me, he went away up the bar to speak to the proprietor. Brisson, I fancy, shared my surprise at this action. A brief exchange of words followed between the pair, and then Brisson himself came along to serve me.

Now, though I had come there to seek traces of de Quettville, with the half formulated intention of giving this man warning of the danger threatening him, I was disappointed not to have a closer look at the man who appeared unwilling to face me. That he knew me seemed now fairly certain; but for the life of me I could not place him. And though I had come across many a queer type, both in hospital and during my service as police surgeon, this chap ought to have been unforgettable. Brisson approached, lifting his eyebrows interrogatively.

"A cognac," I replied.

He inclined his head, and stepped round, to bend swiftly and pluck a bottle from the low shelves under one of the gigantic casks. For all he was so huge a fellow the whole series of actions reminded me of a cat plucking a mouse from its hole. With a twist of the wrist he exhibited to me the Otard Dupuy label.

"You will find this good," he said with a smile of great frankness, as he picked out a glass, blindly, from beneath the counter and set it before me. All his actions were carried through with swiftness and precision, and yet with a marked economy of effort. In a second my glass was filled, and the syphon set to my hand, the bottle being whisked upward as the last drop fell. My eyes were on his dexterous fingers, and I noticed they were covered near the knuckles with short, black hairs. Yes, his finger-tips were certainly too broad to be other than those of a man of huge physique, and I might have said Torode had no need to look further to find the man responsible for hoisting the Neptune on the Perigord gate. But there was this against it: Cæsar Brisson was too deft fingered to need the assistance of any woman in fixing those tennis balls on the trident. That I recognized while lifting the glass to my lips.

"It is good," I said with emphasis.

He showed his fine teeth in a smile as he bowed in his exaggerated French fashion.

"The appreciation of a connoisseur, that is very pleasing to me," he said, patting the bottle before replacing it. "It is not to every one I offer this, you comprehend."

Then I took, so to speak the bull by the horns.

"That man of yours," I remarked, laughing, "seemed to think me unworthy of any kind of drink."

"That man of mine?" he repeated, staring at me with wrinkled forehead.

"Yes, that fellow who kept me waiting. Catulle, I think you called him."

"Oh, yes! Ah, poor Catulle is nervous about his

English, you understand. It is so bad, and he saw you were English. Yes, Catulle, he is so sensitive, poor fellow, and oh, his English, it is so funny!"

Brisson threw back his head and laughed noiselessly and confidentially.

"You haven't had him long, then?"

"Ah, but he is my friend, not my servant, the good Catulle."

After a moment's thought, I said, looking along the bar at the good Catulle wiping a glass:

"Well, you know I have an impression I've seen him before."

"So?"

"But I'm hanged if I can place him."

Brisson was interested.

"Perhaps his name and his occupation will be of assistance to you. His name, it is Catulle Coquard, and he is a wine traveller from Bordeaux, now having, you comprehend, a leetle holiday with his old friend of the road, Cæsar Brisson. That helps— *hein?*"

I shook my head as he stared at me hopefully.

"I must have been mistaken, that's all. But it's of no consequence," I added when Brisson moved away, as I thought at first to call Coquard, but actually to attend to some other customers.

I took out my pipe, and with slow deliberation filled it, my thoughts now working on the problem of how to broach the matter of de Quettville to Brisson. The man must be warned. But the duty called for considerable tact, since the warning could be given only on the assumption that he was believed to be concerned in the setting up of the Neptune over the Perigord gateway; implicated, that is, in the outrage which had driven his brother-in-law mad.

That Brisson already knew of de Quettville's disappearance it was impossible to doubt, for even if he did not read one or other of the local newspapers there were dozens of men coming in and out of the wine shop every hour. I had myself overheard the affair referred to by more than one bystander, although I observed that they did so in lowered tones when the proprietor happened to be within earshot. Then it occurred to me that I could best broach the matter through Coquard. Perhaps I was swayed towards this opinion by my desire to hear Coquard's voice. Anyhow it was not now difficult to attract his attention, for he glanced my way frequently after Brisson's talk with me. So when I caught him at it and signalled, he, being otherwise unoccupied, strolled towards me, manipulating a toothpick, his hairless face rather twisted and contorted by his efforts, as one had to suppose, to reach a back tooth. And all the notice he took of my order till those efforts were crowned with success, was to stand and stare at me out of his screwed up little pig's eyes, a stare curiously malicious and penetrative.

Now in my profession there is one quality which must be acquired if it is not born with a man, and that quality is coolness. So though the fellow's insolence was deliberate, I merely looked him up and down slowly, inwardly wondering as to the cause of the antipathy I divined in him. To the first impression he gave me in the Rue Galette there was little to add except that now, seeing him move, he seemed boneless; and his thinness somehow suggested—it sounds absurd —that his bones had been replaced by springs, for whatever his stamina, he stood upright and was obviously active and muscular.

I badly wanted to kick him for his cheek, and in imagination saw that indiarubber-like body swaying away from the impact of a vigorous boot; yet it would never do to get involved in a brawl in such a place. Besides, there was the counter between us. But it was he who gave me the surprise.

"Before I haf seen you," he nodded at me, replacing his toothpick in a vest pocket.

"Really? Where was that?"

"With that *trompe*, ze ozzer morning."

"*Trompe?*" I repeated wonderingly. The word stirred forgotten memories in me, memories of the Rue Jacob where I studied at the Salpêtrière. In those days we had a familiarity with the thieves' jargon only equalled, I suppose, by the Paris police, and it was for a time the fashion for students to talk in the *argot* of the thieves. So I was just wondering how this wine traveller from Bordeaux knew the meaning of the word when he explained it, at the same time impatiently calling me a fool in another *argot* word.

"*Gonjou,* the lawyer. I see you with that lawyer in the Rue Galette, and I know you haf not come here for to drink, eh?"

"No. As a matter of fact I came here to look for some one."

A sly smirk overspread the hairless face, and his eyes narrowed so that he looked at me through mere slits.

"Ah, then you are a *robeau*—a policeman," he whispered huskily.

This was better still. I felt that it would be easy soon to tell his very age, and the period he had lived in Paris, from his vocabulary; for in Paris not even the fashions in women's hats change so rapidly as the fashion in thieves' *argot*, and, naturally, the slang word for a policeman alters most frequently. In my time *robeau* was the word in fashion when *chardonneret* became *démodé*. All this flashed through my mind as I replied to Coquard.

"No, I am a doctor, looking for a patient who is—" I was about to use the *argot* equivalent to the English "off his rocker," but checked myself in time—"who is . . ." With a forefinger I tapped my head significantly.

Coquard understood, and it pleased him that he did. He snapped his fingers.

"Ah, yais! I know what you mean: one who is of a mentality not very O.K."

"Yes," I agreed, "one who is of a mentality not very O.K."

He opened his eyes to their widest.

"So you come to seek him *here!*" He shook his head sorrowfully. "Ah, monsieur, it is not very *chic*, that!"

Coquard was laughing at me, of course.

"Well, you know," I said, "I have a reason for thinking he may be here."

"Ah, *vous avez raison!* Like ze cat after ze mouse, you know where to look—*hein?* Now I begin to—what you call it?—smell a cat," he cried, rubbing his nose, and looking around for an audience who could enjoy the joke.

"*Vous avez le bec propre,*" I laughed, jeering in my turn.

He stared back at me stupefied, his finger still held at the side of his long, thin nose. At first I thought any reference to his nose must be as delicate a matter to him as it was to Cyrano de Bergerac. Possibly it was more delicate, for Catulle Coquard was certainly a criminal, which Cyrano was not, and all criminals are egoists and stuffed with vanity.

But now, looking back, I think it was the sudden revelation that I was familiar enough not only with French but with his own slang to use the word *bec* and not *nez* for his nose that alarmed him, and set him on his guard. Anyhow, his tone completely changed. As a matter of fact I had myself begun to smell a rat; but not so quickly as Catulle; and, as will be apparent later, it was not the same rat.

Anyway, from that moment Catulle stopped trying to be funny at my expense.

"The patron, I call him. He know where to look for zee man better zan me," he said soberly.

I let him go for Brisson; but as the place by this time had temporarily thinned out its *habitués,* I slid my glass along the bar to a point much nearer to where Brisson stood. And I did succeed in overhearing what passed between him and Coquard. That is to say, I heard many of the words used but learned nothing except that both were past masters in the use of the thieves' jargon, in which hardly a single word retains its literal and natural meaning. That they did not need to be told the identity of the man I was looking for I did, however, infer from the frequency with which the word *tripoteur* was employed. *Tripoteur!* How often had I heard the word in the mouths of poor students. For *tripoteur* stood for *usurer,* and it was as a usurer that de Quettville had been pilloried on his own gate.

When Brisson turned towards me I was holding my glass before the light, examining its colour.

"My friend tells me, sir, you come here to look for some person," he said.

"That is one reason I had for coming," I replied.

"And you have not seen him, is it?"

"Not yet."

Brisson considered a moment and then looked up.

"Possibly he is a gentleman, this one for whom you look?"

"He would certainly expect to be so regarded."

The patron smote his thigh as light came to him.

"Ah, my friend, now one sees the thing! Why, it is only the work people, sailors and such like who come here. Look you, over there, that is where gentlemen go." He pointed to a door at the far end of the bar where, now that the place was half empty, I saw a door which opened into a part of the wine shop apparently reserved for clients of a better class. Brisson smiled, at my dismayed face I suppose.

"So," he went on humorously, "if the other reason was that you needed a refreshment, you go in there and my daughter, she will give it you herself—to console you, if you do not find there him you seek," he added genially.

"Thank you," I said. "I must of course look in there too. But I ought first to give you a warning."

"A warning?" he repeated.

"Yes, it is most probable that the man I am in search of left his house in order to make an attack on you."

Brisson, hearing this, stood back from the counter, leaning up against one of the great brown varnished wine casks. But he was not really alarmed, though Coquard who was affecting to be busy with a napkin and a glass, while struggling hard to understand what was being said, appeared to think otherwise. Then Cæsar, seeing Coquard's startled eyes, laughed sonorously from the depths of his great chest.

"Attack me?" he cried. "In that case, *mon bon jeune homme,* search well for the rascal—search everywhere." He turned laughing to the perplexed Coquard. "Catulle, *mon ami,* see you, here is one who would search this house. Shall we permit it?"

Coquard came forward to stare at me.

"I like your cheeks," he nodded severely.

Brisson laughed till the tears stood in his eyes. He pushed Coquard away.

"But no, it is for one who would harm me he looks, Catulle," he explained, and then turning to me said, "You have no conception where he is, is it?"

"No," I said, "but I've undertaken to find him, and

I mean to do it." Then remembering the avocat's laughter I added, "I mean to find him, even if he is hidden in nothing bigger than the wine cask behind you."

There was a smash of glass. Turning, I saw Coquard staring like a stuck pig, the small towel shaking in his hands, and the glass he had been drying in fragments on the floor.

BRISSON burst into a sudden Gargantuan roar of laughter at the look of horror on Coquard's face. Probably he thought the dismay shown was out of all proportion to the supposed cause. I certainly did. The broken glass could not be worth more than a few pence. Several of the bystanders also laughed. Indeed, there was a very infectious quality in Cæsar Brisson's mirth. A thick-set stevedore in blue jersey and peaked cap, leaning back against the counter, turned his head to him.

"That's the second gone west since I came in 'ere," he observed.

"And the fifth to-day," Brisson nodded.

"Suppose you'll dock it off his wages all right," another suggested.

Brisson glanced playfully at Coquard.

"I might be tempted to if I paid him any," he said with a chuckle. This, however, instantly alienated sympathy from Brisson.

"Mean to say you pay no wages?" the stevedore asked, setting down his tumbler. "My Gawd, no wonder the poor feller breaks your glasses!"

The outburst drew the attention of a couple of ship's stokers standing near, and one of them, at least, seemed to have drunk himself into readiness for any kind of row. A hefty ruffian he looked too, with a pair of fierce red rimmed eyes, and a fringe of red hair showing under his rakish but dilapidated peaked cap. He however took the matter not exactly in the same way as the stevedore.

"What's this?" he cried, coming forward, "what's this I hear? Not take no wages. Let's have a look at the mug what works for nothing."

Laying his two grimy paws on the counter, he bent forward to stare at Coquard who was now standing back against the wine casks.

"What you do it for, eh?" he demanded. "That's what I wanter know. What you work for nothing for?"

His mate, a little man not so inflamed, and scenting trouble, I suppose, from previous experiences, took him by the arm.

"But it's 'ardly work, Ted, old man—handling liquor, I mean; it's not real hard work, not what *we'd* call work at all, is it now?" he suggested persuasively.

Ted, however, waved him aside.

"Sam," he said, "we'd call it a dam' sight worse than work if we had to handle it all day long for others to drink, and well you know it."

My own attention, meanwhile, was chiefly given to Coquard. Comprehending very little of the language used, at first he thought from the laughter that he was being ridiculed, and his eyes had wandered from face to face as he stood, rather like a thin, erect slug in a white apron, with a swaying, watchful head. At least if one can imagine a venomous slug, that would have been Coquard then. But when the bellicose Ted came into the picture I fancy that, while still a little bewildered, Coquard ceased to be frightened. The situation created by the stoker was one he understood. I saw his right hand slip round to his thigh as the drunken, enraged stoker faced him again, the one man full of noise and fury like a wild bull; the other, white and quiet like a reptile.

The stoker smote his fist on the counter.

"You lousy bug of a dago, you'd take the meat and drink out of the mouth of an honest Britisher, would you?"

"Easy on, Ted—not the drink," his friend expostulated.

But Ted took no heed of him, waving to Coquard and leaning as far as he could across the counter.

"Come 'ere," he cried, "come 'ere till I lay you over the bar, and wallop you with my belt."

Laughter followed this sally. No one anticipated real trouble with the counter between the two men. But Coquard did come nearer, face bent forward well in advance towards the other man's, his right hand still on his hip as if protecting the threatened part. The laughter redoubled as the pair faced each other like a pair of fighting cocks. The little fellow, Sam, however, more sober, noted the position of Coquard's right hand.

"Look out, Ted," he shrilled warningly, "the dago's got a gun."

But the big fellow was too far gone to care even had he faced a battery. He made a grab for the scruff of Coquard's neck. As his hand shot out the Frenchman, swift as lightning, struck him a resounding smack

on the cheek with the palm of his left hand. Probably
the stoker had never in his life been so struck. It was
insult more than injury, and as such infuriated him
more than a blow would have done. And Coquard
had not finished his insult. Before his enemy recovered from his surprise he spat full into his face.

"*Cochon!*" he cried, stepping back nimbly so that
the return blow fell short.

Some of those present rejoiced at the prospect of a
bit of rough and tumble when the stoker got one knee
upon the counter to go over the top for his man. No
one appeared to see any significance in the hand Coquard still kept under his apron over his thigh. They
were unused to that sort of thing. But Cæsar Brisson
seemed to know what Coquard kept in his hip pocket.
He called excitedly to me, indicating the angry stoker:
"Stop him, pull him back—queek, queek!"

But I did not move. I had no inclination to lift a
finger to save Coquard from a possible hiding. Seeing
from this that my sympathies were with the prole-
tariat, Brisson, flipping up the counter flap, came round
and got the stoker by the coat collar just as he was
about to drop over to the other side. With one hand
the man was yanked back to the proper side of the
counter. Once there Cæsar slewed him round, and
forcing both arms behind his back, got ready to frog
march him to the door. The stoker, however, was
not yet finished. His right foot swung forward for a
mighty back-heel drive at Brisson's shins. Quick as he
was, Brisson was quicker. For at the very moment the
man stood on one leg he was sent flying to the floor on

his face, all helter skelter, in about as awkward and nasty a tumble as I ever saw. This was too much for his mate, Sam. Lowering his head he ran like a butting ram straight for Brisson as he stood smiling down at the dazed man. And now it was Cæsar who was taken by surprise, for the little man's head got him fair on the pit of the stomach, and down they both went in a heap, the little stoker on top.

That, however, was the end of his triumph. And it must be admitted that there was much to admire in the good humoured way Brisson took the indignity put upon him. Not a sign of temper was visible as he laid one arm over the small man, pinning him down, while he himself got to his feet. Then, picking up the other by the leather belt round his waist, Cæsar carried him to the door much as if he were a coal bucket, to deposit him outside. After that most of us, in open mouthed silence, watched him set the big fellow on his feet with no appearance of extra effort, and lead him, dazed and obedient, to the door. That done, he came back to us with a smile, wiping his hands with a handkerchief.

"They will be good boys next time," he pronounced.

I thought this very likely.

Brisson, instead of returning to his position behind the counter, approached me.

"Very fonny, *hein?*" he smiled confidentially. "But you will see how leetle have I need for a warning." He gave me a familiar—an over-familiar—finger dig in the ribs. "Nozzing to fear from my old brother-in-law, eh?"

I somehow contrived not to flinch. He stood so

close up to me, his black eyes mirthful from utter self-assurance.

"No," I agreed, "nothing to fear from him."

"Good; it is agreed." He took my arm. "Then come and have a drink. This is no place for you."

With this last statement I was now in entire agreement.

"Still," I said as we proceeded towards the superior bar, "you never know, you know. That little fellow you carried out, he took you by surprise."

Brisson snapped his fingers contemptuously.

"But even so did not I carry him out and drop him in the gutter? *Pah*, I know how to—what you call it?—look out for Nombre One!"

For some time, ever, that is, since the good Catulle had dropped and smashed the glass, a vague uneasiness had been gnawing its way into my mind. To define the feeling more exactly, or to connect it with any adequate cause, was at that moment beyond me. At first the feeling of vague disquiet had several causes, but I believe it began with the perception that Catulle Coquard both feared and hated me for no reason then apparent. And this fact, when associated with the impression I had of having seen him somewhere or other before our first meeting on the island, set my head whirling with the wildest speculations. That Coquard was a dangerous rascal admitted of no doubt. His familiarity with the lingo of the Paris *apache* proved it. But that fact about him did not stand alone. Sam, the stoker, had shouted a warning that Coquard had a gun in his hip pocket. He was wrong there.

He had no gun; but he had a weapon, nevertheless; and it was because I knew what that weapon was that I knew just where Coquard hailed from, and what his habits were in such matters.

Yet, struggle as I did, I could recall no previous contact with him; and it troubled me much, for well I knew the danger of being feared and hated by one of his type. It would have meant a speedy end for me in his own *quartier*, even supposing I were no more to him than a passing inconvenience. But by this time I suspected I was much more than that. My head, in fact, was in a whirl with a variety of new possibilities connected with the disappearance of Hilaire de Quettville. And though I felt I might yet find him—felt indeed I had come very near to finding him—not now did I think I would find him alive. But that was a conclusion at which I arrived later in the evening. Had it come sooner it is unlikely that Cæsar Brisson would have been able to lead me so tamely into the room reserved for his better-class customers.

It was, however, neither the room nor the customers that took my eye as I stood on the two steps down into the smaller room. What first took my eye was what would have inevitably taken the eye of any man, and that was the sight of Judith Brisson behind the bar. To say that she, for the moment, banished the thoughts about de Quettville then whirling in my head, is to give the measure of that first impression.

Le Marinel's story about her in that place had aroused my interest. He had told me that Brisson, though proud of the girl, had put her to serve in the bar in order to provoke de Quettville. I now remembered wondering what the girl herself would think about it, and decided that much would depend on whether she had more of the de Quettvilles in her than of Brisson. And now, looking at her talking to a customer as she stood in easy attitude behind the bar, one hand poised on her hip and the other holding a long stemmed red rose which she was coquettishly passing before her lips and tilted chin, I judged her to be all Brisson. A dark, handsome wench would suffice as her description: unmistakably French from her mass of black hair, the colour repeated in her eyes, arched eyebrows and dress, with a dead white skin, and a mouth more vividly red than the rose, but made so by art, not by nature. She certainly did not look out of place there. A small mirror stood on the shelf behind her for consultation when required.

When Brisson shut the door behind me and returned to his own department I hesitated. My notion had been that he meant to present me to his daughter. Besides the man engaging her in talk, a thick-set fellow in plus fours lolling against the counter, there were but three other men present in the snug little room, two at a table with their heads together, evidently intent on some private matter, and a young man by himself at the table in the corner. As I reached the counter the girl turned to me, putting her rose down and raising her eyebrows interrogatively, exactly like Brisson. I had not thought what my drink was to be. Abruptly the man at my elbow shot out a huge fist and grabbed the rose, holding it high above his head as she made a vain attempt to recover it. He stood back, broke off the long stem, and put the flower in his buttonhole, laughingly watching her.

"Oh, Mr. Drury," she cried in dismay, clasping her hands, "you 'ave spoilt it."

"Then you won't want it back?"

"But yes, yes; give it to me."

He lifted a finger at her waggishly.

"Ah, that means you *did* get it from some man."

"Mr. Drury, give it to me," she pleaded.

Mr. Drury shook his head.

"I don't give things away for nothing," he said, lifting the lapel of his jacket to sniff elaborately at the flower.

As if this action conveyed a suggestion, the girl produced and held up a small, squat, glass-stoppered bottle.

"Look," she said, persuasively, "I'll give you some of this for it—*Bouquet de l'Ile*. Give me your handkerchief."

Mr. Drury seemed to see he had gone far enough. He removed the flower.

"Call me George first," he demanded, holding back.

"George," she repeated, eagerly extending her hand. But it was the handkerchief he first gave her; and presently there floated my way, not the crude scent I expected, but a fresh, yet delicate perfume, pervasive yet not violent, that reminded me not of boudoirs or bars but of wild flowers in dewy fields at night. The girl held her recovered rose by the inch of stem that remained.

"It is quite spoiled now," she said.

Mr. Drury laughed.

"Stick it in your hair," he advised. "Just above the ear, that's where the pretty brown girls in the Pacific put their flowers. I've seen them."

She turned to me at last.

"Something soft," I said.

"A Pussyfoot?" she suggested.

"What's that?"

"Oh, grenadine, with orange and a few other things."

"Just what I want. Do I get a straw with it?"

"Yes," she nodded with a smile, "you drink it through a straw."

Mr. Drury gave a grunt of derision or contempt. While she was mixing the ingredients of my drink I picked up a book lying face downwards on the counter, which she had evidently been reading before Mr. Drury began his *badinage*. I remember wondering what the French equivalent would be to the type of fiction favoured by an English barmaid. Gyp or Collette probably. But had the book been the Bible itself I could not have been more surprised, for it was Pascal's *Pensèes*. At my involuntary whistle she turned her head and the man wheeled round and saw me with the volume in my hand.

"A bit naughty, eh?" he sniggered.

He was a big, hulking fellow, in the mid thirties, and his face had that rough, scrubbed looking freshness often seen in the hard liver who drinks too much and tries to wipe out the traces.

"You don't read French then?" I suggested.

"Not me! My dad was a parson, and I had a careful upbringing."

"You don't say so!"

He did not seem to know his own kind of cheap chaff except when he himself used it.

"Fact, I assure you," he replied with a wink to the girl. "But he died suddenly and left me an orphan."

"And his work unfinished?"

The ripple of laughter from the girl set him blinking, and his mood changed from the jocose to the quarrelsome.

"Look here," he said with fuddled gravity, "you go away, I don't like you. What right have you to butt in when I'm talking to this lady?" He waved an imperious hand, raising his voice. "You go away, or you'll find out, as others have done, that I'm not a man to be trifled with."

Well, as I had received my big glass with the straw, and had no desire just then to trifle with any one, I turned away and sat down near the young man at the corner table. Seeing me look about for a place for my glass he pushed aside the ash tray and removed his hat from the table, an invitation in his eyes. He had nice, candid eyes and a sensitive, humorous mouth. But though he seemed disposed to talk I, having a mighty lot to think about just then, gave him merely a stiff nod of thanks, and the almost eager look of expectancy died from his youthful ingenuous face. In a few seconds I had ceased to be conscious of his proximity.

How much must be decided within the next few minutes! All my theories about the disappearance of de Quettville had been shaken since entering the wine shop, and I needed time in which to consider the facts which had disturbed those theories. Indeed, I had to consider whether or no, not my own theories only but also those of Carey and Sullivant were not equally far away from actual fact.

In trying to reconstruct and weigh the various incidents which had happened I began with Coquard's accidental dropping of the wine glass. That rascal dropped the glass on hearing me tell Brisson I meant to search everywhere for de Quettville. No! not for de Quettville, but for a missing man whose name had not been so far mentioned. But Brisson, at least, knew who the man was. I had declared that I intended to search every hole and corner and had added, looking about for a simile and seeing Brisson's background, even if it were a place no bigger than a wine cask. On that the glass smashed to the floor. But was it not a pure accident? Coquard had already, as the stevedore remarked, dropped a glass. There was nothing to prove that was not an accident. I wished I had heard just why and how the first came to be broken. And if Brisson spoke the truth when he said it was the fifth his henchman had dropped that day, it merely revealed the condition of Coquard's nerves, for it was incredible that this could be a daily occurrence.

But though I believed the stevedore about the first glass I did not believe Brisson about the five. But there was something far farther from a natural explanation in the way he had handled the situation after

Coquard's misadventure with the glass. As I saw it, Coquard, listening with all his ears, as he undoubtedly had been, but with an imperfect understanding of English, to what passed between Cæsar and myself, might have come to the conclusion that I knew much more than was actually the case; and the fear previously shown deepened into panic, *because* he himself had some degree of responsibility for de Quettville's disappearance.

It was then that my feeling of active disquiet began, an uneasiness that only deepened when I saw the adroit manner in which Brisson seized on, and developed, the stevedore's intervention to obliterate any suspicion Coquard's panic might have roused in my mind. And if his subsequent talk with me was not intended to see if he had achieved that end, it looked very like it. "Nozzing to fear from my very old brother-in-law, eh?" he had remarked challengingly after throwing out the stoker. He certainly had not in the sense in which I had warned him—if de Quettville were dead. But it was my belief that Brisson spoke as he had to find out if I really did entertain any suspicion of—of what? Foul play? Anyhow I felt glad that I had obeyed the instinct telling me to allow him to show me into the reserved bar. This might well allay any suspicion he might have. That, at least, is what I hoped. For he would not conceive that any one with my suspicion would linger on in his wine shop. So I recognized that it was a sound instinct which had guided me at that moment, although I had felt when the door shut gently behind me much as if it were a prison door, had I not found others also there.

Looking up to reassure myself they were still there, I found the pleasant faced young man staring at me. I was rather abashed when our eyes met, and he pointed to my forgotten drink.

"You'll excuse me," he said, "but it's seldom I see a man in such profound meditation."

This naïveté disarmed me. I took a pull through the straw in the large tumbler.

"I was just thinking."

He bent forward questioningly.

"About how you could get square with that fellow at the bar?"

"No, about what is going to happen next."

"Gee, you must be a bigger stranger to this island than I am."

"Why?"

"Why, not to have seen already that this is the sort of place where nothing ever happens."

Now this was rather like hearing one's own voice issuing out of another man's lips.

"That's what I thought last Thursday."

"And right you were," he nodded.

"No; quite wrong."

He sat up.

"Wrong?"

"Absolutely. It's the sort of place where anything may happen. In fact, such queer things have been happening that, as I told you, I'm left wondering what is to happen next."

He looked me all over, not omitting to throw a swift glance at my glass. Having apparently satisfied himself that I was neither trying to be funny, nor speaking out of an alcoholically stimulated imagination, he seemed yet more perplexed.

"Say," he said plaintively, "I don't know what you're getting at; but sitting there just now you looked as dull and desolate as a Methodist parson considering the collection on a wet Sunday night."

"I was wondering whether I'd be murdered when I stepped outside."

Some instinct told me it was safe to be frank with the clear eyed young stranger; but it was not instinct alone that induced me to speak out. It is said you can never take an American citizen by surprise, and an impulse to make the attempt led me into this recklessness. Surprised he may have been, but he showed more pleasure than surprise. His face lit up like a lamp.

"Reach any conclusion?" he whispered hopefully.

"I did. Do you want to hear it?"

"Sure."

"I believe I'll be all right if I don't leave this place alone."

He shoved his hand across the table.

"Count on me! Gee, this is just like being back home again!"

That was all. The handgrip dispelled the qualm that rose in me the moment after I had so rashly spoken. But it was his clear, candid eyes that made me trust him. The validity of all our judgments de-

pends on our ability to make comparisons; and after
Coquard's shifty little pig's eyes, and Cæsar Brisson
with, as I suspected, all the malice of a devil lurking
behind the affected good humour, I knew I could rely
on this man. Besides, there was no one else; and by
this time I felt I was in deep waters, and had been
ever since I so innocently entered that infernal wine
shop.

My new friend leaned over the table to whisper
rapidly.

"Is it that guy chinning with the girl?"

"No, the two men in the bar, especially the small
man, Coquard by name. He's done something, and
he thinks I know. He's frightened; and I know what
his sort does when that happens."

"It's nothing you've done then?"

"Heavens, no! It's something he thinks I've discovered. But all I actually know is that there is certainly something about him, and about this place, that
needs to be discovered, and I'd be sorry to die before
I've done it."

"Right you are, boy," he replied heartily. "Just say
right away what I'm to do."

That was talking!

"First of all," I said, "go out there as if you were
leaving and see what the pair are up to."

He lit a cigarette and rose.

"That's letting me in easy. But I'll leave my case
here so's I can come back to collect it."

We took leave of each other in the offhand manner
of chance acquaintances, and he bowed to the girl at

the bar on his way to the door. The man with her had of course his back towards us, but he did not turn. I observed his head go up as the girl smiled, and noticed now that the angle at which her mirror stood had been changed. Whether by design or accident, it had been changed so as to include the corner in which we sat. The mirror was there, doubtless, for her own use, but whether or no her companion had been using it to spy on us, I could not tell. If so, its position must have been altered not by him but by the girl. What I did know was that although she had frequently looked over at our corner the man had never once turned, though it was only now when I saw how that little mirror caught the light at its new angle, I knew that to see us he had no need to turn round. Yet in the next breath I was telling myself that all this was no more than the product of an imagination overheated by the night's events. The more probable explanation must be that the girl had taken up the mirror with no more sinister motive than to apply some powder to her nose, and the angle at which it now stood was the angle at which she had set it down not by design but by accident.

So my thoughts flew back to where I then believed the real danger lay. That any attack would be made on me in the wine shop itself was highly improbable, since too many people had seen me there, and if I, too, disappeared the fact of my being last seen in the wine shop would be easily established. There was, in fact, scarcely any safer place for me just then than the wine shop. But the trouble, if trouble there was to be, would come as soon as I stepped outside. So at least the situation appeared to me then; and I began to wonder what was happening on the other side of the door.

I had asked the young American to see what the pair were up to; but now I did not think he would find both men there. If Brisson were the absent one I thought it not unlikely that I might get a knock on the head somewhere in the dark as I took my way along the deserted quay, after which it would be as easy for him to drop me into the harbour as it had been for him to drop the drunken stoker into the gutter. The perception of that possibility made me sit up, remembering Brisson's attempt to get me to interfere with that same stoker. Had this been in his mind as early in the evening as that? Whether or no, it was obvious what conclusion would be formed if my body were found in the harbour after I had been engaged in a brawl with a drink-maddened stoker in a quay wine shop.

Luckily for me, my instinct against Coquard had kept me unresponsive to Brisson's call, and so the attempt to involve me failed. But this, I fancied, only meant that another method would be employed, and a more subtle agent—Coquard probably. Coquard who was as familiar, doubtless, with the latest murder methods as he was with the latest words in the *apache* vocabulary. Of the two I would much rather have to face Brisson. But my conclusion was that Coquard would be the man waiting for his chance somewhere outside in the dark. I resolved to avoid those labyrinthine back passages I had partly explored, and take my way home along the quay which though almost as dark, was much more open.

The next moment my ally came hastily stumbling down the two steps into the room, feeling in his pockets.

"Say, Scottie," he addressed me, "you haven't got your foot on my cigarette case, have you now? I 'pear to have dropped it in your vicinity."

He was evidently enjoying his part. Looking round the table, I picked the case off the seat he had occupied just as the man at the bar wheeled round to look at me, his eyes now fishy from liquor.

"Getting into trouble again, are you?" he said with mock severity, wagging a finger at me. "Bad boy, ver' bad boy. Knew at once you hadn't been well brought up."

"Anyway, I do not put my feet on chairs," I said with affected coldness, handing the case to its owner.

"But what about your nose?" the bully over at the bar demanded. "Don't you occasionally put that where it isn't wanted?"

The American boy's laugh induced me to make an extraordinarily foolish retort.

"Yes, sometimes; but on the other hand I occasionally put something else where it is very badly wanted."

"Such as?" he sneeringly inquired.

"The toe of my boot."

It was the girl who saved the situation. Just as the fellow with clenched fists was about to make a rush at me, she leant forward over the bar and caught one of his wrists.

"Mr. Drury," she cried, "none of that now."

"Let go, Judy, let go."

He struggled to free his hand, and once again we might have had an ugly brawl but for the opportune entrance of a jovial party of friends, apparently anxious to get in a last drink before closing time. They were all talking at once, and under cover of their merry babble Miss Brisson, with a significant look and quick gesture of her free hand, indicated the exit. Although it was to the American she signalled, I obeyed promptly enough when he took my arm. Not that I was afraid of Mr. Drury. All the past season I had played as a second row forward for the Scottish at Richmond, and as I was still hard with training my notion was that I could have sent that drink-sodden ruffian to the floor with one hand behind my back. Fortunately, however, I had also a notion that one must not figure in a public house brawl while looking after another man's practice. Besides, had I not enough trouble on hand already, waiting for me out there in the person of either Coquard or Brisson?

So as soon as the American youth pushed me through the door I looked along the length of the bar with keen curiosity, remembering that whichever of the pair we found absent would probably indicate the kind of danger which, but for the presence of my new-found friend, I would have been compelled to face.

Then the surprise came. Both Brisson and Coquard were there, busily attending to the closing-time rush orders. But not so busy as to miss seeing us as we threaded our way for the exit. Cæsar smiled to me

over the bent heads at the counter. He seemed pleased
with himself.

"Good night," I called back.

"*Au revoir*," he returned with a wave of the hand
and another show of gleaming teeth.

As for the good Catulle, if he did not smile his adieu
at least he no longer scowled; which for him was probably an equivalent.

I left the wine shop feeling very foolish and perplexed. My perplexity arose from the fact that I
could not account for the change in these two men.
Something had happened, something *must* have happened while I was in the other room. If Coquard had
dreaded something before, he certainly had in the interval got rid of his fear. That was my first thought.
But the second came close on its heels—the conviction
that I had made a wonderful fool of myself that night.

We had walked some distance before I became conscious that the young American was at my side, and
the recollection of all I had said to him about the danger that threatened me, filled me with shame. I *felt*
him laughing at me, and at the moment would have
welcomed an attack as a justification for the elaborate
precautions I had taken to get away safely. We had
covered some distance before, I suppose, he mastered
his amusement sufficiently to trust his voice.

"Say," he whispered, touching my arm, "when does
the attack begin?"

But under his solemnity I could detect his mirth.

"Oh, go to the devil!" I retorted, turning away, and
marching off up St. Julian's Avenue. He did not fol-

low. Possibly this black ingratitude left him rooted to the spot. I did not look back to see.

On reaching home I paused on the doorstep, latch-key in hand, debating whether to enter at once, or to work off my depression with a smart walk before turning in. It was late, the house was already asleep, the roads empty. But my sense of fatigue made an easy chair and a book more inviting. I turned round to insert the latch-key. Then, as I leant down to find the keyhole there came an odd kind of thud on the door. It was as if some one on the inside had struck one sharp blow on the panel. Involuntarily I stood up to listen, and as I did so a quick rustle from the laurel shrubbery by the gate made me wheel round. No one, perhaps, escapes that slight thrill of alarm when, in the dark, unexpected noises come, especially if they come from different directions, and the cause is unseen.

For an instant I felt surrounded. I watched the shrubbery keenly. When the silence continued, feeling sure that nothing lurked there but a prowling cat, I turned again to the door—and then discovered what it was that Catulle Coquard carried at his hip. Deep into the panel of the door, and still quivering, stuck a long, thin-bladed knife. Luckily for me, at the moment it was thrown I chanced to bend down to find the unfamiliar keyhole. But for that the knife would be quivering between my ribs.

For perhaps fifteen seconds I stared hard at that knife. Then a flash of thought connected it with the rustling I had heard among the shrubs, and wheeling round, I leaped towards the gate. For I knew from that sound that the skulking scoundrel was bolting after observing his throw had missed.

Out on the road, however, seeing no one I was forced to stop and listen, since I could not tell whether he had gone to right or left. Down the road I heard the sound of feet on the pavement; but the footsteps were those of a man walking, and in less than a minute I could tell he was coming towards me. So my ear went in the other direction: it was the sound of running feet I wanted.

Somewhere up the road a dog suddenly rent the silence by a burst of furious barking. Taking the cue, I headed up as hard as I could go, and when the barking burst out afresh as I shot past a house some two hundred yards ahead, I judged that the hint given me by the dog was a good one.

Confident that I could run my man down, I made the pace as hot as any I had ever pulled out, and flaming with anger, pictured to myself the leap I would take on his back the moment I got within range. Unfortunately, however, it was not a question of speed, or even of stamina since long before I got really tested in wind or leg I had to draw up at the Vauvert crossing to ascertain which of the possible three roads had been taken by the fugitive.

Precious seconds had to be squandered as I again stood straining to catch the sound of running feet. And this time there was no friendly dog to signal to me. So hearing nothing, I had to take a chance, this time with the odds two to one against me. I took the left road because there was a turn in it a little way ahead which might have prevented me from hearing him, and because, unlike the other two, it led back to the heart of the town. But by the time I dropped into Trinity Square I knew pursuit to be hopeless. There were too many twists and turns, too many odd corners, archways, side streets, and garden gates, in that neighbourhood and the odds now were that I was running away from, rather than overtaking, the man. Recognizing this after I stopped for a breather under Trinity Church, I reluctantly turned up Allez Street, towards home. And once the heat of the chase died down I saw that short of catching the blackguard red handed on the spot there was perhaps little use in catching him a mile or so away from the scene of his abortive attempt.

But there was still his knife in the door to connect him with that attempt. That same knife, with certain suspicions I could not now dislodge from my mind, I proposed to lay before the Chief Constable next morning. Coquard, if Coquard it was, had blundered badly in making this attack. I had left the wine shop inclined to regard myself as a fanciful, over-suspicious fool who had been reading sinister significance into words and actions all capable of a natural and innocent interpretation. And now by this attempt Coquard had revived and confirmed my worst suspicions. It was he who was the fool, not me: he was one of that worst kind of fool, the fool who cannot leave well alone. Thus by the time I reached home my self-esteem had triumphantly re-established itself from the shock it had earlier received.

But a new shock awaited me—a shock which proved that I had been fooled after all. And the shock awaited me on the doorstep. For as soon as I reached the step I saw that the knife was no longer in the door! Not for a second did I doubt whose hand had pulled it out. As I stared at the deep incision left where it had penetrated the wood I am bound to say I could not recall a moment in my life when I felt so cheap. Actually I had been got to run away from, instead of after, the would-be assassin. That dog up the road, it was probably only a stray cat in his own shrubbery that had set him off roaring his indignation into space. And all the time there was another cat lurking in my own shrubbery—a cat indeed!

It was long before sleep came to me that night. At first I strove to remember what I knew of knife-throwing. Once or twice in hospital I had come across cases in which, on some foreign ship then in dock, the knife had been so used. Not many cases, for though the art of throwing is difficult, it is, in expert hands, deadly, and the result, nine times out of ten, is merely

a concern for the coroner. But I had always understood that the knife-throwing was practised only in
Southern latitudes. Never had I heard of its use by the
Paris *apache,* partial as he naturally is to the silent
knife in a city so wakeful, so crowded, and so well
policed. Yet how useful in Paris the thrown knife
could be in the hands of one who had elsewhere
acquired the art! Especially among the brethren of
the knife themselves when they fell out. What an
advantage it gave the man who had learned to throw!
He had at his command the virtues of both knife and
gun, with the defects of both abolished. He could,
that is, kill without risking an encounter at close quarters, and yet silently without any noisy detonation.

That had been the notion of how things were to go
with me! And now as certain other matters wove their
way into my mind it did not seem such a bad notion
after all. For if I had not happened to stoop unexpectedly merely to find a keyhole set rather low in
the door and still unfamiliar to me, there was no doubt
in my own mind after seeing the position and depth of
the cut, that the attempt would certainly have succeeded. Then after he had withdrawn the long knife
from my back what would have remained to connect
him with the crime? Investigation would establish,
of course, the fact that I had spent a considerable time
at the Perigord wine shop, that early in the evening
there had been a brawl with a stoker at which I had
been present, that, later, I had myself a quarrel with
another man which led to the intervention of Miss

Brisson who had signalled me to leave, and that I had left in the company of a stranger who appeared to be an American.

Where in all this was there anything to direct one breath of suspicion on Coquard? The American? Catulle could certainly not have reckoned on my making such prompt confidences to a stranger. But supposing this American tourist left next morning, as from his boredom seemed very likely, he would be the first man for whom the police would search, since he was the last in whose company I had been seen. And supposing he repeated all I said to him of my suspicions of an attack by either Coquard or Brisson he would only increase his own danger, for it would be held to be, and would assuredly sound like, a cock and bull story invented to divert suspicion elsewhere.

It amazed me to recognize how suspicion might point to any one rather than Coquard. Evidence could even be obtained that this American had accused me of trying to purloin his cigarette case! Even the bellicose stoker, so obviously spoiling for a fight with any one who would fight him, would be suspect before the good Catulle.

Coquard, no doubt, had perceived all this, recognized his chance and promptly taken it. My respect for him deepened. I had acted like an idiot throughout. Above all when I allowed him to retrieve that knife, which was the one thing that could connect him with the attempt. He had known his danger when his throw failed; but his nerve did not fail, and I was convinced he deliberately made that rustle among the

bushes by the gate, calculating to a nicety the moment
or two it would take me to realize the significance of
the noise, just long enough to let him slip inside the
next gate. Then when he saw me charging past like
an angry bull he coolly returned to recover the one
damning piece of evidence against himself. I had been
no more than a child in his hands. And in admitting
the fact to myself, I set my teeth in the pillow, in helpless mortification, much indeed as a child might have
done.

But that night I did not sleep like a child. For
hours I lay awake, reconsidering the situation, tossing
and turning sleeplessly. Ultimately I reached the conclusion that at whatever cost to my personal pride I
must lay all my suspicions before the local authorities.
But it wasn't going to be easy. For I would have to
begin by admitting I had been totally mistaken in my
assertion that de Quettville was alive. And that admission of error made a poor foundation on which to
gain credence for the theory I had to advance as to the
manner of his death. Indeed, it was a wild theory in
itself, so wild that I myself doubted whether it was not
born out of the distorted workings of a sleepless and
overwrought brain. In a word, I was now convinced
that Brisson and Coquard between them had made
away with de Quettville, that de Quettville's body lay
somewhere in the wine shop when I entered, but had
been somehow disposed of before I left, Coquard having become certain I knew more than I in fact did
know.

Such were the conclusions arrived at as I lay and

considered all that had happened that night; but I wondered whether it would all look so plain in the cold light of morning. I was rather diffident about theories by this time, having formed so many that had gone wrong.

When morning came, however, my resolve to communicate my new theory to Le Marinel stood unchanged. He might turn down my suspicions as he and the police had turned down my opinion as to de Quettville's mental condition. That I could not help. But it galled me to think of that knife! That knife would have spoken for itself! As it was, I had only suspicions, and if in his lawyer-like fashion Le Marinel asked for concrete facts, I had, once again, only opinions to offer.

Then as I sat so thinking I remembered with a thrill of relief that it was Sunday. Le Marinel would not be at his office. Of course I could have as easily gone to his house in the Rue Galette, but I seized as eagerly at a day's respite from a humiliating interview with the lawyer as I would from an equally painful interview with any dentist. On the other hand, a full day's quiet meditation might yield something more tangible than vague suspicions. I knew that to call in the police, and point to a hole in the door made by a knife which I had seen but for a moment while searching for a keyhole after spending a whole evening in a wine shop would be more likely to damage my character than to convince them of that knife's reality. Carey himself, I gathered, thought me too fanciful an alarmist in my theories already.

But the day closed with a curious incident which had unforeseen consequences. I had gone to bed rather early, somewhere about half past ten, and was trying to induce sleep with a book, when the telephone at my bedside rang sharply. A night call is never a welcome sound. I dropped the book and stretched out for the receiver with a groan.

"Allo, allo, is that Dr. Wright?" A voice of high-pitched feminine quality was at my ear.

"No," I responded. "Dr. Wright is away. Dr. Dunn, his *locum,* speaking."

"Then," the voice came quickly and in considerable agitation, "Mrs. le Noury of Rozel, Torteval, she has had another seizure of heart; will you at once come, please?"

Even with less knowledge than I possessed of the island's geography I could have told that Torteval was situated in some remote part where the country folk spoke English with an idiom more or less French. This was hard luck! Wright had told me he had only about three country patients on his books, and this was the second country call, the first being de Quettville, also a night visit, as I well remembered. Wright had taken away his car too. Then as I was remembering all this the voice came again.

"If it is that you cannot yourself come, will you send anozzer doctor, please?"

That settled it. After all, I was there to look after Wright's patients.

"All right," I replied. "I'll come at once. Just ring off and I'll call up the garage for a car."

"Oh, but we send the car for you, doctor."

"You are sending a car?"

"But yais, doctor. Indeed it has already left. It is so—so urgent, and your garage man, he might not quickly find the house."

With a word of thanks I replaced the receiver and jumped out of bed. But as I was getting into my clothes a thought made me ring up the exchange.

"Give me Rozel, Torteval, Mrs. le Noury, please. I'm sorry but I haven't the number."

After a long pause the girl's voice came.

"Sorry, but they do not appear to be on the telephone."

"But," I expostulated, "you put through a call to this number from that very address not three minutes ago."

Another pause, shorter this time.

"The call we put through to your number came from a public telephone office."

"In Torteval?"

"No, Smith Street."

That indeed startled me. Here was something queer. For Smith Street was not more than six minutes' walk from where I stood. Was the call a hoax? Perhaps. There are adult fools who think it funny to ring a fire alarm, and call out the fire brigade, just as there are small boys who ring front door bells and run away. Still, neither doctors nor the fire brigades dares assume any call to be a hoax. So telling myself that the arrival of the car would settle the question, I went on with my hurried preparations. Torteval, I

understood, was about six miles out, and if the car
had already left—a sudden thought made me stop and
straighten up. The next instant I was down the stairs,
and into the consulting room, whirling the pages of the
case-book Wright had left for my guidance. This
brought another fact to light: Dr. Wright had no
patient named le Noury in Torteval. More than
that, Dr. Wright had no patient anywhere of the name
of le Noury.

Uneasiness deepened before the new questions that
now faced me. Why had the call not come direct from
the house in Torteval? Who was the person who
had rung me up from St. Peter Port? How did that
person know that the car had already left? Plausible
explanations of these peculiarities I could perceive;
but I did not believe in them.

Not that I took the call to be a bad joke. That the
car would come I now felt assured. When it did I
would have a good look at it, get its number, and see
who was in it, for I thought it very likely that it would
contain one other besides the driver.

But the car did not come. Till well beyond midnight I stood watching the empty road from an upper
window. The road remained empty. Then I thought
I knew what had happened. This was no hoax. Not
at least, in the ordinary sense. Unlike the little boy,
the caller had not rung my bell and then run away.
On the contrary he had, with admirable caution and
foresight, hung on to the line, overheard my question
to the exchange, heard the information thus elicited,
saw the dawning of my suspicions, foresaw the steps

I would take to verify those suspicions—and stopped the car in time!

But how nearly I had been caught on the hop! If only the sick call method had been tried before that knife throwing incident which had made me so much more alert and wary, I might so easily have walked into the trap. That was plain. What, however, remained inexplicable was why there should be a trap for *me* at all.

Then as I paced up and down feeling helpless and exasperated, I remembered the one man of my acquaintance capable of flooding daylight on the whole business. Wright had suggested I might care to have a friend over for a week or two, and I had thanked him without ever thinking of taking advantage of his offer. But now I recalled the offer with more gratitude. So there and then I sat down and wrote to McNab telling him not only what a delightful place this island in the Channel was, but also giving him enough of the facts about my perplexities to whet his appetite for more.

Francis McNab was not the intimate friend Wright no doubt had in his mind; indeed at our first encounter when I was attempting to shield a blind friend of mine who had got himself into sore trouble, we were in opposite camps. But the respect I had then developed for his talents as a detective made me sure he was the one man I knew with the capacity for the moment's need.

NEXT morning before breakfast I went to the post office and expressed my letter to McNab. At the same time I sent a wire to prepare him for its arrival. Having satisfied myself that the letter would be delivered in sufficient time, if he were free and willing, to allow him to catch the boat train at Waterloo that night and be in Guernsey on Tuesday morning, I strolled home with an easier mind. That he would find the case attractive I did not doubt. Moreover, after reading over the letter in the morning I had added a postscript with reference to the knife-throwing incident and the disappearance of de Quettville which would, I knew, draw McNab as surely as honey draws a wasp.

So I was thinking as I paused on the step to look at that cut in the door, my one tangible bit of evidence, when the gate clicked. Turning, I saw Le Marinel. His haste, a trace of excitement on his face, as well as the early hour, told me something was up. He shook my hand so warmly too, and for that, remembering that our parting had been rather warm in a less pleasant sense, I was unprepared.

"Dunn," he began, "I'm so glad to find you at home."

Wondering, I told him I had not even begun breakfast yet.

"All right," he nodded. "I'll come in and watch you eat it while you watch me eat my own words."

This mystified me indeed. But without more ado I led him inside. I did not however sit down to breakfast.

"First of all," he began with his eyes on the floor, "I owe you an apology."

"You don't for laughing at me last night!" I interjected, disconcerted, since I was now aware how well his amusement had been justified.

He looked up in his bird-like fashion.

"Did I laugh last night? Well, I'm not laughing this morning."

"Neither am I for that matter. In fact I was coming to see you myself if you hadn't come," I said uneasily, preparing to admit my blunder about de Quettville.

Le Marinel, however, seemed not to hear me, and I was astonished now to see he was as uncomfortable as myself. The next moment he was giving me the shock of my life.

"You were entirely right, and Sullivant completely wrong about de Quettville," he said quietly, "he *is* alive."

"Alive?"

"Yes; he has been seen."

After a moment I got back enough breath to stammer a question.

"Where—when—by whom?"

"At Perigord, by the housekeeper, Mrs. Bichard

and the maid, Alice Mauger, at about a quarter to four this morning. He has been in hiding, of course, exactly as you said, and he evidently still is. Even Carey is now satisfied about that."

I dropped into a chair, motioning Le Marinel to another; but he was blind to my gesture.

"Go on," I implored.

"The message from Mrs. Bichard was brought to Carey by a man Tozer, a grower who came in about six-thirty with a consignment of tomatoes for the cargo boat. Tozer said the housekeeper had come round to his place just after five, while he was loading the cases on his cart, and told him she had seen her master in the garden an hour earlier, and asking him to inform me or Carey. My place not being open, Tozer went and saw Torode at the chief's office, and the sergeant rang up Carey who got out of bed and dashed out to Perigord. Well, the old woman's story is that just before dawn she found herself suddenly awake. It was, she said, as if some one had touched her. She could not say what it was, only that she started up out of deep sleep, completely awake.

"She lay awake for some time till, in fact, there was sufficient light to let her see that the hands of her clock stood at five to four. She turned over, and was going off to sleep again, when she heard a noise like, she says, something falling. It frightened her, but she admits she has been jumpy ever since de Quettville disappeared. Anyhow she got up and went to rouse Alice, the maid, whose room is near the top of the

stairs. She found the girl was sitting up in bed ter-
rified. She had heard noises downstairs and now absolutely refused to move.

"The girl's terror communicated itself to the housekeeper, and after locking themselves in Mrs. Bichard
sat down on the bed to listen, while they waited for
daylight. The girl got up after the door was locked,
and was putting on some clothes near the window when
she startled Mrs. Bichard with a sudden cry. The old
woman got off the bed, and hurried to the window
through which Alice was staring.

"It was much clearer outside, not daylight but growing lighter every minute, and she saw a figure crossing
towards the stables. She recognized her master at
once. So did Alice Mauger. Carey found both women
positive about that; and the point to note is that the
recognition was independent; Carey found there was
no suggestion from one to the other as to who it was—
both women independently recognized de Quettville.
They both said they knew him at once. Pressed as to
the points on which she founded her recognition the
girl said she first plainly saw his face and his beard
when he turned as if to see if he were being followed;
while the housekeeper declared she who had known
him for thirty years, could not be mistaken about her
master; and there was light enough for her to notice
that he was wearing the clothes in which, as Carey got
out of her, he must have gone away."

"Carey is satisfied with the identification?" I inquired.

"He cannot doubt it. Mrs. Bichard knows her

master better than any one. Besides, the girl saw
him first and it was her inarticulate cry that drew Mrs.
Bichard to the window. He was thus recognized
simultaneously but independently by the two women."

"But surely they went after him?"

"Oh, yes. At least Mrs. Bichard followed at once;
the girl it seems delayed to get on a few more garments. The out-buildings round the end of which they
had seen him vanish are close to a grassy lane between
high hedges, a lane which if one goes right, passes
Mère Trouteaud's cottage and eventually leads down
to the seashore, while if you take the left, you join
the main road not far from the church.

"Mrs. Bichard scrambled through the hedge and
ran down the bank, but getting no sight of him, waited
till the girl arrived and then sent her towards the sea
while she herself went along in the other direction,
towards the main road. On reaching the main road
without overtaking him the housekeeper stopped, again
not knowing whether he had gone right or left. She
might have taken a chance, but as she had so few
clothes on she was a little prudish about being seen by
any of the growers driving in to catch the mail boat.
So she went back to the house and met Alice returning
from her search which had been equally without result. After putting on a few more things the housekeeper went to Tozer's to give him the message which
had Carey out at Perigord by seven."

"Did he get anything more?"

Le Marinel's eyes flickered at the question, and he
hesitated for a breath or two.

"A little, not much. But he came away with a very definite conviction that we can lay our hands on de Quettville to-night."

"To-night?"

Le Marinel nodded.

"He is convinced of that from what little he did discover at Perigord. It appears that the girl Alice had heard a sound in the house on the previous night. At the time she thought little of it, believing it must be Mrs. Bichard herself. But in the morning Mrs. Bichard found the side door that leads from behind the staircase into the garden unlocked. Now, mark this. When at home de Quettville always did the locking up himself. He was most precise and careful about it. Systematically he went round the house every night, after first taking a turn round the garden, and this door was the first he saw to. He would afterwards go to his study, hang the keys on a nail behind the door, mix himself a glass of hot grog from the hot water Mrs. Bichard always took there a minute or so before ten, after which he went up to bed. All this was a sort of ritual which was invariably followed, every night.

"Since his disappearance the housekeeper has done the locking up, of course, but the study being itself now locked up by me, she has always left the keys in their separate locks, with the one exception of this side door. This key she removed from the lock because it was the one door de Quettville habitually used, and for which he had an extra key on the ring he always carried attached to a chain in his pocket. It was certainly by that door he entered on Saturday night when the housekeeper next morning, finding it open, thought she had removed the key without first turning it in the lock.   And as Mrs. Bichard did not mention her omission to the maid, nor the maid speak of hearing that noise in the night, neither of them divined the truth, though Carey saw it when he put the two facts together."

The avocat eyed me expectantly.

"The truth?" I echoed.

He nodded eagerly.

"Don't you see what it means?   Why, simply that de Quettville has been returning every night *except* the Friday night when we ourselves were there till daylight.   Is it not obvious that he supposes himself surrounded by enemies, that he wants something now in the house, and does not wish to be seen getting it?   If he were in a sane condition he would know that he could come and get what he wants openly.   If it is food, or a weapon, or something out of the study, he finds the door locked against him, and not knowing that the key is in my possession, hunts for it elsewhere in the house on successive nights.   Well, to-night we shall be waiting for him.   To-night, Carey believes, will see an end to all our anxieties."

On that my thoughts flew off in an effort to formulate the new theory necessary to account for Coquard's attack on myself.   For a new theory must now be found since I could not, after this, suppose the attack had anything to do with de Quettville's disappearance.   If that knife came from Coquard's hand it must be on account of some forgotten incident in my Paris days, in which Coquard, or more probably one of his friends, had come up against me, some friend whose grudge Coquard had taken up in the approved *apache* manner. More than one nasty row had come my way in those old, wild days. There was that half-forgotten ugly incident in the Rue Saint Jacques when knives came out; and there was also the affair with the two scoundrels whom I found in the dark hours knocking an old beggar woman about on the Quay, close to the Petit Pont. They had tried to throw me into the Seine. Neither of these had become police affairs. But the police had been very much in that business near the Odeom, when Abercromby and myself, returning from a hospital case, found a gendarme lying on the ground holding on to an arrest while being kicked by four of his captive's pals. In the rough and tumble which followed one of them tried to plant the toe of his boot under my chin; but I taught him that a boot accustomed to kicking place goals could be landed much lower down with greater accuracy. Hugh Abercromby, meanwhile, had also dropped his man, or rather his pair; but in a more genteel fashion, by cracking their heads together. So as the third fellow had bolted, we wound up by helping the gendarme, and the four captives, over to the lock-up. Three of them got long sentences while the man they had been attempting to rescue was sent to Devil's Island.

Le Marinel cut into these flying visions of the past with a cough, a nervous little clearing of the throat that caught my attention.

"There's just one thing more," he said, "and that is the apology I have to make you."

"Apology—what for?" I asked.

"An apology in which Carey joins me. We were both wrong and Sullivant as well, in being so sure de Quettville was dead. You alone believed him to be alive and"—he held up his hand to stop my interruption—"I am to say from Carey that but for his knowledge of the view you have so consistently held, he might never have followed up Mrs. Bichard's message as carefully as he has done."

Had Le Marinel not himself been so uncomfortable in having to swallow his own words he must have seen I was just as uncomfortable myself. For after my visit to the wine shop I had been certain, more certain than any of them, that the man was dead. So I cut short the undeserved apology.

"Never mind about me," I said hastily, "how does Carey propose to catch him?"

"We're going to lie in wait for him at that side door to-night. Carey is making no search for him to-day. He is too well hidden—some one sheltering him of course—and so no police will go out to-day. No need to scare him off, since he will come to that side door himself."

This looked all right if de Quettville remained unaware that he had been seen by the two women, and if he had not got whatever it was he wanted in his own house. A sudden possibility flashed into my mind.

"Suppose this nocturnal visitor were some one impersonating de Quettville?" I said.

The suggestion startled Le Marinel. He stared blankly at me, his eyes a-goggle, vaguely reminding me of an astonished goldfish.

"Impersonating de Quettville," he repeated. "What for?"

"Oh, I don't know."

He came a step nearer.

"But, my friend, what then made you suggest such a thing?"

"Well, he's the last man who needs to enter Perigord like that, isn't he?"

"Possibly; but you are the last man I'd expect to say that."

"Why?"

"Why, because it's your whole argument that Hilaire de Quettville is a delusional maniac who is hiding because he believes himself surrounded by enemies, one of whom at least he intends to kill. Is that not so?" he snapped.

And I could not but admit that so it was. Yet when Le Marinel repeated his question as to what had made me suggest impersonation, and found I had no reason to give, he did not like it at all, insisting that I must have had a reason. Then of course I saw that the suggestion of impersonation I had hazarded had its source in the suspicion born in the wine shop that de Quettville was dead. And it was the last thing I wanted to tell Le Marinel now, after hearing of his and Carey's admiration for the consistency and tenacity with which I had stuck to it that the old man was alive! Lamely enough then, I told the avocat, with a shrug, that my suggestion was meant merely to cover all the possibilities. With that, though he eyed me keenly while I spoke, he had to be content.

"Oh, well," he remarked, rising, "to-night will settle everything." He brushed an imaginary speck of dust from his sleeve, adding, "Carey wants to pick you up here soon after ten."

"Me? He wants me to go out?"

"Certainly. Aren't you the medical attendant? Carey must have a doctor by him when the man is taken, and Carey, I can tell you, thinks the world of you now. Though," he went on, holding out his hand, "what he may think of you if this nocturnal visitor turns out not to be de Quettville I can't tell you."

"You can tell me this: has de Quettville ever lived abroad for any length of time?"

"Abroad?" Le Marinel repeated vaguely.

"Yes, in South America, say, or the Pacific?"

"Heavens, no! He's the regular old type Guernsey-man, to whom Guernsey is the centre of the universe. I doubt if he's been more than twice to England in all his life. Why do you ask that?"

But I was not prepared to tell him the reason just then.

"Oh, I merely wondered. Travel has its influence on the mind, you know," I said, as we reached the door and my eye took a furtive glance at the narrow and deep incision near the edge of the right panel.

And as I sat down to my delayed breakfast my thoughts did not turn on the possibility of a fall in the Chief Constable's new-found esteem for me; nor did I doubt for a moment that the man we should capture that night would be de Quettville. On the contrary, out of the very certainty that it must be de Quettville a new perplexity arose: why had the knife been aimed at *me?*

ALL through that day that question keep recurring. As it chanced, Monday brought a good number of professional calls; but while going from one house to another I could think of little else. That knife stuck in my mind all day, quivering. For the trouble now was to find a motive. Why should such an attack be made upon a harmless medical *locum tenens?* Le Marinel's news that de Quettville was still alive and at large necessarily altered my whole perspective. Knowing what I did of the perversions in judgment and conduct which accompany delusional insanity, I now saw that far and away the most likely person to have made the attack was not Coquard but de Quettville himself. That maniac whom I had seen lying in his bed at Perigord, brooding over his wrongs till his disordered brain flared up into homicidal intent, had included me in the number of his persecutors.

That he had disliked me at the time of my visit I was well aware; but now I could divine the maniacal fury which lay behind those vigorous heart-pulsations on which I had remarked to Le Marinel. He then, of course, had regarded me as the one man likely to thwart his homicidal purpose by getting him put under restraint, and from my experience of delusional dementia I was aware how easily his hatred could be temporarily transferred from the original object of his hate to myself. The workings of a disordered mind are hard to follow, but it is an error to suppose that an insane person cannot conceive, and adhere to, a purpose. There *is* method in madness; and with homicidal lunatics the doctor frequently becomes an object of intense hatred, the first enemy who must be removed before the original murderous intention can be achieved.

The more I thought of it the clearer it seemed to become that in this respect de Quettville's case was similar to others known to me. Even his sudden disappearance now became explicable: he had gone into hiding immediately after my visit because he dreaded another visit from a medical man. If, as seemed probable, the original object of his hate was his brother-in-law, Cæsar Brisson, and if he had seen me leaving the wine shop while he himself was lurking about the dark quay, he would insanely suppose Brisson and myself to be in conspiracy against him. So the knife had come my way first simply because I was the first to leave the wine shop.

The one flaw in all this seemed to lie in the fact that, so far as I had been able to learn from my question to Le Marinel, de Quettville never had lived where the art of throwing the knife could be acquired. For a long time that day this bothered me. True, he had shown no great skill in the art, for the knife had missed me; but the real trouble was to account for his using such a method at all. For long I could make nothing of this problem. Then I recalled what Le Marinel had said about de Quettville's ancestry, and a clue to that problem came.

Normans who had not come over with the Conqueror, he had called the de Quettvilles. Well, now in the hour of this de Quettville's mental collapse, down in the deep unconscious mind where primitive man lurks in the dark, an ancestral impulse had awakened from the sleep of ages, and Hilaire had thrown the knife just as his Norse forefathers had formerly thrown the spear.

That was it! And once the psychological explanation of the knife-throwing became apparent it was easy to explain away the telephone call of the previous night. That call was a mere hoax of the common kind; the car had not come simply because it was all hoax, and but for the knife incident no one would ever have taken it for anything else.

Having reached this unsensational conclusion it will be supposed that my next act was to wire my friend McNab, cancelling my letter. This however I did not do, and to this day I am unable to give a strictly rational reason as to why I did not. Possibly some ancestor of my own whose experiences lived on in my own unconscious, whispered a vague warning that stayed my hand. Possibly it was simply because I had dwelt in my letter so much on the island's charm that I felt that to withdraw my invitation would make me seem not to want McNab, now that he could be of no professional service to myself. Moreover, I knew that once we had the de Quettville case off my mind, McNab and I could have a fine, care-free time together, swimming, sea fishing, or playing golf at L'Ancresse. With these anticipations before me I found myself in a cheerful frame of mind when just after nightfall the Chief Constable's car slid up to the front door.

Carey himself was at the wheel, with Sergeant Torode behind. We moved off at once.

"Le Marinel offered you my apologies?" Carey said after a little.

"Oh, yes," I said, hastily adding, "it was only natural you should prefer Dr. Sullivant's opinion to a stranger's."

Carey replied with quick vexation.

"Sullivant was a fool. So was I."

"Where is Le Marinel now?" I asked, partly to get away from the awkward moment, partly because I had expected the avocat to accompany us.

"At Perigord. We are to meet him at an arranged place when he'll bring us any news. Our plan for catching de Quettville will depend on what he has to tell us," he added, as if warning me not to bother him with more questions. It was a hint I took, content to leave plans in the hands of the police, and, confident that the end of my professional responsibility would soon be over, I yielded myself to the exhilaration of a night ride in a fast moving car.

The route taken was certainly not the most direct way to Perigord. That I let pass without remark, as we headed down the Rohais on the long slope out of the town. Soon we were on a country road raked by our headlights, with the trees flashing towards us out of the blackness at an ever increasing speed. At Cobo, almost as soon as the whitewashed cottages leaped into radiancy, we turned sharp left, following the coast line, along a bare and open road that would lead us ultimately to the mighty headland of Pleinmont. The road was empty of all traffic, but now and then, at some row of cottages facing seawards, our lights would reveal for a second or two a group of figures in fishermen's jerseys either leaning in lazy relaxation against the sea wall, or sitting on it with legs swinging, as they watched us pass.

By this time Colonel Carey's prolonged silence arrested my attention, and it became increasingly evident that he had something on his mind. His silence, in fact, on that empty road brought something of a chill to my own good spirits. Certainly his worries would not, like my own, come to an end with de Quettville's capture. He intended, I knew, to get not only at the identity of the person who had been sheltering the man, but also to discover the identity of the persons responsible for his mental condition through the use they had made of the ship's figure-head taken from Mère Trouteaud's garden. But possibly, the thought came, he had penetrated these mysteries, or at least, as was more likely, now knew just enough of what lay behind to fill his mind with some anxiety, and set all his nerves on edge.

Rounding the L'Eree corner which opens out on the great bay of Rocquaine, I caught sight of a low-hung moon, then just clearing a long stretch of cloud that topped the massive black Pleinmont headland. Carey slowed the car down to a crawl and shut off all our lights. The engine's note was now so soft that it was almost lost in the gentle swishing of the tide beyond the wall. Inland the country looked no more than an extended smear of intense darkness punctured at rare intervals by the small luminous oblong made by a lighted cottage window. To the south, however, beyond the huge mass of Pleinmont, the escaping moon was turning the sea into a long streak of glimmering quicksilver, amid which the jet-black rocks scattered around the Hanois lighthouse lay like a herd of sea-monsters asleep.

Then just as I was thinking the lighthouse itself seemed to be flashing hasty warnings from the midst of that dangerous flock, we turned off the road and began to nose up and up a narrow lane beset with high hedges. Five minutes later Carey swung through an open gate into a field, and the car came to a halt between two haystacks, the radiator touching the hedge in front. Carey at once relaxed.

"So far so good," he said. "But the devil of it all is that all this would have been needless if only we had listened to you."

"You mean about de Quettville's condition?"

"Yes, we gave up the search for him too soon, or rather Sullivant, with his theory of suicide, sent us looking in the wrong places."

So while we sat waiting for Le Marinel's arrival, Sergeant Torode having already gone to the gate to watch for him, I told the Chief Constable of the knife-throwing incident. This I told as a warning of possible danger, but I had it in my mind also to show him that a determined and obstinate man like de Quettville was not at all of the type who take to suicide as a means of escape from troubles. The story certainly made Carey sit up. At first I thought he was stiff from incredulity; but fortunately his experiences in the by-ways of Indian crime had left Carey with a mind which few things could surprise. He fastened, however, on exactly those two features in the affair which had at first puzzled myself: why had the attack been made on me, and why had such a method been used? But my theories on both points he found convincing.

"You have had personal knowledge of his type?" he asked.

"Personal experience," I amended. "And you can take it from me no more determined will exists than the will of a homicidal maniac. It's well also to keep in mind," I added, "that the cunning he develops is only second to that determination."

"Yes," Carey said musingly. "That is clear in this case anyhow. Apart from any impulse derived from his Norse blood, he knew better than to get at close quarters with a man of your physique. And after he missed he had to evade you, and recover the knife which was perhaps the only weapon he had. He knew, or guessed, he could not escape you if he ran."

"So he quietly steps into the next gate, and lets me go blundering past," I wound up, sore with the remembrance.

But Carey's thought had moved on.

"This must modify my plans for to-night. The thing is even more hazardous than I thought. You had better say nothing to Le Marinel. The little man would be scared out of his wits." He laughed softly, adding, "I'll bet he'd never come down that dark lane alone if he knew."

"Has he far to come?"

"Fortunately no. Perigord stands up there on the top of the ridge ahead. The lane we left just now is the lane Mrs. Bichard saw de Quettville making for when she watched him from the girl's bedroom, and it drops down past Mère Trouteaud's cottage which is about a hundred yards nearer here."

As time passed, however, I began to wonder. Carey too revealed signs of uneasiness, or impatience, glancing at the luminous dial of his wrist-watch at more frequent intervals. By now the moon had cleared the headland, and I could see its pale light filtering through the hedge, and flooding the field beyond. The pungent smell of hay was everywhere. It must have been well after midnight when a creak as from a gate being opened made us both sit up simultaneously. Presently Le Marinel's face, looking strangely pale in the shadow of the hayrick, appeared alongside.

"All right?" Carey asked in a whisper.

"I think so," the avocat responded. "You are sure you have not been seen?"

When Carey told him we had taken all the precautions they had arranged and had got there before the moon rose, Le Marinel jumped up into the back seat followed by Sergeant Torode. In the rapid discussion which followed Carey seemed to me unduly anxious about my safety. Whether or no this was the result of the story I had told him I could not decide, but he would not allow me to take the part originally assigned me in the prearranged plan for de Quettville's capture.   And this deviation seemed to irritate Le Marinel.   In his precise lawyer's mind he objected, I suppose, to any late change to the cut and dried scheme already devised.   But Carey was firm.

"No," he said with finality.   "You and Dunn will stay inside.   Torode and myself remain outside in the garden, under cover, where we can watch the approach to the side door.   That will allow us to see whether de Quettville is alone, or whether he is being made use of by others."

"Made use of by others?   What others?   What use?" the lawyer asked after a moment.

"That's what we don't know.   But it's a certainty some one knows more about de Quettville than he has told, since some one is at least feeding him.   That is the fact which has set me *thinking,* Le Marinel."

Le Marinel said nothing for a moment, but I heard him stirring on the back seat.

"Thinking what?" he inquired at length.

"Well, whether something nasty doesn't lie behind the several odd features in the affair."

"My dear Carey, isn't that rather fantastic?   Remember, you are no longer in India," the avocat protested, half amused.

"Well," Carey replied soberly, "that Neptune was fantastic enough, and the gilded tennis balls, and one or two other odd events which may mean much or little.   What is certain is that *some one* is concealing de Quettville, either because de Quettville can put compulsion on him, or because he is using de Quettville for some purpose of his own."

"Is that the only reason you have for reversing our different posts?" Le Marinel inquired.

"Perhaps. Instead of the sergeant and myself waiting behind the door it will be you and Dunn. And now," Carey finished crisply, "it's time we were moving."

We mounted the grassy lane in single file, and not till we reached the top where the gable of the Perigord stables met the lane was another word spoken. Entering the grounds through the gap in the hedge we were still in the shadow cast by the stable wall, and while Carey drew Le Marinel aside for final instructions before we separated, I had a look round the end of that wall at what lay beyond.

The house stood about a hundred yards distant slightly to our left, so that I could see the greater part of the eastern end in shadow, and all its southern frontage white in the moonlight. From where I stood the main door in the western front, approached from the northern boundary of the estate, was not visible, but the path before me, bisecting what must have once been a fine broad lawn, led to a small door in the southern front which I knew must be the door that was to be kept under observation. And I noticed that there was just one position from which this door could be watched from behind cover. The lawn which on my right extended till it merged indefinitely with the tree-studded park, terminated on the left at a ridge of rising ground which ran from the hedge right up to the far end of the house. The highest point in this ridge was quite near to the house, and was occupied by a summer house, the top of which was plainly discernible among a clump of surrounding shrubs and bushes. Here in this summer house though it seemed to face south so as to permit a view of the sea over the top of the hedge, I felt sure was the place from which Carey and the sergeant would keep watch on the door. It was not merely a good place, but the only place among that small grove of bushes where I could also just see the tall stone pillar on which the figure of Neptune had been for a time set. And in fact it was to the summer house on the knoll that the other two turned when Le Marinel led me in a quick dash across the moon-lit lawn, and right up to the side door. Once inside I heard him lock the door and remove the key.

What I did remember about the place in which we now found ourselves was that one reached the side door by a rather narrow passage leading from the hall, and that the slope of the second flight of main staircase formed the roof of this passage. But what I now saw as Le Marinel taking my arm, flashed a hand torch before us, was that just inside the door there was a deep open alcove exactly the width of the stairs which passed overhead. Le Marinel gave me time to see two chairs side by side in the alcove before switching off his torch. We sat down to recover breath. After a little Le Marinel touched me.

"You've got hold of the idea?" he whispered interrogatively.

"I think so. We are to collar him when he enters, and the others are to close in from behind."

"You've seen him; he's not very big. Would it not be better for me simply to light him up with the torch? I know that was what Carey meant to do while the sergeant tackled him."

Now it was true I had seen de Quettville, and though I had not seen him on his feet I had little doubt of my ability, violent though a maniac can be, to lay him on the floor, provided I caught him unawares. Whether I could keep him there depended on the quick following up of Carey and the sergeant. And Le Marinel sounded rather nervous.

"All right," I said; "just be sure to throw the light full in his eyes. Then I'll take him low down, and when he's on the ground we can both sit on him."

He sighed in relief.

"Of course he's quite old, as you know."

That I did know, but I also knew the almost supernatural strength which comes to a maniac of any age, and I wondered what might happen if de Quettville took it into his head to lock the door behind him as soon as he entered. My thoughts turned on my Braxsted days; and it was not good at that moment to remember Braxsted. In spite of me I recalled one man, not a young man either, who had torn the iron bars of his window with his naked hands as if they had been made of soft lead. The only difference age seems to make in such cases is in the time the paroxysm of superhuman strength lasts. Resolutely I turned my thoughts away from the possibilities before me, when the moment had come, and I could hear the key turning in the lock of that door.

McNab would be on the sea now, if he were coming at all. My letter would not have reached him till some time after eight, too late for a reply. Mentally I went over what I had written, re-estimating its powers of attraction for him, and I saw it must draw him if he happened to be free. Then I began to speculate as to the precise amount of annoyance he would show when told that the suspicions which prompted my letter were unfounded, that the problem was merely that of securing a homicidal maniac, and that there was no case for him at all.

After that I found myself hoping either that he would not come, or that there might be something in Carey's notion of some person using the madman for some hidden purpose of his own. This last would offer McNab something to do and so save my face, even though McNab declined the chance. All the same, I hoped that Carey and his sergeant would not spend much time scouring the gardens for this possible second man, after de Quettville entered the house. Not much reliance could be placed on Le Marinel. Already my ear had taken note of the way in which his chair creaked, as if he were fidgeting about with his nerves getting jumpy in the dark. Yet he probably had no experience of how dangerous a man in de Quettville's mental condition can become in moments of crisis. I bent over towards him.

"It is quite safe to talk here, is it not?"

He assented, as with eager relief.

"Oh, yes, I think so, if we keep our ears open too. After all," he added, "there's only four women in the house."

"Four?"

"Yes, Mrs. Blampied and Claire came to-night—in Claire's interests you know." He tittered a little breathlessly. "We may expect other god-children very soon, and no doubt Brisson too, in his daughter's interests."

"The housekeeper knows we are here now?"

"No. Carey would take no risks, and I slipped out only when they had all gone up to bed, leaving me at work in the study."

"You haven't finished with those papers yet?"

This I fancy was said merely for the sake of keeping up the talk. But Le Marinel seemed eager to talk. Again he laughed very softly.

"*Ma foi,* no! For a lawyer there's weeks, perhaps months of work there. But that will come later. At the moment the concern of Mrs. Blampied, and all the god-children, is to discover whether a will has been made, and if so where it is. Sure he must be dead. They are all most positive that a will must exist, since they know he hates Brisson with such rancour that he would most certainly never allow Brisson's daughter Judith to inherit more than he could help. Oh, they have great expectations, these god-children, expectations which, assuredly, were encouraged by their godfather."

"But," I said, interested in spite of the anxiety of the moment, "so far you have found no will."

Le Marinel snapped his fingers.

"On the contrary I found it this afternoon, hidden in a secret recess behind the picture over the fireplace. Indeed I found more, for in the same place I found the draft of a mortagage de Quettville has been arranging on the Perigord estate."

"A mortgage! He was not so wealthy then?" I said at haphazard, my ear on a sound which I fancied came from the outside. The lawyer in Le Marinel seemed to have mastered the man: he was for the moment too full of the legal side of the case to care for any other. Again he snapped his fingers.

"*Poof,* you do not yet appreciate the humour of the situation," he said. "His intention, since he could neither sell nor will away Perigord, clearly was to mortgage it up to the hilt so that Brisson's girl would inherit a quite worthless estate. Some rumour of this appears to have got around, and that doubtless is what has made Mrs. Blampied and the others so eager to see his will."

"But the man is still alive," I said, very conscious of the fact.

"Ah, but they do not know that. Neither do they know how unlikely they are to benefit even if he were dead."

"Because, after all, he has left them out! Another touch of his cynical humour, I suppose."

"Not at all. He has left them everything. But the will is dated on the fifteenth of this month, that is two days before Claire Blampied came on her visit, and, actually, while his earliest god-child, George

Drury, was here. So the question will arise: was he *sane* at the time the will was executed? Some pickings for the lawyers there! Now *we* know—" Le Marinel pulled up just an instant before my warning hand touched him. His ear had also caught the sound. In his professional excitement he had begun to talk rather loudly. Instinctively I had risen and stood listening. The sound came again. But this time I knew it came from somewhere inside the house, somewhere up the passage leading to the hall. It sounded exactly like wood creaking sharply under the weight of a footstep. Then Le Marinel gave me a surprise.

"I'm going to see what that is," he whispered as we stood listening. He moved off at once up the passage, leaving me taken aback by this unexpected display of pluck. To be candid, my own nerve had not held out so well. And I could not help seeing that his had improved, so to speak, as the night advanced. It was true he had, in talking over the legal aspects of the case, freed his mind from the strain I felt in having to listen for the first signs of de Quettville's approach. And after all his job was merely to hold the torch while I overpowered the madman, a thing the lawyer in his ignorance no doubt considered would be easy for me.

I stood forward, then, to listen, one ear on the door, the other on the passage that led into the hall. But from neither direction could any sound be detected, and my thought then was that if de Quettville were as soft-footed as the avocat there was need for even greater alertness than before. There must be no more talk when he returned.

Of course I soon thought I heard sounds after standing listening a few minutes. Somewhere in the house I seemed to detect a door being gently shut, and down the dark, narrow passage there came the sound of voices whispering continuously together. Yet though I knew all this was mere imagination, or if actual sound a thing which could be more sanely explained by the springing up of a night breeze, a puff of air sufficient to move an open window, or flutter some foliage— though I told myself all this the feeling of uneasiness remained. And as time passed and Le Marinel did not return that feeling deepened. At any moment now I might hear de Quettville's key in the lock. Le Marinel knew that too. Why did he not come back? Was it because he could not, because something had happened to him? It could hardly be that, since in the vast stillness of the house, and with my senses on the stretch, no smothered outcry, nor a fall, not even a stumble over a piece of furniture could have passed unheard.

Then I got angry with myself. After all, Le Marinel would not be of much use. Carey and the sergeant would be following up if they were not both engaged in catching the man suspected of being behind de Quettville. In any case, I felt sure I could hold on to the madman, no matter how he bit or kicked. Still, I could not free myself from the influence of that house. Had my watch been kept in a suburban villa at, say, Ealing, I would have felt nothing; but that rambling house, old, empty and uncared for, had an atmosphere to which no one could have been insensitive. It felt at that hour of the night as if it were full of things that peeped at me round corners, and muttered and whispered together. Then something came padding quickly down the passage. I drew back.

"*Hist,* where are you?" Le Marinel breathed.

"Here," I answered; "but where the devil have you been all this time?"

He felt for his chair and sat down.

"All over the house. That noise was nothing—the stairs creaking in the way old wood does when the weather changes. Even a change of wind does it." He began to put on his shoes, and added, "I came as soon as I could."

"You came down the passage as though something were after you," I blurted out. But my annoyance was short lived: I was too glad to have him there once more.

"Oh, well," he replied as he sat up, "that was easy: the keyhole gave me the line."

Turning to the door I saw what he meant. By this time the moon had moved so far round that a thin ray of its light, entering by the keyhole, terminated on the floor in a small but very bright spot, like a new sixpence with a tail to it. It was this that had guided Le Marinel straight down the passage, and his eyes still seemed to be on it, for he said half musingly, as if to himself:

"It will go out when he puts the key in the lock."

Le Marinel of course did not dream how those

words had power to stir my imagination. He did not know what had happened when I had put the key in the lock of my own door, and how nearly my own light had gone out as I did so!

After that we sat on side by side in silence. Le Marinel seemed rather fatigued; his breathing soon suggested he was dropping into a doze. I left him alone; a touch would be enough when the moment came. As for myself, that little spot of moonlight on the floor I found most helpful, for it relieved the strain of constant vigilance by permitting me to transfer the strain from one sense to another, from hearing, that is, to sight. For a while it served to keep me wakeful too; its slow creeping across the floor as the moon moved round was something to watch, the only thing that moved in a world in which even time itself seemed to stand still.

Perhaps sleep had surprised me. I do remember shutting my eyes to transfer my watch from the eye to the ear. My belief was that I had only closed my eyes for no more than a few seconds, when something made me look up. The little spot of moonlight had moved altogether off the floor and was now some way up the opposite wall. The sight startled me into complete wakefulness. To have progressed so far hours must have passed. In a flash, however, I knew this was wrong. The light was not on the wall at all. *That* was not wall-paper on which it shone but cloth —cloth of a narrow black and white stripe.

A man was standing there, doing something, just inside the door. With a shout to the sleeping Le

Marinel I leaped for the man. But he was too quick for me. Missing him as he side-stepped, I went against the door with a bang. Le Marinel, awakened by the sudden clamour, gave a startling scream, like a woman. As I shouted to him to bring his torch to bear there came a rush of feet. Remembering the knife, I ducked and he went down over me, with my right hand closed on an ankle. But kicking himself free, he sent me sprawling, and this gave him time to be first on his feet.

Le Marinel appeared to have quite lost his head, and I dared not again call for the light as I was certain my shout would be followed by a knife throw. I kept still, doubtful where de Quettville was. And as I stood, breathing hard, a whiff of perfume came from somewhere. Not then did I think of the incongruity of perfume in such a moment but merely concluded it was carried by a current of air from the door. If so, that tumble on the floor had reversed our relative positions, mine anyhow, for now I found myself at the entrance to the passage, with him presumably near the door. To be candid, I sickened at the thought of that knife sinking unexpectedly into some part of my body in that darkness. It would be easier to overpower him in the open. Best to let him get outside again. Carey had been mighty slow in following up.

But the next moment there came a hail from the garden, with a rain of blows on the door. I felt just a little bitter: if they had not been asleep de Quettville would not have had time to lock that door behind him. This bitterness however was unfair: had

I not been asleep myself?   Simultaneously with the
shouting another of us seemed to awake, and Le Marinel's torch at last flashed out.   Unfortunately it flashed
on me, and as I stood, blinded by it for the moment
and inactive, something came that struck me down,
though I do not remember going to the floor . . .

When I opened my eyes again it was to find myself
lying on a bed in full daylight.   By the bed sat Le
Marinel—a very dejected looking Le Marinel.   He
did not see I had come round.   I put out my hand and
touched him.   He fairly jumped at that touch.

"Why the devil did you turn the light on me?" I
asked.   It hurt my jaw horribly to speak.   I felt sick
too, but that question I had to get out.   Le Marinel
regarded me with woe and shame.

"I didn't know which of you was which.   That is
why I hesitated so long."   While I pondered over this
he added bitterly: "And in the end I guessed wrong."

"Why didn't Carey—?"

He noticed my hand go to my jaw and nodded sym-
pathetically.

"Ah, that's where he got you with the chair.   It
isn't broken I hope."

His disgust over his own share in the scrimmage
was so plainly written on his face that I could not keep
up my anger.   And obviously it was a fact that he
could not be sure which was de Quettville or which myself after that mix-up in the dark.   He might hear
each of us breathing heavily after the first tumble on
the floor, but it was too much to expect him to distinguish the breathing of one from the breathing of

the other.　And, after all, Carey had failed much more seriously; he had been much too slow in following up de Quettville when he arrived at the house.　Perhaps they also were asleep!

"Carey was very angry with me too," Le Marinel remarked lugubriously.

"What for?"

"For not unlocking the door and letting them in."

"They should have followed up quicker, and not given him the chance of locking them out," I declared.

The avocat opened his eyes wide.

"Oh, but—well, you see de Quettville did not enter by that door at all."

"What!"

"I thought you knew."

"You were asleep; how could *you* know?"

"Because Carey told me—after de Quettville had left by the study window, the way he came in."

This brought me upright, aghast.

"Don't tell me they didn't catch him!"

But that was what he did tell me.　And bad hearing it made, till he told me de Quettville had been seen running across the fields towards Pleinmont.　Two fishermen, one of them my old acquaintance Daniel Sarchet, returning home after a night's fishing off Hanois, had caught sight of him.　That, Le Marinel said, was a few minutes after 4 A.M., for they had just heard the hour striking on the church clock.　Since then Carey had organized a search, and Le Marinel told me every man in the parish, and some of the women were now scouring the cliffs for him.

So, hoping against hope, we hung on for news. The knock out I had taken came, fortunately for me, from the padded edge of the chair, and I could have returned to St. Peter Port an hour or so afterwards but was unwilling to leave at that juncture. About ten o'clock, however, I walked to the local post office, and rang up to see if any calls had come in. No calls had come in, but, the housekeeper went on to say that the friend I had said might be coming had arrived by the mail boat that morning. On hearing this the receiver nearly dropped from my hand. McNab—I had forgotten him! At the back of my mind, I suppose, there had been all along the belief that he would be too busy to come. Meanwhile the housekeeper's voice was telling me the gentleman had gone out to send off a telegram and so could not speak with me then. This I heard with relief. I could not have known how to tell him there was now no case to investigate. But after a moment's thought I told her to send McNab out to Perigord when he returned. After all, although there was no crime involved in the affair, there was perhaps just enough mystery in it to save my face with McNab. As I rang off I remember even hoping that de Quettville would not be caught before McNab turned up at Perigord.

But that hope was not fulfilled.

About eleven while I was loitering in the drive waiting for him, an excited fisherman hurried up with news. Hilaire de Quettville's body had just been taken out of the sea.

It was Colonel Carey the man had come to find. So after eliciting from him enough of the facts to be certain de Quettville was far beyond my help, I told the excited fisherman that the Chief Constable would be found somewhere on the cliffs beyond Pleinmont. I was aware that Carey would want me to view the body; but for a moment or two I stood where the man left me, stunned by the unexpectedness of his news. I felt more than a little abashed, too, in recognizing that, as the event proved, his tendencies must have been suicidal, not homicidal. Sullivant had been right after all.

What would Carey say now? For myself, the professional mortification I then experienced was tempered by the conviction that my opinion had been founded on the evidence and facts available to me. Reviewing those facts as I turned away to make for the lane that led down to the beach, I did not see how in my position I could have come to any other conclusions. Unless there was some flaw somewhere Sullivant's opinion could have been nothing but a guess. It was against the weight of the evidence, unless, I repeated to myself, there was some flaw somewhere. For, to take but the psychological factor in the case, it was preposterous to suppose that a hard man like de Quett-

ville could be mocked into self-destruction by a ridiculous ship's figure-head placed over his gate.

This man was no stranger to public ridicule. From
the day his fiancée fled to the day his brother-in-law set
up his pub and called it "Perigord," he had supped his
fill of mockery. He lived alone: why should he be
sensitive to public opinion? He must have become
absolutely impervious to shame too, not only because
he was merciless to his debtors but even to be a usurer
at all. If there ever had been any softness in him the
memory of it had vanished from men's minds, and
for what he now was men saw him, a hard, embittered,
unlovely, vindictive man, whose whole bent and bias
was for retaliation. He had always hit back. Even
his practice of usury was a method of hitting back. He
had hit back at me fiercely enough. Yet he wound up
by taking refuge in suicide! That was an act so out
of line with his whole past that it made one doubt
whether anything like a science of psychology could
exist.

At this point, when I had almost crossed the lawn,
a series of raucous hoots on a klaxon horn made me
look back. A car had halted some way short of the
house, and a man in grey, standing up, was waving
to me. McNab of course!

I retraced my steps at the run. Not that I was
overjoyed to see him, for it is a fact that I was entirely uncomfortable. I ran simply because it was my
duty to see the body at once, even though I had not
yet been officially summoned. So, our first greetings

over and the car dismissed, I took his arm and started a hasty explanation.

"Afraid your first day won't be much of a holiday," I began.

"Holiday?" he echoed, much as if he had never before heard the word.

"Well," I said brazenly, "the case I wrote about has settled itself, so you'll have nothing to do but enjoy yourself. Ever been here before?"

I felt him stiffen. He replied to my question with another.

"Please explain, will you?"

"Oh, it's simple. The man is dead—drowned himself this morning. In fact I'm on my way to view the body now."

He withdrew his arm, pulling up short, and eyed me almost sternly. In a moment, however, his mouth twitched at the corners.

"You're very uncomfortable about something," he said. "Is it because you have dragged me here for nothing?"

"Yes," I admitted frankly. "Only I hope you won't think it's for nothing. After all, there are few places so restful and interesting for a holiday, and," I added, affecting to scan him with a professionally critical eye, "you look as if you needed one."

"Look here," he said, gripping my arm, "did *any* one throw a knife at you, or was that a hallucination due to your own obvious need of a rest?"

This got my back up all right, and I told him that not only was the knife thrown in the manner I had described but that he could presently see the man who had thrown it. To this he replied in his ironical fashion that since he was there against his will on a restful holiday he did not propose to spoil it by a post mortem inspection of de Quettville, though he would certainly be interested to hear about the man.

So, as we walked down the grassy lane towards the seashore I told him the story, from the night when Le Marinel sent me out to Perigord up to our watch throughout the previous night. No doubt I could have told the story better in other circumstances, but at any rate in telling it hurriedly as I then had to do, I did not gloss over my own mistakes and far-fetched suspicions. These last indeed, I was at pains to stress, since they were the only justification I had for sending that letter to himself. I suppose McNab was familiar with people who harboured unfounded suspicions, for when I from time to time stole a glance at his face I could detect no outward sign of amusement. At any rate not after the earlier part of the story in which I gave an account of the Neptune in the shirt and trident set over the same gate, through which his own taxi had entered.

But there was time for little more than a bare outline of the facts before we emerged from the lane and crossed the road to the sea wall.

From there it was not hard to find the place I had to find. Round a rude boat-house on the beach below us a small crowd of people stood about in little groups. Seeing this, and anticipating my own duty need not detain me more than a few minutes, I suggested to

McNab that he could sit on the sea wall till I returned.

"No," he said. "I'll come with you, if you think this Colonel Carey won't mind."

I did not think Carey would mind any one who came in my company, but it surprised me to perceive that McNab had altered his mind about seeing the body.

While threading our way through the groups of talking women, fisherfolk and farm hands, most of them too interested, with all their heads together, to notice us, I overheard a man explain that the body had come in on the flood tide exactly at the spot where Mère Trouteaud had pulled out the Neptune. Mère Trouteaud herself I did not see, but Daniel Sarchet was there, and pulled a forelock as I passed. He had a portentous look on his weather-worn face, and nodded with solemnity as if to remind me that here was a fulfilment of all the ill fortune the old woman had predicted for de Quettville on the day of the *clameur*.

Inside the boat house we found Sergeant Torode, and the local constable with the three fishermen who had brought the body up from the water's edge. The sergeant in the act of showing the fishermen out after having taken their separate statements, seemed surprised to see me.

"We did not think you would be well enough to come. When we left you didn't look like it," he said, his eyes going to McNab with some curiosity.

Explaining that all I had got was no more than a knock out with what was the equivalent of a padded glove, my own eyes went to the sodden figure on the floor who had laid me out in the early morning. They had placed him on a brown sail, and had folded his arms across the breast. There was dignity and power, more power than I had expected in that long, straight form. He looked, with the pointed white beard lying on his breast, much as one of his Viking ancestors might have looked, like a drowned sea king. For death had brought to his features a calmness and dignity, even a certain air of majesty which had not been there in life.

"We are expecting the Chief and Dr. Sullivant any minute now," Torode whispered.

"Oh, you have sent for Dr. Sullivant?"

"Chief's run in in his car for him, having, as I said, no idea you'd be fit, sir. But he'd certainly want you to be present, if possible, the deceased having been your patient."

Now I was not specially anxious to meet Dr. Sullivant again, but I certainly was still less anxious to seem to avoid meeting him. Besides, I was aware that the procedure followed in these islands differed from English practice, and so did not know how far professional obligations extended. So we stayed on. Presently a car came to a halt on the road above.

In bare justice to Sullivant it must be recorded that if he felt any elation over me in finding his prediction of suicide fulfilled he gave me no outward sign of it. On the contrary, Carey having evidently acquainted him with the knock out I had taken, he was as full of kindly solicitous inquiries as the Chief himself.

While Sullivant and Torode were getting to work

I quietly introduced McNab to Carey as a friend of mine in his own line who had come over for a holiday. Carey rather boggled over the holiday assertion, and the half reproachful look he gave me suggested that I had called in McNab because I did not trust them. However, I left them beginning to talk shop together when Sullivant quietly called me over to his side. He seemed slightly perplexed.

It was Sullivant's job, of course, to decide not only that the man was dead but also to state the cause of death. And if the first was a formality the second was not. For however apparently obvious the cause may be it is never taken for granted by any medical man. A man whose body is recovered from the sea may have died not from asphyxiation but from many other causes, such as syncope, exhaustion, apoplexy, shock, or injuries received before submersion. And as presently appeared, Sullivant's difficulty was to determine the cause of death. Motioning Torode to resume the pressure he had been applying to the chest, he called on me to look.

"There is no froth," he murmured.

The presence of froth, which can be expelled from the nostrils, is a proof of death by drowning. Yet the amount of the froth is in proportion to the duration and intensity of the struggle made in the water. And when I reminded Sullivant that if de Quettville entered the water voluntarily there was unlikely to be much of a struggle, he at once agreed.

"He was most certainly alive when he entered the water," he said, indicating the left forearm. In this

I concurred; for on the arm, as elsewhere, *cutis anserina* was plainly visible, and "goose-skin" is due to the contraction of the skin caused by the sudden cold, which of course only a living body can feel.

"His heart was good too," I said.

Sullivant nodded.

"All right. Asphyxia is what I'll sign for."

At this Carey stepped closer.

"Time of death?" he queried.

The question was quite formal, since we had the direct testimony of the fisherman as to the time he was seen making for the seashore. But just as I had seen Sullivant with Torode's help punctiliously examine the body for marks of external violence, although it was practically certain the man had walked into the water, so now on the question of time Carey wanted an equal thoroughness. Sullivant, holding a hand against the body for a little, then fingered the eyelid.

"Well," he said thoughtfully, "the temperature is certainly very low, not unduly so for one of his thinness and age, while on the other hand rigidity has not yet begun. Not less than six hours dead, I'd say— six to eight hours possibly."

Carey glanced down at his watch.

"Eleven thirty now, so if we said seven hours that would make it about the time he was seen going across the fields to the sea."

Sergeant Torode coughed deferentially.

"And there's his own watch, sir," he said, "it would stop in the water fairly soon."

The sergeant who had charge of the clothes and

personal property found in them, here produced the watch. It was a gold hunting watch, and Carey after flicking it open held it up for inspection. The hands of the watch had stopped at 4.16. Sullivant's extreme estimate had been out by only fourteen minutes! He looked pleased with himself.

"A mere guess though," he nodded, "a mere lucky guess. I might have been out by an hour or two for all there is to go by."

This seemed to bring the proceedings to an end. Carey held out the watch to his sergeant, and Torode, busy with his papers, did not observe the outstretched hand.

"May I look at it?" McNab asked, like one conscious he had no real right to be there.

The watch, as I have said, was a gold hunter, much worn and old fashioned, but good in the old-fashioned way, with a case, as I now saw, perfectly plain on both sides. There was in fact nothing, no monogram or decoration, to show which side one must open to expose the dial. McNab guessed wrong, for he opened the back half, instead of the front. But his head went down as if he had come on something unexpected, almost startling. Then he held out the watch to Carey.

"That is worth looking at, I think," he said.

We crowded round. Inside the case, flattened over one of the key holes was a dark green, feathery fragment which Carey moved deliberately with his forefinger.

"M—yes-s," he said, "seaweed. That, by itself,

would prove he had been in the sea, even if we didn't already know it."

I remember McNab's stare as he heard this. Carey's tone had a touch of raillery in it. My own thought was that McNab's find, in so far as it proved what needed no proof, was in that respect exactly like Sullivant's estimate of the time at which de Quettville was drowned. And the truth is I had begun to be uneasy about that guess of Sullivant's. If I kept that uneasiness to myself it was entirely due to the remembrance of my own previous bad guesses.

So I was thinking, when McNab, watch in hand, turned to Torode.

"Have you the key?"

"No, sir. That wasn't among the personal possessions found on the deceased," Torode replied.

"It hardly would be," Carey commented dryly. "People with the old style watches usually keep the key in their bedrooms, where they do the winding up at bedtime."

"Exactly," McNab said, handing back the watch to the sergeant.

Carey showed signs of anxiety to be gone.

"If we knew where he has slept the last few days we'd find the key," he said. Then turning to me, he added, "We'll want you at the inquest, merely to give evidence as to his condition when you saw him, of course."

Having ascertained when the inquest was likely to be held I slipped outside, and, the tide now being high and within a yard or two of the boat-house, plunged my hand over the edge of the small jetty into the water. As the others emerged Carey noticed my position.

"Looking for the key?" he asked, almost jocularly.

"Yes," I said, well aware of how fatuous the reply must sound.

However, it was not the watch key I meant, but the key to the mystery which had begun to trouble me. As soon as the others left, and the local constable was locking up the boat-house, McNab suggested a stroll along the bay.

Now when we turned our backs on that small, dark boat-house, and faced the wide expanse of blue-green sea asleep in the warm sunshine, I ought to have been feeling relief. My responsibility was at an end. As Carey had said, it was well for everybody and not least for the man himself, that it had ended as it did. The danger was over; no harm had come to any one. All the same, I was disturbed in mind. Possibly disturbed is too strong a word. Irritated professionally —that would be closer to my feeling. And it probably was this feeling of vexation that made me, before we had walked far, and only half conscious of what I did, sit down on an upturned boat and pull out my pipe. Then I perceived McNab's eyes on me.

"Something bothering you?" he suggested.

McNab's eyes were not, as I understand a sleuth's orbs ought to be—of the penetrating, steel-blue variety. There was in fact little about him to suggest the detective, and the impression I took of him when we first met in his flat in the Adelphi remained unchanged.

His clear cut features, lively dark eyes, sensitive hands and lithe upright figure suggested the young doctor— the young doctor with the bloom of youth behind him, who, at the end of prolonged hospital work, in which athletic interests were not forgotten, has just stepped out into his first private practice, and has therefore become careful about his personal appearance. But though his eyes were not of the cold, knife-like sort, they could be keen enough. They were now when he put his question.

"Well, I *am* bothered," I admitted. "Oh, quite a small thing, you know. That's what makes it irritating, perhaps."

"Anything to do with the body?"

I hesitated.

"Well—yes, it's a question of certain contradictory peculiarities about that body; but it's a highly technical matter."

"Oh, I wouldn't venture to express my own opinion," McNab cried with exaggerated earnestness, as if he thought I had been heading him off from putting further questions. After a puff or two at his pipe, he said, "Still, I might be able to follow. In my job one picks up a lot of miscellaneous knowledge, from toxicology to—to watch-making," he added, as he saw me take out my watch. As a matter of fact I was ready enough to talk.

"Did you notice the face?" I asked, beginning with the simplest of the three points.

"I did. It was of an ashy whiteness."

"On the facts given, it should not have been."

"Why not?"

"Because when one is drowning the head, being relatively heavier than the body, sinks lower in the water, with the result that the blood sinks too, and leaves the face livid."

"Invariably?"

"No, there are exceptions. But the point here is that the other two peculiarities can only be accounted for as also rare variations from what normally takes place. Now *one* exception, however rare, would not trouble me; but when we get, as in this case, three together, I *am* troubled to explain them to myself."

After pondering this for a little, McNab suggested that the same one cause might have operated in producing the three peculiarities. When I told him this was impossible he reminded me that impossible was a word that had now almost dropped out of a scientist's vocabulary. That provoked me.

"Very well," I said, "consider the peculiarity of the cadaveric rigidity: how is that to be accounted for?"

"But, Dunn, excuse me, I understood there was no rigidity anywhere."

"Exactly: that is the peculiarity. *Rigor mortis* is a gradual process, extending from a few minutes after death up to about twenty hours, before it is complete. Yet in this case after seven hours there was not a trace of it—not even in the eyelid muscles where it invariably begins—although the onset of rigidity is extremely rapid in water."

"But to this there are known exceptions?"

"Yes; there have been abnormal cases of rigidity delayed up to three days. The last peculiarity, however, is the strangest."

"Go on," McNab urged, suddenly impatient as I paused to think it over once more.

"It is this. You heard Colonel Carey ask Sullivant to give his opinion as to the time which had elapsed since death occurred? And you saw that one of the tests Sullivant used was the body's temperature. He laid his hand on the body. That is not a good test, since the temperature of the hand itself varies in different people, and what seems very cold to a warm hand will feel less cold to a cold hand. Sullivant knew this as well as any one, but he had probably broken his thermometer or left it behind, and did not want to say so. But here again it did not seem to matter much, since they had the evidence of the two men who last saw him alive about 4 A.M. and, as it turned out, the approximate time of death was shown by his watch to be 4.16. Now, notice this! A body loses its heat gradually, beginning of course, with the surface, till it falls to the temperature of its surroundings, where it stays. Now though the test of touch made by Sullivant is not good, by the same test I myself, having taken care to make a comparison, can tell you that de Quettville's body was several degrees *colder* than the sea out of which it had just been taken. And yet I do not consider that in normal circumstances seven hours' immersion is long enough to get a body down as low as the temperature of the sea."

McNab stopped me.

"A moment," he said. "Do I understand you to

say that the body was colder than the water out of which it had been taken?"

"Yes; at least I am almost certain it was. Of course the temperature of the sea is high at this season, higher here than in England, and in the dark boat-house the temperature of the body would fall almost rapidly."

"Beginning with the surface skin?" he interjected.

"Yes."

McNab's face, I noticed, fell at this admission.

"Oh, well, that would account for it," he remarked as he relit his pipe.

"Not conclusively, yet here again one cannot be positive; the conditions did favour rapid cooling, but certainly not so quickly in so short a time. But let that abnormality also pass; there still remains the strangest feature of all."

"And that is?"

"You said that some one cause might have operated to produce all the three exceptional features."

"I suggested it."

"Well, it was not a good suggestion, as I believe, now that we have set out the facts, any layman can recognize. To put it quite simply: cadaveric rigidity and decrease in temperature are two processes which go on together. As the body cools the muscles stiffen. Yet in *this* case the body is cold while the muscles remain pliable. It is incredible that any one cause could operate to produce such different results. In fact, if there is any one circumstance which can produce such opposite effects recorded in post mortem manuals it is unknown to me."

He looked up through narrowed eyes.

"You mean, of course, a body dead for no more than seven hours?"

"I do."

Having thus got all I had to say off my mind I set a match to my own pipe, and let McNab make what he could out of the facts. We had the beach to ourselves. Nothing within sight moved; even the sea itself seemed asleep in the noonday sunshine. In that translucent air objects at a great distance took on a sharpness of detail and outline which gave one the illusion of an increase in one's power of vision. Away out in the bay, from the rocky islets the silence was broken for a moment or two by a sudden clamour of seabirds, excited apparently by the discovery of some wandering shoal of small fry.

But McNab had withdrawn to a world of his own. He had drawn his legs up almost under his chin, and maintained them in position by encircling his knees with his arms. His pipe had gone out again, and its position in his mouth seemed as precarious as his own position on the side of the boat, while his hat, thrust to the back of his head, seemed as likely to drop over the other side. His furrowed brow, and lidded eyes, as well as his abandoned attitude, told of troubled thought.

As for me, I had had enough of thought. So I let him get on with it, and squatting on the sand leant my head back against the boat till sleep overtook me— sleep of which I had not had anything like enough.

"Dunn," McNab began, "is there anything known to medical science which would account for it?"

The question was the one I had been expecting. But it had been a long time coming. After I awoke, and found McNab still perched on the boat, still quite as oblivious of his surroundings as I had just been, I dragged him off to the little hotel on the cliffs at Pleinmont for lunch. Not till lunch was over did the heavy drowsiness induced by my sleep in the hot sun leave me. And not till then did McNab make one reference to the matter which preoccupied our thoughts. That is why I was well aware of what his question meant.

"You are referring to contradictory post mortem appearances?"

"Yes. Is such a condition unknown?"

At that I let the fact appear, the fact that had bothered me so much.

"Not at all in a body dead for about three days."

He glanced up, startled.

"Three days! As long as that?"

"Not an hour less, especially in cases of death from asphyxia. Any time after three days, however, the rigidity passes off, while the coldness of course remains."

He nodded slowly, abstractedly stirring the coffee I had ordered as an extra stimulant to thought.

"Yes, so I understood; but you see what it means?"

"Of course; that's what I've seen all along."

"But he died by drowning."

"Certainly. Sullivant will be right in signing for asphyxia. But believe me that body has not been three days in the sea."

"Eh?"

"It has not been three days in the sea," I repeated.

"Why are you so sure?" he demanded.

"Because when I made my examination I found its temperature was so much lower than that of the water. It could only have been in the sea for a relatively short time before it was found, too short a time for the sea to raise it to its own temperature."

McNab leant across the table, his eyes ablaze.

"If that is so we can take it, then, that this Daniel Sarchet and the other man who say they saw de Quettville walking towards the sea about four this morning are either lying now, or were mistaken then?"

This was only part of the problem, as I reminded him, which was so perplexing.

"But what about Mrs. Bichard and the girl Alice Mauger? They also saw him yesterday morning. And, if it comes to that, I saw him myself before the two men, and just at a time which tends to confirm their story."

"No," McNab interrupted, "we must, at any rate, leave you out. To be exact, what *you* saw was a leg merely, and that may have been anybody's."

On this, however, I had to correct him. For though it was true that through Le Marinel's blunder in throwing the light on me I had not actually seen de Quett-ville, yet the leg I had seen was certainly clothed in the same pattern cloth as I had seen in the boat-house. To this he assented without seeming to attach much importance to it at the moment.

"If you are right in saying he had been dead for at least three days then neither Daniel Sarchet nor his friend, neither Mrs. Bichard nor Alice Mauger saw him. As for yourself, you cannot have it both ways. You must make your choice. You must be either, like them, mistaken in supposing you were at grips with him in the dark, or you are wrong in asserting that that body has been dead for three days."

It was not hard to make my choice.

"That body has been dead three days at the very least," I declared. "Quite probably more, but three days at the very least. Not all the eye witnesses in the world would make me believe that that body has been capable of voluntary movement since Saturday morning."

"All right, Dunn. As a matter of fact I agree with you for reasons of my own. But you see what it means? It means that if he has been dead since Saturday morning it was not he who threw the knife at you on Saturday night."

McNab was right. But, so far, the fact had not occurred to me. I had been so obsessed with the dis-crepancies between Sarchet's statement, my own as-sumption that I had actually had my hands on the man, and the post mortem appearances, that I had not yet thought back as far as Saturday. But McNab was right. For a moment we stared at each other.

"Of course it's somebody masquerading as de Quettville," he said.

In ordinary circumstances such a conclusion would have seemed far fetched, even absurd; but on the balance of probabilities it won easily, as McNab made me recognize.

"When one is faced, as we are now, with a straight choice between the incredible and the improbable," he remarked, "one naturally believes that the truth will be found somewhere in the improbable. Later it may turn out that the incredible was only apparently incredible, just as later the improbable may turn out to be only apparently improbable; but it is to the improbable one first goes for the truth. And after all," he went on, "when you think of it, it was not so difficult for the man to masquerade as de Quettville in the way he did. No one spoke to him in the character; and no one even saw him except at some distance, and in no very good light either."

"But," I insisted, "for what purpose did he do it? Robbery? Was he simply taking advantage of the fact that de Quettville was known to be absent?"

McNab's fist came down on the table.

"No: all the time he knew where the body was. He put it back into the sea this morning, if all you have said about that body is right. And he also—" He broke off suddenly and pushing away his yet untouched coffee got to his feet—"Look here," he said, "this is a horrible affair; it makes me sick to think of it; let's get outside to the fresh air and sunshine."

After settling the bill I found him seated on a bench, absent-mindedly over-stuffing his pipe from an old rubber pouch, his eyes looking seaward. Magnificent, however, as was the prospect from that terrace, I doubt if he took in much of the great sweeping contour of the bay, or the vivid colouring among the tumbled cliffs. Nor did my own taste at the moment incline towards scenery. The number of possibilities now opened out in connection with the case seemed endless, and to guess where any one of those possibilities would lead was beyond me.

McNab, I gathered, did not believe de Quettville had died by his own hand. But his belief seemed to be held on other grounds than those which had weighed with me. Accidental death? The body left above high water mark, where it was found by some one who concealed it for some end of his own? To me this seemed a possible explanation. But quite clearly McNab, reading more from the known facts than I, had already dismissed the theory of accidental death. And at this point I saw that all I had said about the abnormal appearances of the body must have merely served to confirm a suspicion already existing in his mind when he began to put his questions to me after we left the boat house. He had himself seen something more than had met my eye. Suddenly I recollected the incident with Carey and the dead man's watch and McNab's inquiry for the key. But how the absence of the key could have aroused suspicion

I could not guess. McNab's voice recalled me to externals.

"You look mighty worried," he said, "standing there as if sudden bad news had turned you into stone. Maybe you're no' aware," he added, "that you've been glowering at me for the last ten minutes with your empty pipe in one hand, and your matchbox in the other."

This was a tone familiar to me; but I had not heard it since his arrival. All the same, in spite of this chaff I observed that his own pipe had just been set going.

"I can make neither head nor tail of it," I said, sitting down, and regarding him with some hope. He laid his hand reassuringly on my knee.

"Laddie, it's simple, though. We've only picked up a clue out of its right order and position, that's all. What we need is an earlier clue, one nearer the start of the business, before we can understand this day's work."

"It's exactly like beginning a serial story in the middle," I asserted.

"Ay," he agreed, "that's what it is; we've come in right in the middle of the story. A very interesting story, I'm thinking, though maybe not exactly edifying. But wait a bit, we'll get our hands on the—well—the synopsis before long."

"Before the next instalment is due?"

McNab stirred uneasily.

"That I can't say," he hesitated. "There's just one man who might help us to a quick answer."

"The man who threw the knife?"

"I was thinking of this lawyer, Le Marinel. A talk with him is the first step, if a talk with me can be contrived naturally."

After some discussion as to how the talk could be arranged it was agreed that Le Marinel should be asked to come up to see me that night, if in the meantime he did not, as was quite likely, communicate with me over the matter of the inquest on de Quettville. When this was fixed up McNab knocked the ashes from his pipe.

"What about a swim now?" he suggested.

It was a suggestion I took with alacrity, as if it were the one thing I wanted but had not happened to think of. In a few minutes we had left the road, and were on a grassy path that took us, deviously, among the huge tumbled masses of rock lying, like fallen giants, about the base of the headland. Ultimately in a lonely cove, the access to which was sufficiently laborious to ensure us of undisturbed possession, we stripped. Before I was ready, however, McNab called to me.

"Have you got your thermometer?"

"My thermometer?"

Remembering how in my school days the temperature was always taken by the careful matron, to my disgust, before we were allowed to bathe, the absurd notion flashed through my mind that McNab wanted the temperature taken before he took the plunge. He put his head round his rock, his shirt arrested on its way over his head.

"Yes," he said, "your thermometer. Or have you left it behind, like your colleague, or broken it?"

Now the fact was that in my pocket case I had both a clinical and a bath thermometer; but it wasn't going to be easy to use the low register instrument there. I looked down at the water, which was easy to reach by a dive, but, though the rocks were smoothed by the tides of ages, it made an awkward climb down even if one carried the thermometer in one's mouth.

"I must be certain about it," he said.

I understood. He had seen me outside the boat house putting my hand in the water. And it was quite true that there, the temperature of the water coming in on the flood over the hot sand would be considerably raised in the process; but for all that, as also for other modifying factors, I had allowed an ample margin. Indeed, after I entered the water and McNab had followed hard on my heels, it did not take long to prove to him that the margin of difference I had allowed for the shallower water at the jetty was more than adequate. Out in the deeper sea where I submerged the thermometer I let him have the first glance at the reading. Rubbing the water from his eyes, he examined it carefully. The mercury indicated 64.3° F., which meant that my previous estimate had erred on the safe side by several degrees.

After a long swim, from which we both emerged panting and blowing, we climbed to a high niche among the rocks, and lay down to get dried by the sun. The smooth rocks were full of a soft heat garnered from the many hours of sunshine, and up at that height a little drift of air, finding us out, played intermittently over our prone bodies, touching the skin into little delicate spasms of alternate coolness and warmth. It was too good a moment to waste in speech. We lay a long time without a word, almost, on my own part, without thought. But when McNab rose silently, and after padding down to where we had left our clothes, returned with his tobacco pouch and box of matches and his little book of cigarette papers, I recognized he had thought of the one thing that could better that halcyon moment.

Deft as his fingers were I watched impatiently. He had a foible for rolling his own cigarettes. Like myself, he was more given to a pipe, but he instinctively knew that at that perfect moment a pipe would have been wrong, almost indecent. Lying propped on my elbows, I watched him as I smoked, himself now seated tailor-wise, finishing off his own cigarette. There was a question I frequently wanted to ask him. For long I had wanted to ask him how he came to take up work as a detective and private inquiry agent. Some obscure form of delicacy restrained me, however; for such a question might imply either that I considered him too good for his job or too bad at it. But something made this occasion propitious, and the question blurted itself out, almost pleadingly, so great was my curiosity.

"McNab, do you mind telling me how you came to be a private detective?"

In the act of putting the edge of the paper to his lips, he looked at me, amusement in his eye.

"Och, no, I don't mind telling you that," he said.

"It was because my father married a little scrap of a woman belonging to Callander."

"What?"

At first I thought he had misunderstood my question.

"In other words, I am a private detective because, not having the necessary height or weight, I cannot be a public one." He sighed as he struck a match. "If only she had just passed on her wits to me, and left him to supply the physique! But she was like that you understand—one of those women who think a thing never well done unless they do it all by themselves. Not, mind you, that he hadn't brains too. He must have had, since he rose to be a chief superintendent of police in Perthshire, which is the most law-abiding county in the whole of law-abiding Scotland."

"Well," I said clumsily, "no doubt there's scope in this county for both the professional and the amat— and the unofficial detective."

But my correction came too late. McNab nodded at me.

"An amateur is one who does for love what a professional does for money. Now I get quite a lot of money out of it, as you will probably believe later on. In fact, if a Scotland Yard man gets as much joy out of his job as I get money, we can cry quits in the matter of names. Besides that," he added, "if I were in an official position it would be impossible for me to do my *Record* newspaper articles on crime, or to pick and choose among the cases offered me."

But that was an end to our badinage for that day, for he began to put me through it pretty thoroughly in regard to the present case, and all the people who might be even remotely connected with it. He himself, however, would not commit himself to anything in replying to my questions; and that is why he got far the largest share of the many new cigarettes he had to roll while listening to my replies. One glimpse, however, he did give me into the line he proposed to take first in his investigations. When we climbed down to the corner where we had undressed his first act was to jot down in his note book certain facts I had supplied. At least that is what I believe he did, for as I glanced over his shoulder while busy with my collar, I observed he was using some kind of shorthand of his own. But one entry proved intelligible, and this he asked me to verify:

Average temperature of a living body.............. 98.4° F.
Actual temperature of the sea that day............. 64.3° F.
Estimated temperature of body recovered from sea....   45° F.
Average rate at which heat is lost after death in the
    first three hours (slower after that)............   3.5° F.

"You accept these figures?" he asked.

"Yes, they will do."

"All right, see what we extract from them." He began to write with great rapidity. When he had finished he handed me the book while he was dressing.

1. The body could not have been in the sea for seven hours only.

    Because it takes about twenty-four hours to reduce the

temperature of a body to the level of its surrounding medium.

But:

2. The body when found had a lower temperature than its surrounding medium.

Therefore:

3. The body has been lying since death in some place the temperature of which was several degrees lower than the sea.

Further:

4. The fact that cadaveric rigidity had passed off by the time the body was recovered from the sea supports this conclusion

And:

5. Indicates that death must have occurred *not less* than three days earlier.

"How does it strike you?" he inquired, eyeing me keenly while busy with his braces.

There might be more in this note than met my eye, but one thing I saw:

"This incriminates nobody," I said; "he may have first been drowned, either by accident or his own act; then his body might have been washed ashore, left among the rocks for three days or so till carried out once more, and then in again by the higher tide of this morning. There is no evidence that any human hand ever touched the body."

McNab's face relaxed as he began to pull up his tie.

"And suppose you offer this evidence at the inquest to-morrow you can anticipate the verdict?" he asked.

"They probably won't ask for any of this from me—that side is Sullivant's affair. What they will ask me about is de Quettville's mental condition when

I saw him last Thursday night, on the eve of his disappearance. But I can tell you what the verdict will be on this evidence: Found drowned, with nothing to show how the deceased came to be in the water."

He stared hard for a moment or two at me, hesitated, and then said:

"Of course there is the evidence of his watch for the approximate time at which he was drowned."

"Yes, Carey will no doubt mention that, and at the same time produce the watch," I said.

Again McNab stared at me so that I wondered if he had not something on his mind he wished to ask me.

"Look here," he said at length, "it seems to me the verdict may be suicide. This housekeeper—what's her name—?"

"Mrs. Bichard."

"Yes. Well, she will say that in consequence of his odd behaviour all that Thursday, his talking to people who were not there, and all that, she became alarmed and sent for a doctor. This will be corroborated by the parlour maid and Miss Blampied?"

"Yes."

"And the lawyer Le Marinel can also testify to recent eccentricities?"

"No doubt."

"And the opinion you formed will substantiate all this, as well as Dr. Sullivant's opinion when he was placed in possession of the facts?"

"Yes, we agreed as to the man's insanity: our only difference was as to the acts to which his condition might lead."

"Dr. Sullivant suggested suicide; don't you think the verdict will be with him?"

"Not if it can be avoided.   Even in England they are unwilling to return a verdict of suicide, and on a small island like this they probably will be still more anxious to avoid the stigma of suicide.   You'll see, they'll give an open verdict of 'Found Drowned,' glad to find there is no direct evidence to justify any other."

"No direct evidence?"

"No; it's scarcely even presumptive evidence, since an insane person wandering about is no more immune from accident than any one else; he may fall over the cliffs into the sea and be drowned like any one else."

McNab took over his note book.

"Yes," he said thoughtfully, "it looks all very simple."

"Yet we know it is nothing of the sort," I said.

He nodded assent.

"Quite.   The trouble of course is that we have got hold of a clue entirely unintelligible till we light on an earlier one which will explain it."

He spoke so confidently that I asked him what his next step was to be.   I gathered that he hoped for some light in the talk with Le Marinel I was to arrange for that night.   Meanwhile he wanted me to take him back to Perigord and introduce him to the housekeeper so that he might have the run of the place for the remainder of the afternoon.   This suited me well enough, so long as I did not myself have to stay on, for there were two or three patients I already had on my conscience and on whom I must look in sometime that day.

On the way to Perigord we fixed things up. He could have a look round the house and grounds, see Mrs. Bichard and the maid, Daniel Sarchet, Mère Trouteaud and her Neptune, and catch the six o'clock 'bus from Pleinmont back to town.

When we had scrambled clear of the rocks he asked me how I proposed to explain him to Mrs. Bichard so that he might get the run of the place. It clearly would not at all suit his ends to say he was there because an attack had been made on me. And just as little would the old housekeeper understand any one seeking to probe about in order to obtain material for an attractive contribution to the *Daily Record*. Indeed it became self-evident that, as far as possible, McNab's real business must be concealed, especially with the case in its then undeveloped state, lest essential evidence should in the meantime be destroyed by any one who had something to conceal. Finally, we arranged that I should present him as a surveyor, a designation vague enough to impress the simple old housekeeper, and sufficiently elastic to cover the closest inspection of the Perigord property inside and out.

How vividly I recall that walk along towards St. Pierre du Bois, under trees whose exuberant foliage formed a green shade through which the afternoon sun laid a network of golden tracery on the road. The very air seemed asleep. From the chimney of a little white farmhouse that stood gable end to the road, a thin spiral of blue smoke drifted and wound its way upward with an appearance of infinite languor. A little fawn and white Guernsey cow, slowly rubbing her neck on a low gate, stopped the operation to regard us with placid, kindly eyes as we passed. When we approached Perigord I wondered whether we should find Le Marinel there, and others perhaps who might make it difficult for McNab to get on with his investigations. The simple-minded country-folk would present no obstacles. Indeed, they would accept him on what might be called his face value, and once they grasped his object, a rather lengthy process since they first thought in their Guernsey French and then spoke in English, he would be left undisturbed. But if others were about the house, Mrs. Blampied, say, keeping an eagle eye on her daughter's interests, it would be hard for him to hide his real object.

Luck, however, favoured us at the start. From Mrs. Bichard, red-eyed and shaken, we learned that Mr. Le Marinel had left only half an hour earlier, but that not only had Mrs. Blampied been there too but Mr. Brisson in his daughter's interests, and Mr. George Drury as well. All the local arrangements had been left in the hands of Mr. Drury, she told us, since he lived in the neighbourhood, and being on the telephone could communicate with Mr. Le Marinel direct. McNab's intervention she appeared to accept as just one more among the many unusual and upsetting things such a tragic event thrusts on an ordered household.

When I left McNab was well on the way in his conquest of Mrs. Bichard. He was like that : he inspired confidence. I knew his methods, for I had myself

been under his treatment.   All the same, I hurried
away convinced in my own mind that if he unearthed
there the clue he wanted, it would lead him to the
other Perigord, where Cæsar Brisson had much good
wine in his big vaults alongside the Quay.

LE MARINEL rang me up just after eight that Tuesday night. At first I thought the call would be from McNab, since he had not yet returned from Perigord. But when the avocat's voice came through telling me he wanted to talk over a rather private matter I was, for a moment, at a loss for a reply. It was better that Le Marinel should want to come to see me than that, as arranged with McNab, I should call him in to see us. But McNab had given me no indication of what the nature of his proposed talk with the avocat was to be; and, in any case, McNab was not there. So I answered that I was disengaged, and that he could come over at once. My thought was that I could probably keep the lawyer in talk till McNab turned up. And, while I waited, my mind turned to resume its speculations on de Quettville's death. The one fact about which all the consideration I had given subsequent to seeing the body made me convinced, was that he had been dead for days. Beyond that I remained in a fog.

To make the inference that whoever had been impersonating the dead man at Perigord must have been some one who knew him well did not carry me far, since on a relatively small island people were very familiar to each other. But whether this masquerader were also a murderer, and what his motive could be, these were questions to which I had no answer. On the body there had been no indication of any external marks of violence. And if an autopsy had been arranged Carey had not called for my presence. He would of course ask Dr. Sullivant to make the post mortem examination, not only because he was his usual aid but also, I suspected, because Sullivant appeared to be right in his prediction of suicide, while my strongly expressed opinion that de Quettville had become a homicidal maniac was now demonstrably wrong. It need not be said that I felt thoroughly unhappy and uncomfortable about the whole case, not least on account of Dr. Wright whose *locum* I was. Both Carey and Le Marinel appeared to think I ought to have seen the man's mental condition when I first saw him on the Thursday night. And it was only the discovery of the nocturnal masquerader, supposed to be de Quettville, which had seemed to prove my opinion right that had re-established my professional reputation, and won me their respect.

Well, my latest opinion that the man had been not less than three days dead would certainly not do anything except justify Sullivant once more, since instead of wandering about inflamed with a desire to kill some one, as I had suggested, it would show that he had simply risen from his bed to throw himself into the sea.

I have said the one fact of which I was certain was that de Quettville had been dead for not less than three days. This is wrong. There was another fact following from the fact on which I was necessarily equally sure: the man who had been taken for de Quettville by four people, who would no doubt testify at the inquest to having seen him, was certainly not de Quettville. But who was he? And what game was he up to? Then just as the door bell rang it struck me that McNab out at Perigord must be making progress towards an answer to both questions, since he was now a good two hours overdue.

Le Marinel seemed tired. He dropped rather heavily into a chair. I guessed that only some urgent matter would have brought him to see me that evening.

"Inquest is fixed for to-morrow at noon," he said.

"I know; the notice was waiting for me when I got back."

He waved a weary hand.

"Yes, I fancied Carey would want your evidence. That's why I'd like to know what your evidence is going to be."

"In advance?"

"Why, yes, if you don't mind."

"It will of course depend on the nature of the questions put to me."

He sat forward abruptly.

"I can tell you that. The questions will relate to the condition in which you found him when you visited him professionally last Thursday."

"Well," I said, "you know that both Sullivant and myself concluded him to be of unsound mind."

Le Marinel waved a hand, more alertly now.

"Sullivant will not be asked as to his mental condition. Sullivant did not see him alive. You alone saw him alive as late as Thursday night, just before he disappeared."

"Very well. I shall state that I formed the opinion that de Quettville suffered from delusional dementia."

"And that the opinion was formed on Thursday night?"

"No; that would be untrue. The opinion was not formed till after he had disappeared, and we heard of his strange behaviour from the housekeeper and Miss Blampied, when we went to Perigord on Friday night."

"Exactly." Le Marinel nodded. "And, if I remember correctly, the opinion you expressed to me on the Friday morning when we met outside my house was merely that you had found de Quettville a taciturn and bad-tempered patient. You were, in fact, rather indignant at having been asked to go out and see him at all."

Pressed in this fashion I could only admit the correctness of the lawyer's memory. It was true that at the time de Quettville was seen by me no suspicion of his sanity crossed my mind. As I made the admission a gleam of—no, perhaps not triumph but—satisfaction came into Le Marinel's eyes, and that satisfaction was also manifest in the way he softly rubbed the palms of his hands on his knees.

"Look here," I blurted out, "what is all this for?"

"Oh," he said, "all this is rather important in view of to-morrow's inquest. You see," he went on as he lifted one of his hands to examine a finger nail, "it might be awkward if you were to state that on seeing him you detected no traces of an unsound mind, and then had to add that—well—that Mrs. Bichard got you to change your mind about her master's sanity. That would not look well, *mon ami*—to be so influenced by an old woman's gossip, eh?"

Did he intend to be offensive? I stared at him in wonder, and his eyes rose to meet my own.

"My concern is for your reputation, Dunn," he said with some eagerness. "Consider that, after all, you judged the man's mental condition not by what you yourself saw but by what the old woman said. Therefore, though to-morrow, before the Court, you may say de Quettville was insane, the real and only authority for that declaration will be that imbecile old Mrs. Bichard, speaking through your voice."

"Do you suggest that what she told me was untrue?" I demanded hotly.

"About hearing him talk to himself? No, an old man often does talk to himself, many who are not old also, particularly in moments of agitation. About shutting himself up in his room? No; it was natural if he was afraid of some one. And let me tell you de Quettville was in great fear. That is why he fled from his own house. That, indeed, is why he only ventured back at night."

Now the logic of all this would have hit me with shattering force but for the fact that I *knew* de Quettville had not been coming back at night. For I knew what Le Marinel did not know; and that was that de Quettville had been dead probably from the night of his disappearance, and certainly from the night after

he disappeared. And had Le Marinel not irritated me
quite so much I probably would have then and there
acquainted him with the fact. As it was, I kept it up
my sleeve, intending to flatten him with it afterwards,
when I discovered what the real object of his visit
might be. For I did not believe that he was there
solely, or even chiefly, out of concern for my professional reputation. Yet I saw it was quite possible de
Quettville had gone in fear of some one, and indeed
that such a fear might even be the cause of his mental
collapse. Had the avocat somehow discovered the
identity of this person? If so this might be the earlier
clue we needed, the absence of which left us feeling
much as if we had begun a serial story half way
through.

"Well," I said deliberatively, as if I had been considering his words all the time, "I see no evidence that
de Quettville went in fear of anybody."

"Don't you?"

"No."

Le Marinel laughed.

"Why, it's plain enough, it's written over all his
actions; it's the one fact that can explain both why he
shut himself up, and why he ran away."

"He ran away to drown himself, you think?"

The lawyer writhed with impatience over my suggestion that he could think anything so stupid.

"No, no, no!" he almost shrieked. "Why in
Heaven's name should he take his own life? Who-
ever he feared could do no more to him than kill him.
Why should he himself do it for him? No; what

really happened must have been that after reaching the Pleinmont cliffs towards which Sarchet and Nicolle saw him running, he *fell* into the sea and was drowned. There is no more need to presume suicide than there is need to suggest insanity."

Well, of course I knew Le Marinel wanted to stop me from suggesting at the inquest that de Quettville was insane. I would have been as dense as he supposed me if I had not seen that from the first. But what I did not yet see was his object in trying to prevent such evidence being given. I might have put a straight question to him about that, but the truth is I had become sensitive to the fact that our relations with each other had altered in some subtle way. Frankness was at a discount that night. He had come to influence my evidence, while I, on my side, annoyed by seeing him suppose I was blind to his purpose, had kept my own secret, and let him talk as if I believed de Quettville had been drowned that morning. Still, if we were fencing with each other it was by his choice, not mine, and, after all, it served to keep him there against McNab's return.

"Of course," I said, "if one could be certain his actions were dictated by fear it might well alter one's opinion as to his mental condition, especially if one had proof of the identity of the person who terrorized him into such strange actions."

Le Marinel promptly replied in a way that revealed a taste for the dramatic. He leant forward, touched my knee with his forefinger, and then pointing at me, whispered one word:

"Brisson!"

If he expected to startle me he was disappointed. Brisson was my own suspect, aided by the good Catulle, of course.

"And the proof?" I inquired.

He spread out his hands in quite the French fashion, elevating his dark eyebrows.

"Oh, my friend, just consider. The hatred between the two, it is a thing notorious for years. And the climax came when Brisson somehow got wind of de Quettville's intention to mortgage Perigord, and so do his daughter out. Why, if de Quettville had been murdered instead of drowned I, who know much of the relations existing between the two men, would not hesitate to suspect Cæsar Brisson of the deed."

I had not hesitated myself to hold that suspicion; but I did not tell Le Marinel so. It impressed me, however, to find that he could share such a suspicion; and seeing this he tapped my knee and continued.

"You will remember what I told you while we watched last night. I have no doubt, now, that the will I discovered was drawn up in the hole and corner manner, and kept a secret even from me, because he had developed a fear of his brother-in-law. That will he could keep secret, since the two witnesses were witnesses of his signature only, not of its contents. But the mortgage he could not keep secret if the holder of the mortgage talked; and that he must have done, or one of his clerks. Now you see what will happen if to-morrow Hilaire de Quettville is declared to have died by his own hand. The question of his sanity will arise, and if he is declared insane then the will is void, and then that nimble rascal Cæsar Brisson steps into everything."

In his indignation Le Marinel rose to pace the floor. Presently he stopped, turned to face me, and as he paused I heard the door bell ring. But Le Marinel was too preoccupied to hear anything. He did not even hear the quite audible knock that next followed on the door behind him.

"Dunn," he cried with great solemnity, "there is but one thing that can prevent Cæsar Brisson from stepping into the dead man's shoes: the verdict to-morrow *must* be Death by Misadventure."

The concluding words, at least, were overheard by McNab as he was shown into the room.

"Not by misadventure," he said, his hand still on the door.

Le Marinel wheeled round as if suddenly stung.

"I beg your pardon," he stammered, taken aback and nonplussed.

"By violence, not misadventure," McNab repeated quietly.

For a minute the two men stood staring at each other. Then McNab looking past the other, caught my eye and nodded.

"Ring up the Chief Constable. Ask him to come at once. Say the matter is urgent."

IN my haste to get at the telephone I omitted to make the two men known to each other. This placed Le Marinel at a disadvantage, for while McNab from my talk about the avocat could easily divine his identity, McNab must have been a complete puzzle to Le Marinel. But by the time I got back McNab appeared to have explained himself to the other. Later I gathered that when I had been holding the line while Sergeant Torode was trying to pick up the Chief at one or other of his haunts, Le Marinel had, in his lawyer-like way, hinted his doubt about McNab's legal standing in the affair. But McNab had brushed this aside by the blunt statement that professional negligence having been suggested against me in regard to de Quettville, he himself was acting in my defence. To this Le Marinel could say nothing, since he had made the suggestion himself when I met him on the Saturday night just before I went to the wine shop. And of course McNab knew as well as the lawyer that this charge of professional incapacity or negligence might be revived to-morrow.

To my relief the interval during which I had been out of the room appeared to have been occupied in settling this technical point. But as soon as I explained that Torode would get in touch with his Chief, and send him up to us as soon as possible, Le Marinel proceeded to question McNab. He wanted to know how he could be so sure that de Quettville's death was due to violence, and not to accident. Here, however, McNab turned the tables on the lawyer, coolly reminding him that this was a matter for the Chief Constable, with whom would rest the decision as to whether Le Marinel would at that stage in the case be told anything at all. After that the avocat sobered down. But he did not sit down. The sudden turn the case had taken was, I suppose, too much even for his self-control. It certainly was so for my own; and I could well gauge his impatience for Carey's arrival by my own feelings. If McNab were right this meant murder. If McNab were right the murder must have been committed at least three days before the body was found. If McNab were right how had the murder been done so that no traces had been left on the body? And in a body taken out of water it is known that even the smallest *ante mortem* bruise remains visible.

But McNab had not called it murder. He had simply said the death was due to violence. Had some one, attacked by the insane man, killed him in self-defence? In that event some mark of external violence must have been visible. And yet I could swear to it that there was none.

Now Le Marinel, as he hung about, hands deep in his pockets, and a frown on his face, may have been preoccupied with thoughts along other lines; he may have been considering whether in a case of death by violence the question of insanity would arise, since it would be clear that de Quettville had not committed suicide. In which case the will would presumably stand valid. But if he was doubting the correctness of McNab's assertion that was a matter on which I knew more than he could know. McNab had all the proverbial caution of his race, perhaps a trifle more. And when I recalled his handling of the Kinloch case in which I had found myself against him, and how I had actually laughed in derision when he told me exactly how he was going to find a blind man who did not, as I knew, then exist! Well, he had been right about that. And I had no doubt that he was right now about de Quettville.

"Mr. Le Marinel."

"Yes?"

"Why did you have a new catch put on the study window?"

McNab's question broke the tension. Le Marinel revealed this by sitting down on the nearest chair.

"You mean at Perigord, I suppose. Well, it was because the old one was worn out, and the window frame so shrunken with age that the catch could easily have been pushed open by inserting a knife between the sashes. You see," he went on, expanding as if at the sound of his own voice, "I hadn't been long among the de Quettville papers before perceiving that there might be a good many people on the island who would be glad to get in among them. He had an astonishing amount of money out on loan, and on terms which made it plain why he kept these transactions to himself."

"You mean the terms were harsh?"

Le Marinel nodded rapidly.

"Precisely. At interest so excessive that no *écrivain* in the island would have acted for him. So any one of his numerous clients might have held himself justified, if he could force an entry in de Quettville's absence and destroy the evidence of his debt. That was a risk I couldn't take, when I saw that one or two of his debtors were—well—very tough customers."

"So you had this new catch fitted—yesterday?"

Le Marinel stopped in the act of tapping a cigarette on the gold case.

"Ah, you got that from the housekeeper," he said.

"No, nobody told me; it merely followed from something I noticed."

"Well, anyway, I could hardly have had the job done sooner, you know." He glanced at me. "We first saw the papers on the Friday night, and as it was Saturday before I began to read them—well—there was no time."

"Had you any reason for suspecting that some one had entered the study?"

"Yes. On the Sunday it seemed to me the papers were not as I had left them. But I had made no special note of their order, and so could not be sure. When, however, the housekeeper reported seeing de Quettville in the garden, my idea was that he had entered by the study window, the one key of the door being in my possession, and so, though he could enter the house by means of the side door key he himself had on his ring, he could not enter the study."

"But once in the study he could leave by the door?"

"Yes, it is a latch lock."

"Any one entering by the window could snap the catch back, then leave by the door, pull that behind him and leave no evidence of his presence?"

"Quite. That's what de Quettville did. But when the new catch was on the window I hoped to force him to enter by the side door. Colonel Carey knows all about that. That is how we hoped to take him last night. The new catch, unfortunately, does not seem to have been as strong as I believed."

Le Marinel in a disappointed way struck a match and held it to his cigarette. McNab waited till the operation was completed.

"Mr. Le Marinel," he said, "your new catch was very nearly strong enough. But if it had been ten times stronger you would not have taken de Quettville last night."

The avocat threw up his head.

"What—what's that you say?" he cried.

"You could not have taken de Quettville, simply because de Quettville was not there."

The avocat's face, with its dropped jaw and arched eyebrows made an almost comic picture of utter bewilderment.

"Not there," he echoed. "But—but—" he looked over at me, "but somebody was there, as Dunn knows."

"Oh, yes; it was no shadow that knocked him out."

"Then who was it—who in Heaven's name was it?"

"That is what we want to find out, with your help," said McNab.

After a moment Le Marinel slowly shook his head.

"There are so many—twenty at least among those

debtors who might have—" He stopped abruptly as if one name suggested itself as more likely. Then again he shook his head. "No, *not* Brisson," he murmured. "Brisson owed him no money, so had nothing to gain by entering the study, so long as de Quettville was alive."

"And if he were dead at the time?"

"But he wasn't."

"But suppose he was."

The lawyer's gesture indicated that he considered this childish. When McNab persisted, however, he replied:

"Brisson, in that case, would have everything to gain. He must have heard, like others, about the mortgage, and although he could not know whether it had yet been implemented, that did not matter, since he had only to get at the will and destroy it to inherit not only the money raised by the mortgage but everything else as well."

For a second or two McNab looked keenly at the lawyer, then he spoke.

"All right, Mr. Le Marinel; he *was* dead when the man came to Perigord last night."

I fancy the avocat did not credit his ears; either that or he thought McNab had gone crazy.

"Eh?" he whispered blankly. "What did you say?"

When McNab repeated the statement he looked at me for confirmation.

"He must have been dead for three days before he was taken from the sea," I said.

And slow as he had been to grasp the medical facts

he was mighty quick to recognize the legal implication. I saw it in his eyes before my explanation ended. Then he leaped to his feet.

"By God!" he cried, "that means that if Cæsar Brisson was the man who entered Perigord last night he already *knew* de Quettville to be dead."

McNab nodded his assent and approval.

"That seems to follow, since he would otherwise have nothing to gain by destroying the will while his brother-in-law was still alive."

Le Marinel straightened up to stare at McNab. We felt, I think, that a moment of crisis had arrived. All along, of course, my suspicion had centred on Brisson and his ally Coquard. But how much could McNab prove? This question appeared to be in Le Marinel's mind also.

"And if he knew he was dead, how did he come to know? Had he made sure he was dead by—?"

McNab held up a protesting hand.

"That does not follow. He may have found him dead."

"But you suspect him," I asserted, for it did seem far-fetched to suggest that Brisson might, somewhere, have come upon the body of de Quettville, and then cut away to Perigord to hunt for his will. Yet my assertion had an effect on McNab as strange as it was unexpected. He turned on me.

"I'll tell you what I suspect," he said. "What I suspect is that you could tell us a great deal more about this than you have done."

"Me?" I cried, utterly taken aback.

"Yes."

"I've told you absolutely everything."

This brought a vigorous negative.

"No! You told me what you saw and heard; but there was something you did not see or hear, something you must have missed, Dunn. It was thought you had *not* missed it, though. And that's why that hasty knife attack was made on you."

"You mean that?" I asked.

"Certainly; the attempt on your life is not to be accounted for otherwise. And I'm sure Mr. Le Marinel will agree with me."

The avocat's pale face, however, reflected the uttermost surprise and bewilderment.

"Knife attack!" he repeated. "What knife attack? This is the first I have heard of such a thing."

On that I had to give Le Marinel the story, as already reported to the Chief Constable and McNab. At first he resented having been kept out of this fact so long, as he appeared to think that it was only through McNab's mistaken assumption that he must have known all about it that he was hearing about it now. But before I finished the frown disappeared, and when I frankly related the suspicions roused by my experiences in the wine shop I could see he was entirely with me there. For those suspicions, like his own, pointed straight at Brisson. Although I had laid no stress on the thieves' *argot* I had detected in the vocabulary of the good Catulle, Le Marinel fastened instantly on this feature. Its significance was not lost on the avocat in him, and the fact that Coquard used the thieves' slang was accepted as convincing proof that Coquard belonged to the worst criminal class in Paris. We had it all our own way when it came to discussing *argot* French, and McNab had never a word to say. Indeed we almost forgot he was there, lying back in his chair listening.

Le Marinel did not doubt the attack had come from Coquard, and could not understand why I had given up that belief.

"Well," I said, "I knew the *apache* does not throw the knife. It would be a useful accomplishment in a city like Paris if he could. He likes his knife because it is quiet, but he never seems to have learnt the art of killing at a distance with it."

Le Marinel pondered this, fingering his chin.

"Well," he said, "it is strange the trick isn't known where it would be so useful."

Then an explanation occurred to me. The *apache* is no traveller. Indeed, he seldom goes further afield than the outer boulevards. But occasionally he is made to travel, even as far as the French penal settlements. Still, though the art of knife-throwing has its home in these islands I could hardly visualize the French authorities providing their prisoners with knives, much less supplying them with native instructors in the art. So any degree of proficiency implied a sojourn, and a rather long sojourn too, among the natives, free from all official interference. Now the fact that the knife was thrown was equivalent to a proof that the man who threw it had lived for some time in the southern latitudes of the world. Le Marinel at once agreed when I put this to him.

"It would simply mean," he remarked, "that this Coquard is a transported criminal who escaped from Cayenne."

At this McNab woke up.

"But," he said, "isn't that begging the question? Aren't you assuming as true what has yet to be proved: that Coquard is the man who threw the knife?"

Le Marinel hesitated.

"I was merely assuming it for the moment," he said, "as a possibility. You yourself, I am sure, as a detective have often followed the method of elimination. And surely in this instance we can rule out as beyond suspicion all who have never lived for some considerable time in those regions where knife-throwing is practised. Now," he went on quickly as McNab stirred as if to speak, "all I say is that Coquard as a Paris *apache* might well have been sent to those regions, and if he is an escaped prisoner it would account, not only for his ready use of the knife, but for his taking refuge here with Brisson."

"But why attack Dunn? If you think it was because he happens to be one of the men Dunn has told us about, one of the four he helped to arrest five years ago in Paris, then that attack has no connection with de Quettville's death."

Before replying the avocat glanced at me deprecatingly.

"Well, since you put it like that," he said, "I'm

afraid I must agree with you that Dunn was attacked
because it was supposed he knew something which he,
in fact, did not know. I think, further, that it was
something he said, or saw, or overheard, in the wine
shop that frightened Brisson, who promptly availed
himself of the new talent his friend Coquard had acquired in a distant hemisphere."

This brought McNab forward in his chair.

"And now we can go back to the suggestion that
Brisson may have found de Quettville dead, and concealed the body in, say, one of his empty wine casks
till he had time to go through the documents. Does
that theory sound tenable now?"

The question was put to the avocat.

"Absurd," he promptly replied. "Quite absurd, unless de Quettville had been murdered."

"Then in that event the attack on Dunn would be
accountable—if they believed he knew something that
made him dangerous?"

"Then, and then only," Le Marinel agreed.

"All right." McNab turned to me. At the very
moment, however, the 'phone went off in a shrill ring
and on lifting the receiver the voice of Sergeant Torode came through to tell me they had run the Chief
to earth out at the Vale and he was now on his way
to us. When I returned with the news I found McNab
playing the host with my whisky. Indeed, Le Marinel
was protesting against the stiffness of the peg McNab
had poured into his glass.

"Remember," he was saying, "whisky here is one

third stronger than you are allowed to drink it in England."

McNab was greatly surprised.

"Do you tell me!" he cried, elevating the decanter to stare at the contents, "a third stronger?"

"And less than half the price," Le Marinel nodded. "Didn't you know?"

McNab shook his head, as he lifted his own glass and winked at me.

"Not me, and I doubt if the fact is generally known. I'm sure at least that not even a rumour of it has reached Scotland."

"Oh, I don't know," Le Marinel responded, "they do say there's a Scotsman or two on every boat that comes in."

"That's nothing, man. If what you tell me about the income tax, the whisky and the tobacco were generally known in Glasgow, nothing less than a direct boat service from the Clyde would meet the need."

The sudden change in the atmosphere indicated by this jocularity was astonishing. We had all been on the strain, and, I suppose, were ready to relax for a moment or two on any pretext. Le Marinel seemed to have thawed. With a gleam in his eyes he nodded like a wagtail at McNab.

"You know," he said, "I believed at first when you began to question me that you even suspected me of being the man who was masquerading in the dark as de Quettville."

McNab laughed.

"Why shouldn't I? You were on the spot last night, you wandered about the house alone, and for all Dunn here could see you might yourself have knocked him out with the chair."

Le Marinel laughed too.

"After throwing the light of my torch in his eyes to see just where he stood."

"Exactly. And we must not forget that, after all, no third person did enter by the door while Dunn watched it."

"Of course! I didn't need to; I was there already. That's where Carey and his sergeant were dished. No wonder you considered the possibility."

McNab waved a hand.

"I might have gone further than that but for one thing that cleared you," he said.

"What was that?" the avocat cried, greatly interested.

"The scented handkerchief."

"The what?"

"Oh, it was a small thing," McNab smiled, "but it was none the worse evidence for that—all the better, in fact, since it was unlikely to be thought out beforehand."

"What on earth are you talking about?" Le Marinel cried in round-eyed amazement.

"Just this. Dunn here, in giving me the facts about his watch in your company last night behind the door, happened to say that while struggling with the man, and before he was knocked senseless, he became very conscious of a perfume which pervaded the whole place. Well now, that was quite reliable evidence that you were not the man. You don't see it? Well, consider the pervasive qualities of perfume. Had it been on your handkerchief, Dunn, with whom, as I understand, you sat side by side for hours, would have noticed it sooner. But as he only became conscious of it when he was grappling with the man, it indicates that a *third* person was then present."

How much further this sort of talk might have gone I cannot say, but just then a sharp ring on the door bell brought the badinage to an end. At the sound of Colonel Carey's voice in the hall McNab turned to the avocat.

"Now," he said with seriousness, "we return to the new window catch you fitted to the window."

It seemed we had dragged the Chief away from a dinner party. But to judge by his pleasant and inclusive nod it had not spoilt his humour; and in any case he must at that hour have got his dinner before the call reached him.

"It's about that attack on Dr. Dunn," McNab presently began. "I wanted to show you something I found this afternoon, below the study window at Perigord."

Producing his pocket book, McNab extracted from between its pages a silvery, pointed object about four inches long: the broken end of a double-edged knife.

"Unfortunately for us," he added, "the maker's name must have been placed near the handle."

Carey turned over the length of blade, and nodded.

"You suggest this was the knife used against Dr. Dunn?"

"I have reason to believe so," McNab replied, "but we have not yet tried it in the hole in Dr. Dunn's door. The point was broken off in forcing the new catch put on the study window."

Carey glanced at me.

"If it does fit it confirms our guess that the attack came from de Quettville," he said. "Not that there was much doubt about that," he added. "Still, now I am here, we may as well test it."

In the tone more than the words there was an ever so gentle reproach which implied that we had called him from pleasant company to confirm something which needed no confirmation. In that respect Carey, I fancy, considered the fractured blade as a parallel to the fragment of seaweed McNab found in the watch, which McNab had exhibited as proof of what needed no proof: that the man whose body had just been taken out of the sea had been drowned in the sea.

McNab, however, now, as then, made no comment; and at a gesture from him we followed Carey into the hall. The Colonel himself, on his knees, fitted the blade into the hole. There could be no doubt about it: this was the blade that had come at me on the previous Saturday night. We all tried it in turn, and found that it fitted perfectly and firmly, like a blade in its sheath. But the significance of this was to Carey nothing like what it was to us. To him so far it merely meant that this undoubtedly was part of the knife de Quettville had in his insanity thrown at me; and as de Quettville was now dead the incident might be regarded as closed. To us, who knew that de Quettville had been dead before the knife was thrown, it meant —well, perhaps only McNab could tell us that.

Carey was about to take his leave when McNab stopped him.

"We know the knife was not thrown by de Quettville," he said.

Carey lifted his head, staring vaguely.

"What?" he said, in an effort at apprehension. "Not thrown by de Quettville. How can you know that?"

"Because he was dead at the time."

Carey peered at us standing behind McNab in the dusk of the hall.

"But de Quettville was drowned this morning," he said.

"Not this morning, sir," McNab said with confidence, "not less than three days ago."

"Who says so?" Carey demanded crisply, now master of himself.

"Dr. Dunn found demonstrative evidence of the fact in the condition of the body."

"Dr. Dunn, eh? Well, forgive me, but an assertion of this nature sounds—well—needs support. Dr. Sullivant saw the body, assigned the cause and hour of death, which the watch confirmed, and though doctors can, like the rest of us, make mistakes, Sullivant made no mistake last Friday when he predicted suicide."

For all the hasty rush of words the thing could scarcely have been more delicately put. Carey had deftly drawn the contrast between Sullivant and myself, calling attention to my previous mistakes, as he thought them to be, without mentioning them.

"But this does not rest on Dr. Dunn alone," Mc-Nab was saying.

"No? Who then supports his view?"

"I do. What Dr. Dunn as a medical man saw in the body's condition only served to confirm a conclusion I had previously reached," McNab declared.

The stiff formality of his tone may have impressed the Chief Constable.

"Really? You yourself, independently of Dunn, saw something that convinced you he had been three days dead?"

"More than that," McNab replied. "I had not been ten minutes in the boat-house before I suspected the man had been murdered."

"Murdered?"

It was almost a cry. His eyes went from face to face. Nobody spoke. Neither Le Marinel nor myself had anything to say. And McNab looked as if he had said his say. Then the Chief Constable pulled himself together, put up his hand and quietly shut the door.

COLONEL CAREY was a changed man by the time we got back to the room. His eyes had lost the glint of humour usually there, and the hint of a smile usually about his mouth was no longer discernible. He pulled up short, and wheeled round sharply.

"Le Marinel, you have heard the facts on which this suggestion of murder is based?" he asked in a voice that had an edge. Even his easy fitting dress clothes had somehow taken on the rigidity of a uniform.

Le Marinel bowed.

"Some of them."

"Speaking now as an avocat, do you consider the suggestion of murder tenable?"

"Tenable, yes, certainly. But not yet proved," Le Marinel replied promptly.

On that Carey with a gesture sent us to our chairs. He was going to examine the evidence for himself. He nodded at McNab.

"State your case," he said in a grave, official tone new to me.

McNab's statement of the case included the facts already known to us; but he handled and marshalled them in a way that to me at least strengthened conviction. He began by showing that though de Quettville met his death by drowning, he had not been drowned that day. The discrepancies in the post mortem symptoms were decisive against that possibility. What the physiological facts proved was that de Quettville had been dead for not less than three days, which was about the time when *rigor mortis* begins to disappear. But the body could not have been in the sea all that time, since, if it had, its temperature would have been the same as that of the sea. Wherever the body had been in the interval between death and the time at which it had been transferred to the sea, that place must have been a place with a lower temperature than the sea, because the body when found was at a lower temperature than the sea. And this fact also proved that the body had not been in the sea long enough to be raised to the temperature of its surrounding medium. Thus obviously, since a dead body cannot move itself, some one had put it into the sea a few hours before it was found. Yes, there *was* evidence of contrivance and forethought in the time chosen for transference to the sea. It had been put there exactly at the time when cadaveric rigidity began to pass off, and thus the impression would be conveyed that the man had been drowned only a few hours earlier, since when found cadaveric rigidity, which normally lasted about three days, would appear to have not yet set in.

"Whereas it was really over?" Carey nodded.

"Exactly. And," McNab went on, "as the only way of harmonizing the absence of rigidity with the low temperature is to conclude that death took place not less than three days earlier, it follows that it was not de Quettville who came to Perigord last night, nor was it he who was seen by the two fishermen making for the sea that morning. Again, you see, some one is offering us an appearance for the reality."

"And the reality?" Carey questioned as McNab stopped to pour himself out a drink.

"Looks like murder."

"Looks like! Appearances again?" Carey frowned.

McNab set down his glass.

"Is not the attack on Dunn enough to suggest it can be no less than murder? The man who made the attack risked his own life to do it. What his motive was we cannot yet tell; but that it had some connection with de Quettville's death is made certain by the discovery that the blade found under the window at Perigord fits the hole in the door of this house."

There was a prolonged silence in which Carey stood holding his chin, eyes on the carpet, considering this argument. We all watched him. Finally he looked up.

"No," he said, "there's nothing decisive in all this. Suppose I accept the medical evidence that the man has been dead three days, we can account for everything if he was drowned three days ago after which his body was left by the tide in some crevice or corner among the rocks till it floated out again this morning by the higher tide."

This was a possibility I had myself seen. And now it occurred to me that a body among the rocks, and out of the sun's heat might have a lower temperature than the sea.

McNab rose from his chair.

"My dear sir, your suggestion, pardon me, is simply preposterous," he said.

Carey obviously did not like this; he became rather pink about the gills. I imagine he had allowed more of the old Indian official to come into his manner and tone than he knew. He curbed himself now with apparent effort.

"There is no evidence whatever that I can see that any human hand touched the body," he declared.

"You are forgetting the man's watch," McNab said.

"The watch?" Carey lifted his eyebrows.

"Yes, the watch; its evidence is eloquent and blows your tide theory sky high."

"I don't quite see that," the other man said calmly.

"No," McNab nodded. "You didn't see it this morning either."

Carey looked at us with a patient, fleeting smile as the memory came back.

"I remember you drew my attention to a piece of seaweed in the watch case."

"And what did that tell you? That de Quettville took out his watch to see at what time he was going to drown himself? Do you believe that? I should have thought that, at such a moment, he would be less concerned with Time than with Eternity." McNab began to get a trifle excited. "Oh, that watch just fair shouts things at you. The hands of it had stopped at 4.16, a quarter of an hour or so after de Quettville was seen by the two fishermen hurrying towards the shore. But if his body had been lying among the rocks for three days, as you suppose, it could not have been him they saw. But it is easy to see who he was—the man who *opened* the watch to set the hands at 4.16 in order to suggest that de Quettville had been drowned at that time that morning. That is the evidence that some human hands *had* touched the body that morning. No one could have known, in advance, at what time to set the hands. But after this man had been seen, he, aware that a renewed search would follow, and knowing where the body was, went straight to it to get it into the water. At the last moment, with the body already among the seaweed, the thought came to him to alter the hands of the watch in order to confirm the tale he knew the two men would tell, and so establish the fiction that de Quettville met his death by drowning at that precise time."

Carey seemed, like ourselves, rather overwhelmed by McNab's rapid and vehement presentation of his evidence. His tone changed, and we recognized with relief that a breeze between the two men had been avoided.

"I suppose," he suggested diffidently, "it would be too miraculous a coincidence if the watch had just happened to stop at that exact time on the day on which he actually was drowned?"

McNab shook his head.

"Miraculous coincidences do happen," he admitted. "But you see, sir, in this instance the watch had been *opened*—opened to alter the hands. That was what first caught my eye in the boat house. I thought it odd that de Quettville who was then supposed to have drowned himself, should trouble to correct his watch.

Then when Dunn spoke of the peculiarities and anom-
alies in the body's condition, it became self-evident that
it was not de Quettville who had opened the watch at
4.16 that morning."

"Suppose it is murder, have you any idea who the
murderer is?"

"No evidence," McNab admitted. "But where no
evidence exists we usually begin by asking who profits
by the death."

"Ah," Le Marinel cut in, "an ancient practice that.
The principle of *cui bono* which the Roman law immediately applied in such cases."

Carey turned to the avocat.

"All right, you apply it now."

The avocat sat forward, nothing loth, although he
began guardedly.

"Supposing the evidence has established this as murder, and speaking merely as an avocat whose duty it
is to make out a case, the main relevant facts to which
I would draw your attention are these: the bad feeling known to exist between the dead man and his
brother-in-law, Cæsar Brisson; the deepening of this
feeling into hatred when it became known that de
Quettville proposed to mortgage Perigord solely with
a view to make it a worthless property when it passed
to Brisson's daughter at his decease, and the fact that
only de Quettville's immediate death, before the deed
of mortgage was executed, could prevent this."

Carey nodded.

"Yes, I agree that Brisson had very strong motives.
That is so apparent that any one could see it."

McNab's brow puckered as he stared at Carey.

"Ah, you mean that any one having a grudge against de Quettville could count on that as cover for himself?"

"I do," Carey assented. "Any one with a grudge against de Quettville *or* Cæsar Brisson," he added significantly.

This startled us all. It gave the affair a new turn, opening out possibilities not before visible. It was Le Marinel who first recovered himself.

"That's all very well," he began, "but there are certain indications which point straight at Brisson."

"You didn't mention them just now," Carey said.

"No, I was dealing with motive. Yet though what I have in mind might be called straws, they have their proverbial value as indications. For example, the murderous attack on Dunn, which from the knife blade we now know to have *some* connection with the nocturnal entry into Perigord, followed immediately on the visit he made to Brisson's wine shop. Again, I am convinced that there is some direct connection between de Quettville's death and the erection of the figure of Neptune on the gateway at Perigord. I think the story begins with the setting up of that figure, and my notion is that we shall never get at the truth about this affair till we know more about the Friday night on which that figure was erected on the gate. But what is clear is that it was transformed into an effigy of a moneylender with the three golden balls to upset de Quettville. And it did upset him, making him take to his bed, and all that. Now the erection of the Neptune over the gate was held to be merely an act of mockery. But suppose there was a deeper calculation in it. Suppose it to be part of a scheme to worry and harass this man into exhibiting what could be taken for symptoms of insanity. Why then, in that event, not *only* would the Perigord property be saved if he died before the mortgage could be completed, but if evidence of an unsound mind could be produced, the will by which he left his money elsewhere would become null and void, and Brisson's daughter would inherit all."

Here Carey protested that Le Marinel was recurring to motive and pleading his case like an avocat for the prosecution, whereas he had promised facts which pointed directly at Brisson. This was admitted by Le Marinel.

"But," he said, "I have given you one fact, and I was only leading up to the other. Do you agree that the affair probably began with the erection of the Neptune on the gate?"

"That is what I have believed all along," Carey replied without hesitation.

"Very well. Now consider this rather delicate point. One of the pointing straws, I called it, and as it involves a point in psychology, a mere matter-of-fact person might be blind to its significance."

The Chief Constable smiled at this challenge.

"Try me," he said.

But Le Marinel remained very serious.

"Carey, what known act of Brisson's would you say most annoyed his brother-in-law?"

After a little consideration the reply came.

"Well, I'd say it was when he put up the word Perigord in huge gilt letters over the entrance to his wine shop."

Le Marinel, his dark eyes sparkling, snapped his fingers.

"And the figure of Neptune, with the three gilt balls put up over the entrance to Perigord, that too had the same intention: to bring de Quettville annoyance, derision and contempt. And my contention," the avocat concluded, striking one fist in his open palm, "is that both actions bear traces of the same mentality behind them."

For a second or two, while we watched him, Carey said nothing. Then I observed a flicker come to his eyes and he turned to McNab.

"And what is your opinion on this last point?" he inquired pointedly.

"An excellent point," McNab said with enthusiasm, "delicate, subtle and almost convincing."

This did not satisfy Le Marinel.

"Why not quite convincing?" he demanded.

McNab fidgeted in his chair.

"Well, its one weakness is psychological. The Neptune was transformed from a sea god into a moneylender. That implies that whoever did this was thinking of de Quettville in terms of usury, and how many might be doing that you alone can tell us," McNab replied.

"As to that," the avocat admitted, "there are thirty-five who owe him very large amounts, but only three who might have—well—gone to extreme lengths to escape their obligations. Still, none of the three is, I should say, imaginative enough to have conceived the notion of erecting the Neptune over the gate. There is something so palpably Gallic in its satiric humour and mockery, that, even if we had nothing else to go on, would connect Brisson with the affair."

Here Carey intervened brusquely.

"Dismiss the notion, Le Marinel, once for all. You see," he added quietly, "I *know* that, whoever murdered de Quettville, it was not Cæsar Brisson. I know it because, all along, we have been trying to trace the person who put up the figure on the gate since we believed that person to be morally responsible for de Quettville's supposed insanity. The most promising clue we had was the set of finger prints left on the gilding on tennis balls, and as the first person suspected naturally was Brisson, I had a glass stolen from the wine shop which he had just handled. The finger prints on the glass were not those on any of the tennis balls. But that is not all. Brisson could not possibly have murdered any one on this island at the time supposed. For he was in France at the time. He left by the *Foam* for St. Malo on Thursday at nine A.M. This I put beyond doubt by questioning both the master and the steward of the *Foam,* both men, of course, knowing Brisson well. And both vouch for the fact that Brisson returned with them when the *Foam* returned and berthed at the Albert Quay about five P.M. on the Saturday. Now as de Quettville was undoubtedly alive *after* Brisson left, and as according to your own contention de Quettville must have been dead before his return, is it not clear that whoever murdered de Quettville it was not Brisson?" Then as no one had any reply or comment to make, Carey, with a touch of his old raillery, himself suggested an explanation. "Unless indeed, Brisson, like Sir Boyle Roche's famous Irish bird, has, unknown to us, the faculty of being in two places at one time."

At this jest Le Marinel visibly writhed, and McNab sat as if turned to stone. For myself I could suggest no other explanation which would involve Cæsar Brisson. For I had undoubtedly seen de Quettville alive at 10.30 on the Thursday night, and I was no less sure from the state of the body that the man must have been dead before Brisson's return. And though de Quettville could have been dead for more than three days, he was certainly not dead on the Thursday morning when Brisson left on the *Foam*.

"No possibility of a return between Thursday and Saturday?" McNab inquired.

"None. Dismiss the notion. We absolutely *know* that Brisson slept at the Hotel de Provence, St. Malo on Thursday and Friday night. My own suspicion that he was behind the Neptune outrage was so strong after de Quettville disappeared that I have investigated all his movements during the past ten days. I got the *Chef de Police* in St. Malo even to verify his identity and trace his movements while he was there."

Le Marinel looked up wanly.

"They ought to know him. He formerly ran a low sort of café in St. Malo."

"So I understand," Carey said. "Anyway, it was

established that he spent both Thursday and Friday evenings playing *boule* at the Casino."

Thus did Carey put the lid on our suspicion of Cæsar Brisson. And to clear Brisson was to clear Coquard also. This was at once recognized just as we saw that to involve Brisson would have implicated Coquard. For de Quettville had undoubtedly met his death by drowning, and homicide by drowning is, except in the case of new-born infants, the rarest of crimes. For the very good reason that murder by such a method is next to impossible for any person to carry out alone. And Coquard was a smaller man than de Quettville, much younger no doubt, but probably nothing like so vigorous. Moreover, he was a stranger to the island, would not know his way about, and we had no evidence that he had ever set eyes on de Quettville. Was it conceivable that he alone, while Brisson took advantage of his help in the wine shop to transact a little business and see old friends in St. Malo, could have murdered de Quettville by drowning? It was not.

While these thoughts were passing through my mind as the others were talking, a word of the Chief Constable's caught my ear. He was saying something to the effect that if it could be proved de Quettville had been three days dead he would be more certain than he then was that a crime lay somewhere concealed in the affair. That roused me.

"By to-morrow," I said, "no one who looks at the man's face will be able to believe he was drowned this morning."

They knew what I meant, and the talk ended. Then Carey looked at his watch and rose.

"Till to-morrow then," he said with a sigh. "At present we have reached an *impasse.*"

When he and Le Marinel were gone we did not feel like going to bed. So McNab, drawing up his chair to the table, produced his notebook and gave me some account of his afternoon and evening's investigations at Perigord. Mrs. Bichard had talked freely to such a sympathetic stranger, and shown him over the house. He had also seen the Neptune, which by Mr. Le Marinel's order had been restored to Mère Trouteaud. She too had talked to him in her garden while he examined the figure-head, and told him of the bad luck which had followed its loss, and of how her little dog Mimi had barked at sight of it on the pillar in the Perigord garden, when she had stolen in to see if the story of its being there was true, and of how the little dog—many other instances of whose wisdom he had to listen to—had been taken ill with grief over the loss of the holy figure and had died the following night. And how on the following morning she had gone out to find a sheet she had left on the line to dry torn in shreds as if by evil spirits.

Then, when he succeeded in escaping from Mère Trouteaud, he had seen Sarchet who could not be shaken in his story of seeing de Quettville making for the sea that morning. After that he had returned to Perigord, to make some measurements such as a surveyor might be expected to make, and it was while pacing out the distance between the pillar by the summer-house and the study window that he had discovered the broken knife blade among the weeds under the window. Having recognized from its shape and double edge that it might well be the balanced type of knife used for throwing, he had come away almost satisfied that it established a connection between de Quettville's death and the attack made on me.

"And now," he commented wearily, "I suppose there's nothing for it but to seek for the man among those debtors the lawyer told us of. Let's have another drop of that cheap whisky," he said with a sigh, beginning to fill his pipe.

While I was getting the decanter he went on. "We'll just have to get a list of debtors the wee lawyer mentioned, and go through them on the *cui bono* principle, and a fine lengthy business that's likely to be. You'll notice, Dunn, that *cui bono* doesn't mean who profits *most,* but just who profits. That's where the Romans showed their good sense. For the man who, like Brisson here, stands to profit most by de Quettville's death, may not *need* the profit as much as another who stands to profit less. And, after all, that's making the big assumption that this is a case of murder for gain, which is only one among the many motives that incite to murder."

But McNab seemed to cheer up after a sip or two of whisky. As soon as his pipe was drawing well he asked me for a sheet of paper on which to set down his clues.

"A big sheet," he said with much gravity. "I like

to write them big, it seems to make them easier to read."

Now it did not appear to me that he had yet obtained enough in the way of clues to make it worth while to set them out on paper. And so after hunting out a sheet of quarto size it was with the keenest curiosity I placed myself behind his chair. Here is the list in the order he set it down, as I read it over his shoulder:

Body recovered three days later.

To account for this the possible clues are:

1. Fragment of seaweed.
2. Ship's figure-head.
3. Watch stopped at 4.16.
4. Four gilt tennis balls.
5. A torn sheet.
6. A stolen rope.
7. A broken knife blade.
8. A barking dog.
9. A scented handkerchief.
10. A broken clock.

Having completed this surprising list of clues, he cocked his head to one side and regarded his list critically.

"Doubtless I've overlooked some items," he remarked, "and probably some I've set down are without significance; but I have a notion that if we could sift out the worthless items, and set the remainder in their right order and relations, we would not be far away from a solution to the riddle."

But if this were true we evidently did not get the separate items into their right order that night, for by the time we went to bed no glimmer of a solution had dawned on our befogged minds. A glimmer, however, came just when the actual dawn began to filter in at my window. I remember sitting up, fully awake, as a light percolated into the focus of my consciousness. I sat still for one moment to marvel why I had not thought of it sooner. The next instant I was out of bed and into my friend's room.

"McNab," I shouted at him, "McNab, *now* I see it."

McNab sat up rubbing his eyes. But it did not take him long to get fully awake. He listened to my story with his arms behind his head, and I poured out the facts at a speed which afforded him no chance of getting in a word. When I finished I sat down on his bed to hear his comment. He was kindly, considering how stupid I had been.

"Memory," he moralized, "is a queer faculty. For while it's perfect in itself we blame it because there's a deficiency in our capacity to recall some particular memory from the depths of our minds. But the impression is always there if we can find it. And for stimulating memory there's nothing to compare with a perfume. One whiff of a remembered scent, and you are back in some old garden you had forgotten for half a lifetime."

"But it wasn't a garden but a pub; and it wasn't a lifetime but only last Saturday night."

"Oh, quite," he returned with a yawn; "it's only the very aged who can go back a lifetime and forget what happened in a pub last week."

This was hardly fair. I had told him very much of what had taken place in the wine shop. Only, in concentrating on Brisson and Coquard, I had overlooked Mr. George Drury, since by comparison he seemed a person of no importance. And, as a matter of fact, it was the handkerchief rather than the perfume that had stimulated my remembrance of that scene between him and Judith Brisson. This scene I had now to repeat in great detail to McNab. The mere recital, above all the particulars of the absurd quarrel between Drury and myself, served to open my eyes, now that Carey's vindication of Brisson compelled me to look somewhere else. And the moment, as it were, I looked behind Brisson and Coquard, there stood Mr. Drury, in his plus fours, with his shifty eyes, and the red rose in his button-hole. It amazed me to see how, once my gaze fastened on him, all the facts tumbled into a coherent whole like the separate pieces in a jig-saw puzzle. To McNab I began with the perfume.

"I can see the girl now on the Saturday night," I said. "She touched his handkerchief with scent from a small squat bottle."

"And on Tuesday night it was still going strong! Marvellous!" McNab interjected. "I'd like to take a bottle away with me. You didn't hear its name?" he inquired.

I wasn't sure he wasn't laughing at me. But I could laugh now myself.

"Oh, his handkerchief would have frequent chances of fresh applications since then," I said.

"And did she put the rose in her hair as girls do in the Pacific islands?" he asked in mock seriousness, to which I responded in the same vein.

"No, but he nearly put the knife into my ribs as the men do in the Pacific islands."

"And supposing his godfather should be judged insane when he made his will, how much does Mr. Drury stand to lose?"

"He stands to gain if he brings it off with Miss Judith."

"So he might win both ways?"

"He is safe one way, if not the other."

"What does he do for a living?"

"At the moment he's a tomato grower and exporter. I understand he was trained to be an engineer, but like so many sons of the clergy he went on the stage."

McNab opened his eyes with delight at this information.

"To play old men's parts, I suppose?"

It was amazing how it all fitted together. Undoubtedly, had my mind not been preoccupied with suspicion of Brisson and Coquard, I could never have missed the truth. Apart altogether from the question of an alibi, to impersonate the dead man obviously needed some one perfectly familiar with the inside of de Quettville's house and the country around, which Coquard certainly was not; and the notion of a bullock like Brisson dressing up to masquerade as his brother-in-law—well, his very bulk would have made the attempt grotesque. I could have kicked myself to see how blind I had been. All this, of course, was what McNab had meant when he declared I could tell them much more of the affair than I had done.

McNab lay on, arms behind his head, with his own thoughts, when I returned to my room.

Over breakfast, some hours later, we discussed the

new situation.   McNab, who must have spent the interval in cogitation, now had his list of eleven clues
propped up against the sugar basin under his eyes.   As
presently appeared, he was trying to rearrange the
separate numbered items into a sequence which might
tell its own story.

"It seems to me," he said, "that the time of death
must be the Thursday night, soon after you saw him."

"Why not Friday?" I inquired, that being the time
I had all along considered most likely.

"Because it would mean that he was detained alive
somewhere all through the Friday, a needlessly risky
proceeding, which would almost certainly involve the
necessity for having one confederate at the very least."

"But Drury may have had an accomplice."

"Certainly.   But I have learned never to assume an
accomplice in murder till facts force me to do so.
Murder in modern times is usually a lonely crime: to
have another in it doubles the risk and halves the
gain."

"In that case he was not murdered at Perigord."

"Right; he was not.   One man could hardly have
removed the body from the house to the seashore.
But then even two men could not have forced him
to rise from his bed and dress himself as he did without making an outcry, or leaving some signs of a struggle in the room.   He must have been inveigled into
going away on some pretext, though heaven knows
what at that late hour it could be, unless it had some
pretended connection with his money-lending transac-

tions. We'll try for something that may bear on that from the housekeeper, after the inquest to-day. Then possibly we may learn who could have got into communication with him at that hour of the night. It could not be by a 'phone call since Perigord is not on the telephone."

After breakfast I left McNab to himself while I set off to get in a round of visits before leaving to attend the inquest at midday. Returning about eleven I found McNab in a state of extreme impatience and unrest, the cause of which was a call that had come through from Colonel Carey from the hotel at Rocquaine. Carey wanted us both at Perigord as soon as possible, and though McNab had tried to get from him the reasons of his request, he had been unable to elicit anything; yet although it had been easy to divine from the Chief Constable's voice that something new had occurred, all Carey would say was that what he had to tell us could not be conveyed by 'phone. But the mention of the place from which the call came was sufficient. Carey had gone to the boat-house and had seen what I told him he would see.

We might have been late for the inquest had not the inquest itself been late in opening. When we reached Perigord we found the big hall occupied by what must have been the whole of the parish's adult population. Those connected more directly with the proceeding I picked out from the retired position near the door into which we had slipped. The first person to take my eye was the massive Brisson, who sat beside a sharp-faced man at the far end, near the coroner's table. Daniel Sarchet and the other man, Nicolle, were also there, as well as Mrs. Bichard and the frightened-looking maid Alice Mauger. At the end of the table, the only person on his feet, stood Sergeant Torode, like an expectant statue. Among the others the only ones known to me were Mrs. Blampied and her Claire, both in deep black, and Mr. George Drury seated in a corner. Opposite him, on chairs placed along the wall flanking the table, sat a dozen or so of men whose appearance suggested that they did not belong to the type of simple country folk among whom we sat. I had just decided, after puzzling over them, that they must be a selection of de Quettville's clients when the door leading to the study opened and Carey appeared, followed by Dr. Sullivant and a little man, whom I judged to be the district coroner, with glittering gold pince-nez and a little tidy white moustache.

A gesture from the coroner as he was about to take his seat brought Le Marinel to his side, the avocat apparently having been seated where I could not see him behind Mrs. Blampied. Then Carey, who had been talking to Torode with his eyes all the while searching the room, caught sight of us, and with a hurried word to the sergeant, he stepped quickly in our direction, nodding towards the door as he passed us. We took the cue and followed him. He was waiting for us on the steps under the immense Georgian portico.

"No need to wait," he said; "the coroner is going

to adjourn after Brisson has given the formal evidence of identification."

"For further inquiries," I suggested.

"Yes," he said, eagerly yet amiably, taking us each by an arm. "Come where we can talk in peace. I've got two really big things to tell you."

We walked round the house, across the neglected land to the tree-studded park beyond. But he did not wait till we reached it.

"You were quite right," he said to me as soon as we were clear of the house. "Sullivant instantly supported your assertion as to the time of death when he saw the body this morning."

And though I knew Sullivant must agree, it meant much to me, then, to have Sullivant's backing. The unusual glow I felt on hearing the news was evidence of that.

"The fact that the man has been dead for not less than three days will not come out in court to-day?" McNab asked.

Carey assured him that nothing at all could come out in evidence that day. No one would object to the adjournment except possibly Brisson, who had attended with his own avocat to establish de Quettville's insanity. This information made me welcome the adjournment with real fervency; for I had an idea that if Brisson remembered half of what I had said to him in his wine shop that sharp-nosed avocat of his would call on me for evidence in support; and, if he got an opening, would put me through it if I had to testify as to de Quettville's condition when I visited him on the Thursday night. The mere sense of relief was so intense that I forgot Carey had mentioned a second piece of news. But McNab had not.

"And the other news item?"

The reminder brought a beaming smile to Carey's face. Out came his cigarette case.

"Ah, that is so good that I wish it had been better. I'm not complaining, though. It's something that will show you we can accomplish a thing or two ourselves, and aren't going to owe everything to you." He held out his case to McNab. "But perhaps you despise the cigarette," he said. McNab accepted the offer.

"Not at all," he said. "I like a cigarette when I'm not smoking."

This sample of McNab's dry humour was new to Carey, and after staring a moment he laughed. But his light heartedness which indicated his satisfaction with the progress made in the matter of de Quettville, made us more impatient to hear what his discovery was.

"It came about in this way," the Chief began. "Last night Brisson and his avocat, Simon, were out at Perigord ostensibly, since Brisson's daughter is heir at law, to see to the arrangements about the identification, but really, there can be no doubt, to ferret out any facts which would tend to establish de Quettville's insanity. For, will or no will, Judith Brisson inherits Perigord. That fact gave Brisson his standing. But they found Mr. Drury there, and some others, among them the two trustees, Mrs. Blampied and Claire, as well as other expectant godchildren, and several of de Quettville's clients who had come to see Le Marinel. At one point something like a scene threatened between Drury and Brisson; but it ended with the pair agreeing to treat the company to some of de Quettville's cognac, which they got from the housekeeper.

"That is where the story begins, really. You see, Torode happened to be out fixing things up for to-day's inquest, and Mrs. Bichard, upset by the way she had just been put through it by Simon, she besides being quite unused to entertaining guests when it came to drinks all round, let the sergeant take over management, with the assistance of Alice, the parlourmaid. Torode learned to be a handy chap in India. And in India he learned more than how drinks should be served. In our life out there he learned to develop his imagination. And, aware of the search I'd been making to trace the originals of the finger-prints on the tennis balls, every time Alice brought back an empty glass he gave her a fresh one, and stealthily slipped the other into his brief bag. For he argued that among all this assembly of people interested in, or connected with, Perigord there very likely would be the one individual whose identity interested me. He was right too. The man concerned in putting the Neptune over the gateway was there. We got the same imprints on one of the glasses as we already had on the tennis ball."

"But not those of the woman concerned?" McNab asked.

"No, but her identity is bound to come out, now that we know who the man is," Carey rejoined with the air of one who expects to startle his hearers.

"Ah," McNab said, "so Mr. George Drury's game is up."

Carey caught his cigarette as it dropped from his mouth.

"Good Lord, how did you know?" he cried.

McNab soon rattled off the story, and Carey, who was quick to perceive how every detail answered to the needs of the case, listened with eyes that glowed satisfaction.

After that we put our heads together over the next step to be taken, and it was decided that Carey alone must interview Drury. There was to be no suggestion of murder, not even that Drury was concerned in the attack on me. But as it was generally known that Carey had been endeavouring to trace the person or persons responsible for the erection of the ship's figurehead, he was merely to seek an explanation from Drury as to how and when he had handled the tennis ball placed on the trident. And as this act did not constitute a criminal offence, Drury was to be left to suppose that he was in for no more than a reprimand as one responsible for a joke in very bad taste.

We did not return to the house with Carey, since that might well have suggested to Drury when approached by the Chief that he was going to hear something about the knife-throwing incident, a much more serious affair, which he would be ready to deny. And our talk with Carey had taken place too far from the house for us to be observed from the windows.

We ourselves, after telling Carey where to find us,

went off in the direction of Mère Trouteaud's cottage, McNab bent on another talk with the old woman. As we made for the lane I felt that the rope was already as good as round Drury's throat. He was a type I knew. This son of a calculating clergyman he had learned to hold life cheap during his sojourn on some Pacific island. He had been staying with his godfather at the very time the will was made, and no doubt in an expansive moment the old man had told him of its contents and thereby sealed his own fate.

"What did you think of this man Drury when you met him?" McNab, who had been silent, abruptly inquired.

"A truculent brute," I promptly replied.

"He is a native of this island?"

"Well, he happened to be born here I believe, son of a popular preacher imported from England. Been abroad for some years, comes back to despise the untravelled natives, whose intelligence he rates at about the level of a Solomon islander."

McNab shook his head.

"It's going to be hard to bring anything home to him," he said.

Mère Trouteaud's home was a white-washed one-storey cottage of the humblest type. But it had a fair-sized garden, facing south, and out of its fertile soil, and the hen run abutting the cottage, no doubt most of the old woman's living came. A stone path led across to the sun-blistered door on which McNab knocked. Getting no response to a second knock he tried the latch, and found it locked. We resolved to wait, having told Carey where to find us, and after a look round the garden sought for something on which to sit down. But the domain boasted no garden seat, Mère Trouteaud probably having no time in which to rest in her garden. So we sat down on the coping of the well beside the gate, and I reverted to McNab's assertion about the difficulty of bringing home the crime to Drury. But he reiterated his opinion.

"We have no direct evidence at all to connect him with any crime," he said.

"What about the knife?" I asked.

"The knife blade, you mean. Nobody could identify that as his property. It would be another matter if we got the handle. But he would hardly retain that."

"Well, there's the handkerchief on which the Brisson girl put the perfume; he certainly kept that, for he had it when I tackled him in the dark, which probably means that he is keeping it for sentimental reasons."

This suggestion McNab received with impatience.

"Och, man, that probably only means that his laundry day comes later in the week," he cried in contempt.

After that I refrained from further suggestions.

"You see," he resumed, "it's the method of the murder that creates the difficulty. The man was drowned, and as I heard you say yourself, homicidal drowning is one of the rarest methods used in murder. No doubt because it is so difficult. But this man managed it very cleverly. That is what is bothering me. Don't tell me he isn't clever. Short of getting a confession I do not see how we are to get a conviction."

Just then the gate opened with a squeal of rusty hinges and Carey appeared. I could read nothing on his face.

"Well?" McNab said as he stood over us.

"A flat denial," Carey nodded. "It's hardly credible. I told him we had his finger-prints on the ball, and he told me he didn't care a damn, he had never touched any tennis ball."

"That means he's alarmed."

"He's not. Angry if you like, but not scared in the least, believe me. What's more, with the utmost self-assurance he instantly produced an alibi. Said he couldn't have handled the ball as he went to Sark on the morning of the Friday on which the figure-head was put up, and returned only last Saturday evening."

McNab smiled.

"A very neat alibi that! It exactly covers not only the Friday night on which the Neptune was stuck up, but also the following Friday on which we believe de Quettville was murdered."

"Yes," Carey nodded. "I noticed that; it looks rather too pat and neat. I was asking him only about the first Friday, and, as if he knew what lay behind, out came an alibi for the whole affair."

"You are testing it?"

"Oh, yes. As a matter of fact, Torode is now going hell for leather to catch the afternoon Sark boat. He'll stay the night in Sark, for his inquiries so as to make sure of catching his people at home. But even

so the results may not be decisive, for Drury said he
spent much of his time fishing, and after all there's
only seven miles between the two islands."

"Night fishing, I suppose?" McNab suggested.

"Yes."

"From a boat?"

"Yes."

"And alone?"

"No," Carey unexpectedly replied. "No, he said
he went out with the brothers Bongourd, Nicolas and
Henry."

This jerked up McNab; it was as if he had hit himself against a rock.

"Oh," he said, recovering after a minute. "Well,
I'd like to see the brothers Nicolas and Henry."

"You think there's a hole in the alibi?" Carey asked
hopefully.

"There must be. But is your Sergeant Torode likely
to get his finger into it?"

"Certainly; he has all the necessary local knowledge
at his finger-tips; knows all there is to know of tides,
and distances, and times, not to mention the family
of Bongourds."

"Anything against them?"

"Nothing whatever; they belong to a well-known
Sark family, their ancestors have fished the sea, and
done a little farming there for centuries probably."

McNab jumped from his seat on the well.

"All right: the alibi is a fake. Drury knows we
are on his track for actual murder; he's frightened;
he did not give you credit for being up in finger-print

work. The adjourned inquest alarmed him first of all; so when you came, he named these well-known Bongourds to give himself time to get away before you could find out the truth about his alleged trip to Sark."

"I'm overlooking none of that," Carey replied; "but as for giving himself time to make his get-away, you overlook the difficulty of that on an island like this. One officer alone, at the White Rock, would stop him going aboard any boat. But it is a fact that Drury was in Sark part of the time at least, for you see I saw him there myself last Wednesday, just a week ago to-day."

McNab, however, was unshaken.

"Very well," he said more quietly, "I'll go to Sark myself. There's some sleight of hand in all this. Not, this time, the sleight of hand displayed in knife-throwing, but the kind that may well know how to throw dust in the eyes of Sergeant Torode."

And go to Sark we did. Although the *Courier* had left before we could reach the quay, McNab was too keen on the scent now to wait another day. We promptly hired a motor launch, and were soon skimming over the pellucid sea, with the water sounding a rapid plip-plop at our bow, and a hissing stream astern. Soon we watched the enchanted island grow steadily in size and detail, and in what seemed an incredibly short time we were slipping along under its vast cliffs, with wheeling sea birds high overhead, showing like wind-blown snowflakes against the dark mass of the cliffs.

But that day neither of us had an eye for the beauties

of nature, our thoughts were too much preoccupied with the one example of the ugliness of human nature whose movements we had come to investigate. McNab was on edge all the way, and had been ever since he jumped from his seat on the coping of the well in Mère Trouteaud's garden. He had been frightened, I think, that Drury would after all slip clear in some way he could not divine. Carey had spoken of the complete self-assurance with which Drury had produced his alibi, and I knew it was the self-assurance rather than the alibi that troubled McNab.

It did not take us long to discover the ground on which Drury's self-assurance was founded. For as soon as we shot through the tall narrow entrance of the little Creux harbour we came on Sergeant Torode and a fisherman, engaged in examining a boat standing on the slip. Torode was doing some head scratching as he listened to the other man, who with outstretched palms was laying off explanations at a great rate in a querulous high-pitched voice. The sergeant took our appearance without surprise.

"This is the boat," he said. "Nicolas Bongourd, here, says they were out last Friday night, on the northeast of the island."

We examined the boat, a mere rowing skiff without fixtures for sails, or for fitting on an out-board motor.

"Speaks for itself, don't it, sir?" Torode mumbled.

"But it has been calm weather for a week or two, hasn't it?" McNab suggested.

The sergeant smiled pityingly.

"You mean rowing? Yes, there's been no wind, but

the tide don't stop running fourteen knots out there, between the islands." He gave the little boat a kick. "If you was to try it, you'd find yourself near the Casquets on one tide, and somewhere off Jersey on the next. But you can try, if you like."

We knew the sergeant was suggesting not that McNab should try to row the seven miles to Guernsey and back but that he could try to overturn the alibi. And this he did try, Torode conducting us over the ground he had already covered. We interviewed people at the hotel, inspected the books, talked with both the brothers Bongourd later on; and never once did the shadow of a discrepancy appear.

"You can't break that alibi, sir," Torode said as we left the Bongourds' cottage; "it's an alibi as water-tight as the Lower Head buoy. It can't be broke, because it's right what Mr. Drury says about his being here when he says he was."

And with half an eye I could see that McNab himself had now reached the same conviction.

As we descended the long hill towards the harbour dusk was falling, and from the slope on either side of the road there reached us the greeny smell of dew-drenched bracken and gorse. Deep in the gloom of the high granite quay our launch sat waiting. By the time we were under way the darkness had swallowed up the larger island. But away in the far distance, across the waste of black waters, I could see the Hanois light which marked the southern coast of Guernsey, and its rapid succession of flashes made it seem like a knowing eye, winking derision.

For several days the case was at a standstill so far as we were concerned. I tried to put it out of my mind, and if McNab thought about it, as I have no doubt he did, he gave me no indications beyond an occasional brooding and gloomy absent-mindedness. We played golf at L'Ancresse in the afternoon, went for a swim in the early mornings, did a good amount of walking, and had one glorious sailing trip among the smaller islands.

Gossip about the de Quettville affair floated around the town. Occasionally I had to listen to some of it from my patients. But no suggestion of any crime leaked out, the gossip relating exclusively to the fight expected between Brisson on the one hand and the legatees, of whom the chief were Mr. Drury and Mrs. Blampied, on the other. Brisson, it was said, disputed the will on the ground of de Quettville's insanity on the date it was executed.

Thus the time passed till the eve of the day on which the inquest fell to be resumed. Public interest was now roused over the result, it being said that the adjournment had been for the purpose of obtaining the real facts about de Quettville's mental condition, since so much hung on the verdict. In the interval stories of de Quettville's strange doings just before his death got into active circulation, and it was generally held that the verdict would be one of suicide during temporary insanity. There were those, indeed, who asserted that de Quettville never had been of sound mind since the day his fiancée ran away with his younger brother.

Of Le Marinel I was then seeing little or nothing, he being so continuously engaged in the legal work entailed by the expected dispute over the succession to the estate. As for Chief Constable Carey, he might now have reverted to his original theory of suicide for all we heard, though I had an idea he was working away at inquiries about the movements of the more shady characters among de Quettville's debtors.

It will thus be seen that with the complete establishment of the alibis of our own principal suspects the case came to a standstill. To a standstill that is, so far as action was concerned, but certainly not so far as concerned thought. I found it impossible to keep the thing out of my mind. And though he said little or nothing, I judged McNab to be in the same condition of mental turmoil, and I knew that, later on, he spent his mornings when I was professionally engaged, doing some quiet investigation about the town.

Then on the eve of the resumed inquest he spoke, abruptly, yet so naturally that I could see how continuously the subject had been occupying his thoughts.

"Dunn, there's just one absolute certainty I hang on to," he said.

"Yes?" I replied, well aware he referred to the Perigord murder.

"Finger-prints cannot be faked. Drury beyond all doubt did handle that ball."

"But you were satisfied with his alibi," I said.

"Entirely. Brisson's too; for if Drury couldn't do seven miles from Sark, Brisson couldn't do the fifty from St. Malo. It's another alibi that bothers me now—that of the corpse itself."

This time I did not credit my ears.

"The what?" I cried, horrified.

"The corpse—you would call it the cadaver, no doubt—I'm sure now that the secret is concerned with de Quettville's body. There was no hanky-panky about Drury's alibi, but I fancy it's a trick with the body that will explain how we've been fooled."

"But—"

"Wait a moment," he cut me short almost fiercely. "I'm going to see Drury presently, to see if I can find out just when he set his fingers on that gilded tennis ball. I'm going to set that ball rolling to-night, Dunn. To-night I'm going to start that ball rolling, and see where it leads me."

"Where do you suppose it—" I began, but again he stopped me.

"No, no! Your questions can wait: mine cannot wait. Now carry your mind back to the time we entered the boat-house. You said the first thing that surprised you was that de Quettville's face showed no discoloration."

"And I told you why. In cases of drowning the blood flows into the head and produces a flushed appearance."

"And if de Quettville had been, say, laid on his back and somehow maintained in that position, perhaps at low water till the tide came in, would that account for what you saw?"

"Yes."

"Or if he had been drowned in an upright position?"

"That too would account for it."

The replies appeared to give McNab immense satisfaction. He bent forward to run his eye over the list of clues entered in his notebook, and I guessed he had got something that made him more hopeful of rearranging them in a more illuminating sequence. But the next question in his catechism surprised me.

"When exactly did you arrive in Guernsey?"

"On Monday the twelfth of this month, by the evening boat."

"And your friend, Dr. Wright, he left next day, I take it?"

"No, he stayed on till the Thursday. He wanted to show me the ropes, and introduce me to such patients as needed particular attention."

"But de Quettville was not one of these?"

"Oh, no. Wright only introduced me to a few patients in the town, chiefly old ladies who might be touchy over a stranger. Besides, de Quettville was not ill when he left."

"So Dr. Wright left, of course, on the day before the Neptune was set up over the gateway," McNab said, half to himself. "Good! And there it stood till Tuesday when it was taken down by de Quettville's order, put on a pillar in his garden out of reach to keep it from again being used to mock him. Then on the Tuesday night Mère Trouteaud slips into the garden as soon as it is dark, and her dog Mimi barks at the figure," McNab ran on, staring down at his note-book, passing a hand through his hair. He looked up at me suddenly. "Why did the dog not bark on the Wednesday night?"

"You forget, McNab, the dog was dead on the Wednesday."

"Ah, yes—the poor little noisy dog was dead on the Wednesday, and that, if I remember, was the beginning of much bad luck for Mère Trouteaud."

At this point I became quite sure McNab had got on to something. In fact I remember that the way he uttered the word "noisy" made me catch my breath for a second and sit up.

"Yes," I said, "the old woman's catalogue of her misfortunes is easily remembered: the clock fell off the wall, the lamp burst, her baking got burned, or something, on another day—"

McNab stopped me.

"Never mind what happened inside her house, it's what happened outside that is important."

"Oh, well," I said, trying to keep calm, "only two things happened outside. Some neighbour stole her well-rope, and tore up a sheet or two she had left out to dry overnight. But I forget what day that ill-luck belonged to."

"The Thursday, the morning after the dog died, and the same morning on which Miss Blampied, looking out of her window, saw the Neptune had gone from the pillar."

"Does that mean much?" I inquired.

He snapped his notebook and began to smooth down his ruffled hair.

"It hangs together. But it is the old woman's wee doggie that sets me on the trail. Do you not see anything yet, Dunn? No? Well, I'll have to give you an explanation when I come back. Not that I see everything myself yet."

I got to my feet in protest.

"You're not going to leave me out?" I cried.

He held up his hand.

"No, certainly not. But I'm going now to see Mr. George Drury at one of his haunts—not the Perigord these days—and as you and he parted on pretty warm terms, he would be very quick to suspect my purpose if I approached him in your company."

Something odd in his manner of saying this caught my ear.

"McNab, there's some danger in what you're going to do to-night," I asserted.

"Danger?" he repeated, savouring the word slowly. "Man, my kind of work has always that possibility in it. But I've noticed that the precise amount of danger is usually determined by the way a thing is done. In my work as in your own, tact is an indispensability."

After that I could of course say no more. It was clear he considered my presence would increase his danger; but the fact that danger had now to be faced left me very uneasy. After he had gone I sat on recalling the separate events, chiefly the knife which had so narrowly missed me on the night of my quarrel with Drury. Fortunately just then a 'phone call, which I expected might come next day, took me off to a case, and presently my thoughts were occupied with the beginning of life rather than with its end.

It was some two hours later—eleven-twenty by my watch—before I found myself free from the case, and in a position to think of anything else. Outside I found the night as sultry as the room I had just left, the night air coming hot and heavy to the lungs. Straightening myself as I began to walk down the road I saw the sky overcast with great, rolling masses of deep violet cloud, shot with sulphurous patches here and there. It looked as if before morning the hot spell was going to break in a rackety thunderstorm.

But it was anxiety to hear McNab's news that made me quicken my pace almost to a run. I made sure he would be back in the house again. Almost three hours had gone since he left. Then I wondered what I could do if he had not returned. Before reaching a decision my latch-key was in the lock. As I set down my bag and looked at the hall table on which notes were left for me, I saw one envelope so propped up as to draw immediate attention. Believing it to be a 'phone call to another case which had been taken down by the housekeeper, I picked it up, saw the message was in McNab's neat little handwriting, and was headed by the printed address of the chief constable's office. It read:

If you want to be in at the death come to Perigord and be prepared if necessary to give professional assistance.

Never have I jumped to any call as I did to that! My first act was to ring up the garage, and then when I had got together a set of emergency dressings and other professional necessities, I got on to the police office for fuller particulars. The officer in charge knew about the message to me. He himself had brought it up after McNab had called me on the 'phone and learned I had gone off to a case. This was about ten minutes before eleven. But beyond telling me that the Chief, accompanied by the sender of the message, Sergeant Torode and three constables, had left in two cars, he could not, or would not, say any more.

I knew they must have gone off to make an arrest. Quite apart from their numbers the very fact that McNab had sent his message from the chief constable's office was itself significant. He must have gone there hot foot with information that led Carey to take instant action, as I saw before my own car reached the outskirts of the town. And McNab's message by itself was decisive, implying that Carey found the evidence McNab had obtained that night and placed before him, to be conclusive. McNab had read the riddle: this was the end!

My driver did not go fast enough for me. He must have been resentful over a tip from his last fare. I had to wake him up.

"Is it a matter of life and death?" he asked.

"Death," I replied; and though this may have befogged him, he got a bit more out of his engine. I knew the road now, and marked the stages pass. Then just as we slowed down to take the curve through the Perigord gateway a figure in policeman's uniform stepped into our headlights with uplifted hand. As he came along I recognized him for a St. Peter Port officer I'd seen about the streets.

"Dr. Dunn?" he inquired at the window.

"What is it?" I returned.

"He's got away, sir, and we're scattering after him. I was to use your car, if you turned up, to get towards Icart Point."

He was soon in beside me, and the driver, now aware he was on a livelier adventure than a sick call, at once began to show us the wonders he could get out of his antique vehicle. The officer gave me the facts, so far as they were known to him, but this he had to do, as it were, in spasms, during the brief intervals when we were not whirling round corners or negotiating hairpin bends, in narrow lanes, which threw us now to one side, now to the other of the rocking car.

"We hadn't enough men," the officer admitted, "not for such a big rambling old house. All the same my idea is he must have got wind we were coming."

"You didn't try to surround the house?"

"Not what you'd call surround it. I was outside myself; so was Brache and Falla; but we reckoned to get him unawares, really. It was Falla sees him drop from the window, before the others were well inside the house or we had got properly set, as you might say." Here he clutched at me involuntarily as the car just cleared a perilous corner. "Lord, good the rain's not started, or we'd be standing on our heads in a ditch that time," he declared. "Well, sir, as I was saying, Falla sees him all right, but coming so unexpected like, and so quick, took Falla by surprise, and the man was off like a hare across the park before Falla got back breath enough to shout. They reckon he'll make for Saints' Bay to get one of the boats moored there. That's where the sergeant and Falla have gone, and the idea for us is to lay up on Icart Point."

"Icart?—on a night like this a brigade could hide on Icart," I said.

"Yes, sir, but they reckoned the moon would be up as soon as we reached it, and the idea was that laying there we might sight him as he came on; and if we all missed him there'd still be the sergeant and Falla watching over the boats."

Just then a sound like the distant roll of drums came to our ears, and the torn, sulphurous-edged clouds I had already observed told me it was not drums but distant thunder.

"Looks as if we may presently have something stronger to see him by than moonlight," I said.

The officer, letting down the window, craned his neck to get a look at the heavens.

"It may pass us by," he said, "there's no wind nor rain."

As if to belie this hope a second peal, louder and longer, broke the silence, and a short tattoo of heavy raindrops sounded on the roof of the car. But nothing more followed, and before long we left the hedge-bordered road, and were travelling over an open space, on a rougher road bordered by gorse and bracken.

The vague feeling of being on a great height came to me just as the officer told the driver to pull up.

"Reckon the headlights can be seen for miles out here, and we dursent go on without lights," he murmured to me as we got out.

"You can turn here," he said to the man, "then you can be off home."

The man's face, he was a young fellow, looked appealingly back from the gloom of the car.

"I'm in no hurry, Mr. Dorey," he said.

P. C. Dorey turned on him.

"What's the idea, Tostevin? Think you're likely to pick up a fare here, eh? You be off."

"Can't I stay on and see the fun? Who is it you're after?" he pleaded.

But Dorey was adamant, telling him we could have no loitering there, and threatening him with the loss of his licence. When he had gone we left the road and set off across the headland.

Icart Point I had previously seen but once. That was during an afternoon walk with McNab a few days earlier. Then I had been struck with the wildness of its plateau, dotted all over with gorse, bramble bushes and bracken, intersected with sheep and rabbit runs. Towards the sea the ground began to slope down, and across this slope ran a narrow pathway, safe enough in daylight and dry weather, but safe only then, for in many places the path passed close to the edge of the cliff, and to slip, or miss the path in the dark, was to be lost, since a yard or so away there came a drop of about two hundred feet. But no one would go there in the dark, I suppose, for the path seemed to exist entirely for the magnificent view it opened out seawards.

I recalled that path as we threaded our way among the gorse, making up my mind that though I might watch it, nothing would induce me to set foot on it that night. Before we had crossed the level ground, however, the storm which had been threatening so long, broke out at last. It came with the impetuosity and fury of a roaring monster enraged by long detention. The sudden detonation right over our heads sounded as if the heavens had burst. We had forgotten the sky in our keenness to watch the earth. As we pulled up involuntarily, the lightning flashed past us in silent brilliance, dazzling our eyes for a second, and then leaving us in darkness. But no rain fell, and we pushed on to get nearer the bigger bushes which Dorey said grew close to the slope above the cliff's edge. It was among those bushes we had meant to post ourselves, since from there we had a clear sight of the path which crossed the bare slope, Dorey's idea being that our man would take this path, as nobody else would be willing to do it then, and he only because it was now neck or nothing with him.

Reaching the point where the bushes ended and the bare slope began just as another terrific clap of thunder went off into echoing reverberations, we came to a halt. We knew that here a wide expanse would in ordinary conditions lie before us; but at that moment it looked no more than a wall of inky blackness. The next instant, however, the whole world seemed to leap into intense distinctness as a rod of forked lightning went by, hissing like a rocket. Then darkness fell again and the thunder, like salvos of artillery, shook the ground beneath our feet. But the exhilaration of the storm took hold of me, and the air, which had been so hot and dead, now tasted fresh and vital. It was impossible that any one could pass along the cliff path unseen, for the flashes came too frequently, following at once on the thunderous uproar, which indeed seemed almost continuous.

"It's right overhead," Dorey said.

"And here comes the rain," I answered.

Dorey dived for a clump of bushes growing around a small tree as a sudden sluicing sheet of rain dropped on us, and I followed. It was poor shelter, and in a few minutes we were both so wet that further wetting did not matter. However, it was this deluge that led to what followed. A hurried consultation with Dorey convinced me that now the cliff path was impassable. It simply could not be used. And any one caught on it in the midst of that torrent of rain would be forced to cut up the slope to the more level ground. This reduced our chances, and it was simply to make the most of such a chance as remained that I agreed to leave Dorey to patrol northwards, while I myself took the opposite direction, the understanding being that we were both to return to the spot where we then were, which was marked by the tree among the bushes, every twenty minutes. An hour passed in this way and we met thrice. Then something happened.

It must have been about half past two. At the

moment I had reached the extreme limit of my beat, and was standing facing the slope watching a zig-zag flare of lightning go fizzing and crackling seawards, when in the death-like silence that followed I heard a slight sound behind me. But I was not quick enough: darkness fell like a shutter and I had to wait for the next flash. The intervals were longer now, for the storm was working southwards. Probably, I told myself, I would see nothing. There could be nothing to see. Even if it had only been a rabbit breaking cover I would not see it now. And all the time I was telling myself this I knew it was not a rabbit, and waited for the next revealing flash. I thought it would never come. Indeed, my eyes, now no longer unfocussed by the frequency of the blinding flashes, were beginning to see better, and I wondered whether the dawn was at hand, or was it the moon, no longer entirely blanketed by cloud, that was throwing out this faint, watery light?

I dared not look up to see. I dared not take my eyes away from the direction from which the small sound had taken my ear. But before the light came I think I knew who it was. Something in the blood warned me. And when, between two breaths, the lightning, little more than a quivering reflection now in the first streaks of dawn, lit up the earth, I found myself staring into the eyes of Catulle Coquard.

He was peering at me out of a bush. I had time to see there was murder in those eyes and that he had the necessary instrument in his right hand: a pistol whose barrel shone for an instant like quicksilver. I just saw the muzzle veer straight at me and jumped as the shot rang out, and darkness again fell. Then after dodging round the nearest bushes, and running a little way, I caught my left foot in a rabbit hole and almost pitched over the edge of the slope above the cliffs. But the rabbit hole held me, though in coming down I twisted round on my back knowing too well what that wrench on my ankle meant.

The bone was not fractured and for a moment I rejoiced in this knowledge, till I remembered that it would not matter either way since Coquard had only to come round the bush to finish me off. I remember striving to see the corner of the bush round which I expected him to appear. But he did not come. Had he missed seeing which way I had jumped, and gone to look in the wrong direction? Did he think his bullet had found me, and that there was no need to look anywhere? No, it was not that! Somewhere near a twig snapped and I knew he was searching for me.

But a thought came to me, and I managed to get my foot clear of the hole. My one hope was to sham death, and, although it took me nearer the edge of that perilous slope, I wriggled over so as to hide the rabbit hole from view. For to allow him to see what had brought me down would make him shoot again.

It took him a long time to find me. Find me however he did at last. After hope had risen almost to certainty of escape I saw him him come round the bush, no more than a creeping shadow which stopped the instant he caught sight of me. The storm had entirely passed now, and the steady increase in the light showed me it was not moonlight but the dawn. I did not want to die, and tried not to think of it. After the storm a hush seemed to be on everything. Under my eyelids I saw Coquard draw nearer. He was not sure I was dead, nor whether I had a weapon. But he did not come very near. As he stopped his arm went up, and under my half-closed lids I could see the muzzle of his pistol pointing straight at my face. The impulse to move was almost irresistible; but I knew I could neither get away nor get at him. So I lay shamming the stiff, awkward position of one who has tumbled dead to the earth. He did not fire at once. There was a hesitation which was to me as unaccountable as it was agonizing. The weapon was lowered and raised more than once. Then with a thrill I understood, and the first ray of hope came so suddenly that it was a miracle I did not betray myself by a movement.

He did not want to fire. If only he were sure I was dead. He did not want to fire now, in case the shot would be heard. In the midst of the storm a pistol shot was nothing, but now in this great quietness it was another matter. Abruptly, he seemed to make up his mind that there was no need for a second shot, for he came right up and stood over me, considering, I suppose, what might happen if my body were found there. It did not take him long to perceive the best method of dealing with me. When I felt a kick land on my ribs I knew he was going to send me hurtling down that slope and over the cliff to the beach below. He found me, however, much too heavy to be sent over in that fashion. All the same he did not at once stop kicking me. Dead as he thought me, he liked sending his toe hard against my ribs too well for that.

At last he did what I had hoped he would do: he pocketed his pistol and then bent down to roll me over the edge. That was the moment I had waited for, prayed for, died three times over to bring about. At last he was safely within reach. I got him by both his wrists as he was in the act of stooping—got him entirely off his guard, and almost defenceless in the shock of his surprise. But I did not prolong his agony though he had prolonged mine. My fierce desire for instant satisfaction was too great for that.

Shifting one hand to his ankle as I drew him over me, I heaved myself up, and sent him hurtling over before he had time to do more than made a despairing grab at me with his free hand. I only saved myself from going over too by getting my undamaged foot into the same rabbit hole which had landed me.

At first he rolled down that slope, which from where I lay looked like the steep slope of a high-pitched roof. I could see his arms flying in frantic clutches at the turf. The next moment he spun round when he struck some inequality in the ground, and I saw him as he slid forward, endeavouring to check himself by wild digs of his heels at the earth. But the momentum he had gathered was too great to be arrested by anything less solid than the granite boulders two hundred feet below. And the last sight I had of Catulle Coquard was when, a mere small black object in the distance, he shot like a bird out into space, over the cliff, and dropped like a stone towards them. Then I must have fainted clean away.

IT was in my rooms that night that we settled on the evidence which was to be offered next day at the inquest. They had to come to me because I was on a couch with a twisted ankle and two broken ribs. P. C. Dorey had found me lying on the cliff's edge, and after rendering first aid had gone off for help to transport me home.

"Well," Le Marinel was saying, "all along I said the Chief would get them by the finger-prints." He looked over at me. "Didn't I say that on Saturday before you went into the wine shop? Of course the fellow didn't suppose that the little island of Guernsey could boast a finger-print expert like Carey."

Carey looked at McNab apologetically.

"Forgive this outburst of local patriotism," he said. "We all know that without your constructive imagination my technical knowledge would not have carried us far."

Now this kind of talk was all very well between Le Marinel, Carey and McNab. They had been together all day, and were in full possession of all the facts. But I had been out of things since Dorey took me home that morning, and knew nothing of the day's developments. So I cut in to the talk.

"If there's to be a vote taken on the question of pre-eminence," I said, "may I remind you that I am not in possession of all the facts?"

"As to that," Le Marinel nodded, "there's something I don't know either; but what I do know is that the problem was to destroy the alibis, and that this was accomplished, in the end, by our Chief Constable's intimate knowledge of finger-print technique."

Carey would not have this.

"No," he declared firmly. "You've got it by the wrong end, Le Marinel. My technique, as you call it, was applied merely to find out who was concerned in annoying an old man by erecting his effigy over his gate. The notion of crime never entered my head, not even when the evidence was thrust under my nose in the boat house, over the man's body."

"Not evidence," McNab protested; "that scrap of seaweed in the watch was merely an odd thing that called for explanation. The first real evidence came from Dunn, when he convinced me that the man apparently then just drowned must have been dead for not less than three days."

"Ye-s—not less than three days," Le Marinel murmured.

They exchanged glances, and I divined they shared some knowledge between them which had not yet been disclosed to me. As I wondered what it could be, and was resolving to drag it from them, McNab continued:

"Dunn's evidence suggested crime of some sort. For here was some person masquerading as the dead man, entering the dead man's house, wearing, mark you, the clothes in which the body was afterwards found. Quite apart from the knife throwing incident of which Dunn was the intended victim, this last fact impressed me by the determined purpose which I felt must lie behind it.   For by the moonlight entering through the keyhole Dunn observed the very pattern of the cloth the man whom he tried to overpower was wearing; and Dunn saw those same clothes taken from the body a few hours later.   But they must have been worn by some one else, who stripped and re-clothed the body between the time Dunn saw them in the house, and the time when they were found again on de Quett-ville's drowned body.

"Now when you think of it, to strip and re-clothe a body like that is a thing no one is likely, to put it grossly, to do for nothing.   In fact it would have to be a man of a very callous nature to do it at all.   Here, then, was presumptive evidence, not only of some crime, but of a crime which might, from the cold-blooded character of the perpetrator, well be of a very brutal kind.   So far, however, we had no evidence of murder. But that evidence was not long delayed.   And it also came from Dunn."

McNab paused with his eyes on Carey.   But I had got tired of the repetition of my name, and felt that there was something defensive in the way McNab was making it recur.

"Oh, leave my name out," I cried.   "No one is more conscious of the blunder I made than myself."

This time the three avoided looking at each other. But McNab looked across at me with kindly eyes.

"Credit where credit is due," he said.   "But for you, this murder might have gone undetected."

"So far as concerns myself, I entirely concur in that," Carey nodded.

"Well," McNab resumed, "where was I? Oh, yes, I was saying that as yet we had no evidence of actual murder. But that came the moment I got further facts from Dunn, bearing on the facial discoloration of the drowned. This discoloration is caused by the fact that in a floating body the head sinks lower because of its greater weight. But de Quettville's face revealed no discoloration, therefore his body had *not floated*. I ascertained that no discoloration would occur if the person, prior to death, had been held either in a flat or upright position. It did not take long to decide which was the position in de Quettville's case. First, he had *not* been drowned in the sea at all. The body, when recovered, was of a lower temperature than the sea out of which it had been removed, and never could have fallen to that lower temperature unless it had reached it in some medium, or place, colder than the sea. The body could only have been placed in the sea very shortly before it was recovered, since sufficient time had not elapsed for the sea to raise it to its own temperature. Where, then, had de Quettville been drowned? The place ought to be obvious the moment one asked where a man could be drowned in water much colder than the sea. The answer is, in a well of spring water, some fifty feet deep, in which he was held in an upright position by the rope they threw back into the well where they drew him out again."

"Mère Trouteaud's well?" I cried. "And you

knew that when we were sitting on it the other day?"

"Oh, it was obvious. They must have got him when he took his usual look round before locking up. Possibly the reserve tennis ball was thrown through his window to draw him outside. Once outside they used the sheet taken from Mère Trouteaud to throw over his head, and stifle any outcry. You see at the time we sat on the well I was not wondering how it was done but who did it."

"Yes," Carey said reminiscently, "the alibis were too good—both sets. Drury all the week in Sark; Brisson from the Thursday till the Saturday in France, and it was manifestly impossible for Coquard to do the thing single-handed."

This sat me up on the couch, exasperated.

"Look here," I said, "if I have any rights in the matter, if I deserve any credit at all, will you explain just how you discovered who did it?"

"Ah," Le Marinel cried, "that is where our Chief Constable comes in."

McNab nodding assent to my question looked over at me.

"You remember I left you last night to go and see Drury about his finger-prints on the tennis ball? Well, I put it to Drury that finger-prints cannot lie, and that somewhere or other, at some time or another, he must have handled that particular tennis ball on which his finger-prints appeared. He denied it in a manner stamped with sincerity, and since he had told the proved truth about his Sark visit, I believed him. Then as delicately as possible I suggested the possibility that he might have touched it when in a certain condition. I may mention we were then drinking together, though not in the Perigord, bad blood having arisen between himself and Coquard over Brisson's daughter, each man supposing the other stood in his way, Drury's stock besides being down with Brisson on account of de Quettville's will.

"Still I got no reaction from his memory, and, in despair, I repeated suggestively, 'A gilt ball, a yellow ball, a golden orange ball.' Quite suddenly a spark lit in his dull eyes. Before he spoke I knew something was coming. 'Ah,' he said, 'now I've got you! By Jove, yes, I was rather tight that night. It's mighty vague, though; it's like trying to remember an old dream. Let me see, I was crossing to Sark next day, and when Judy said she would not give me another drink, not even a lemon squash, I got over the counter to frighten her. That made her cry out and run, and when she was away I saw what I took to be a plate of lemons on the shelf under the counter, and made a grab at one just as Coquard got me by the neck.' "

Carey smiled.

"Talking about giving credit where credit is due," he said. "Notice that if Drury had not got drunk he would never have mistaken a gilded tennis ball for a lemon, and we should never have traced the ball through Drury to Coquard."

"But that wouldn't convict him of murder," I said, aware there was more behind. "Surely Coquard didn't bolt for that?"

Here was a matter for an avocat's handling.

"No," Le Marinel admitted, "but it didn't stand alone. He knew we had begun to examine the well, and that sooner or later we should discover there the handle of the knife which he tossed into it when running down the lane on the morning the body was found, and that it could be identified as his property. And he knew that though de Quettville might have lowered himself into the well and so drowned himself, he could not afterwards raise himself out of the well. And he also knew that we suspected him of being an escaped criminal from Cayenne, and that alone would make him fly to escape the Chief's clutches."

"But why fly to Perigord?"

"To look for Brisson."

"But was Brisson at Perigord?"

"No fear! Brisson made straight for the boats at Saints' Bay while we were actually interviewing Coquard about Drury's tale of the lemons, for Brisson knew his Catulle, and had no doubt that Coquard, once cornered, would give him away."

"But," I protested, "that's like telling me Brisson is the murderer."

"Assisted by Coquard, yes."

"But Brisson was in France on the night of the murder. Did he somehow contrive to pass from France to Guernsey and back on the Friday night?"

To my further amazement no one answered this question. And as I waited I saw how they looked at each other. Here, then, was the thing they were keeping from me. Then McNab spoke very quietly.

"Hilaire de Quettville was not murdered on the Fri-

day night.   He was murdered on the Wednesday night,
two days earlier."

"That is nonsense.   I myself saw him on the Thursday, and he was certainly alive then."

"He certainly was not," McNab said.

I looked at Carey and Le Marinel in turn.
On neither face was there any surprise.   McNab's
astounding assertion was accepted in silence, though
both looked uncomfortable.   But McNab looked unhappy, and attempted to disguise it by an affected light
tone when he had to resume.

"We've been talking about where the chief credit
should go," he said.   "I'm not sure that most of it does
not belong to a little dog, a little dog I never saw.   For
when I was at a complete deadlock over that alibi of
Brisson's it was the little dog's bark that gave me the
necessary hint.   You remember how on the Tuesday
night, when the old woman went to see if it was true,
what they told her, that the Neptune had been put up
on a pillar in the garden, her little dog barked at it.   It
was a bark that cost the dog its life."   McNab stopped
as if taken by a sudden thought.

"There was a time when I wondered whether this
was a murder of premeditation, or whether it was more
or less accidental.   The torn sheet, for instance, might
only have been taken to the garden to redeck the figure
in the similitude of de Quettville again, to replace the
shirt, where it and the false white beard were removed
before de Quettville re-erected the ship's head in its
proper character.   But no!   The evidence of scheming
and contriving is too overwhelming; and part of the

evidence is the little dog's death.   For the dog saw
what his mistress, in the obscurity and with her old
eyes, could not see—that it was a living man who
knelt on the top of the pillar, a living man who must
have been in terror when he heard the barking.   The
old woman, however, did not understand what the little dog was trying to tell her, and so the danger for
the watching man passed.   What was he watching?
Maybe more things than one, but one thing I can tell
you, and that is that from the top of the pillar you can
see right into the study.   Now you know the position
of the well in the old woman's garden, nearer the gate
than the cottage.   Little risk of her hearing them, but
great risk of that alert little dog.   So it died on
Wednesday, the same day as de Quettville but earlier,
some hours earlier.   They wanted to be quite undisturbed while they were using the well."

Now all this would have been really interesting if it
had not been for the fact that it could not be true.

"Look here," I cut in, "again I have to remind you
that I saw de Quettville alive on Thursday."

Then out it came.

"Dunn," Le Marinel began, "do you remember on
the Friday morning in the Rue Galette, when you met
me outside my house?"

"Quite well," I replied, surprised at his solemn tone.

"You remember that when you saw this man Coquard you said you thought you had seen him before?"

"Yes."

"So you had."

"Where and when?"

"In de Quettville's bed on the Thursday night."

All their eyes were on my face. I felt that. And they were quick enough to read what they soon began to see there. It did not take long.

Le Marinel was right. Some truths win conviction from us gradually; others blaze upon us as by a flash of lightning. And this truth was one of these. Le Marinel was right: Coquard it was.

McNab rose to come and sit down on the end of the couch.

"Don't blame yourself, Dunn," he said. "If it's any comfort to you I'll admit that I would have been taken in myself. You had never seen de Quettville before. They counted on that, and had chosen a time when Dr. Wright was away. Mrs. Bichard did not enter the room with you, and even if she had he could have carried it off, since she already believed him to be queer. But he didn't bargain on your being sent for. That must have been his second moment of terror. No wonder you found his heart going above the normal. It would be the false beard that he was afraid of. His head was all right since his hair was covered by the night cap; but that beard was only meant to take in the housekeeper and Miss Blampied, and them he could, and did, keep at a distance. He could not keep you at a distance. Still, you had only the light of a single candle, and he must have thought all was well till he saw you enter the wine shop on the Saturday night."

Here Carey intervened in a matter of fact voice, as if to take the talk away from anything that might reflect on me.

"I was greatly puzzled as to why Coquard should occupy the bed at all," he said. "It was to search the room for the will, I suppose, and obtain the freedom of the whole house at night."

"Probably," McNab asserted. "And also to create a suspicion of de Quettville's insanity by odd behaviour. A master stroke that, since even if they failed to unearth the will and destroy it, the same object would be achieved by establishing insanity." He turned to Carey. Since you haven't been rung up by the office yet I suppose there's no news of Brisson?"

"I doubt if we'll have further news of him," Carey said. "If he hoped to get picked up by a French trawler, the storm last night would shatter that hope before he got far."

He rose and stretched himself in a way that somehow suggested content.

"I'm very sorry about my failure to identify Coquard," I said to him. "I *knew* I'd seen him before, but I started trying to connect him with some incidents in my old Paris days and that put me on the wrong scent."

"You needn't blame yourself," he said, shaking hands. "Wait till you see that false beard to-morrow; it was no impromptu affair, I can tell you." He hesitated, and then looking at me said, "I envy you last night. We got him this morning, and settled one last question that would have left us otherwise rather bothered. The woman's finger-prints, you know. They were not those of a woman at all, but Coquard's.

Among his other attributes his hands had the long thin prehensile fingers of the thief."

"Yes," Le Marinel said as he got up. "I, too, envy Dunn his chance last night; but we cannot grudge it him when we remember all the tricks Coquard played on him."

Here, still feeling sore with myself I blundered out something rather ironical and bitter about having been more successful in taking life than in saving it. This brought up McNab.

"Man, you're just havering. Whose life did you want to save?" he cried in mock indignation. "Not de Quettville's; he was dead before ever you saw him. As for Coquard, I've a notion that when ye tossed that slimy devil over the precipice last night ye did more for human welfare than you've yet done with all your pills and poultices."

Le Marinel, his eyes twinkling, held out his hand.

"As to that," he said, "we, on this island, must also be grateful that Dr. Dunn's action saved the States of Guernsey the expense of a gallows."

"True!" McNab eagerly assented. "Both in its economic and its ethical aspects, Dunn's prompt action with Coquard was more than justified."

A CATALOGUE OF
SELECTED DOVER BOOKS
IN ALL FIELDS OF INTEREST

A CATALOGUE OF SELECTED DOVER
BOOKS IN ALL FIELDS OF INTEREST

RACKHAM'S COLOR ILLUSTRATIONS FOR WAGNER'S RING. Rackham's finest mature work—all 64 full-color watercolors in a faithful and lush interpretation of the *Ring*. Full-sized plates on coated stock of the paintings used by opera companies for authentic staging of Wagner. Captions aid in following complete Ring cycle. Introduction. 64 illustrations plus vignettes. 72pp. 8⅝ x 11¼. 23779-6 Pa. $6.00

CONTEMPORARY POLISH POSTERS IN FULL COLOR, edited by Joseph Czestochowski. 46 full-color examples of brilliant school of Polish graphic design, selected from world's first museum (near Warsaw) dedicated to poster art. Posters on circuses, films, plays, concerts all show cosmopolitan influences, free imagination. Introduction. 48pp. 9⅜ x 12¼. 23780-X Pa. $6.00

GRAPHIC WORKS OF EDVARD MUNCH, Edvard Munch. 90 haunting, evocative prints by first major Expressionist artist and one of the greatest graphic artists of his time: *The Scream, Anxiety, Death Chamber, The Kiss, Madonna,* etc. Introduction by Alfred Werner. 90pp. 9 x 12. 23765-6 Pa. $5.00

THE GOLDEN AGE OF THE POSTER, Hayward and Blanche Cirker. 70 extraordinary posters in full colors, from Maitres de l'Affiche, Mucha, Lautrec, Bradley, Cheret, Beardsley, many others. Total of 78pp. 9⅜ x 12¼. 22753-7 Pa. $5.95

THE NOTEBOOKS OF LEONARDO DA VINCI, edited by J. P. Richter. Extracts from manuscripts reveal great genius; on painting, sculpture, anatomy, sciences, geography, etc. Both Italian and English. 186 ms. pages reproduced, plus 500 additional drawings, including studies for *Last Supper,* Sforza monument, etc. 860pp. 7⅞ x 10¾. (Available in U.S. only) 22572-0, 22573-9 Pa., Two-vol. set $15.90

THE CODEX NUTTALL, as first edited by Zelia Nuttall. Only inexpensive edition, in full color, of a pre-Columbian Mexican (Mixtec) book. 88 color plates show kings, gods, heroes, temples, sacrifices. New explanatory, historical introduction by Arthur G. Miller. 96pp. 11⅜ x 8½. (Available in U.S. only) 23168-2 Pa. $7.95

UNE SEMAINE DE BONTÉ, A SURREALISTIC NOVEL IN COLLAGE, Max Ernst. Masterpiece created out of 19th-century periodical illustrations, explores worlds of terror and surprise. Some consider this Ernst's greatest work. 208pp. 8⅛ x 11. 23252-2 Pa. $6.00

UNCLE SILAS, J. Sheridan LeFanu. Victorian Gothic mystery novel, considered by many best of period, even better than Collins or Dickens. Wonderful psychological terror. Introduction by Frederick Shroyer. 436pp. 5⅜ x 8½.
21715-9 Pa. $6.00

JURGEN, James Branch Cabell. The great erotic fantasy of the 1920's that delighted thousands, shocked thousands more. Full final text, Lane edition with 13 plates by Frank Pape. 346pp. 5⅜ x 8½.
23507-6 Pa. $4.50

THE CLAVERINGS, Anthony Trollope. Major novel, chronicling aspects of British Victorian society, personalities. Reprint of Cornhill serialization, 16 plates by M. Edwards; first reprint of full text. Introduction by Norman Donaldson. 412pp. 5⅜ x 8½.
23464-9 Pa. $5.00

KEPT IN THE DARK, Anthony Trollope. Unusual short novel about Victorian morality and abnormal psychology by the great English author. Probably the first American publication. Frontispiece by Sir John Millais. 92pp. 6½ x 9¼.
23609-9 Pa. $2.50

RALPH THE HEIR, Anthony Trollope. Forgotten tale of illegitimacy, inheritance. Master novel of Trollope's later years. Victorian country estates, clubs, Parliament, fox hunting, world of fully realized characters. Reprint of 1871 edition. 12 illustrations by F. A. Faser. 434pp. of text. 5⅜ x 8½.
23642-0 Pa. $5.00

YEKL and THE IMPORTED BRIDEGROOM AND OTHER STORIES OF THE NEW YORK GHETTO, Abraham Cahan. Film *Hester Street* based on *Yekl* (1896). Novel, other stories among first about Jewish immigrants of N.Y.'s East Side. Highly praised by W. D. Howells—Cahan "a new star of realism." New introduction by Bernard G. Richards. 240pp. 5⅜ x 8½.
22427-9 Pa. $3.50

THE HIGH PLACE, James Branch Cabell. Great fantasy writer's enchanting comedy of disenchantment set in 18th-century France. Considered by some critics to be even better than his famous *Jurgen*. 10 illustrations and numerous vignettes by noted fantasy artist Frank C. Pape. 320pp. 5⅜ x 8½.
23670-6 Pa. $4.00

ALICE'S ADVENTURES UNDER GROUND, Lewis Carroll. Facsimile of ms. Carroll gave Alice Liddell in 1864. Different in many ways from final Alice. Handlettered, illustrated by Carroll. Introduction by Martin Gardner. 128pp. 5⅜ x 8½.
21482-6 Pa. $2.50

FAVORITE ANDREW LANG FAIRY TALE BOOKS IN MANY COLORS, Andrew Lang. The four Lang favorites in a boxed set—the complete *Red, Green, Yellow* and *Blue* Fairy Books. 164 stories; 439 illustrations by Lancelot Speed, Henry Ford and G. P. Jacomb Hood. Total of about 1500pp. 5⅜ x 8½.
23407-X Boxed set, Pa. $15.95

THE SENSE OF BEAUTY, George Santayana. Masterfully written discussion of nature of beauty, materials of beauty, form, expression; art, literature, social sciences all involved. 168pp. 5⅜ x 8½. 20238-0 Pa. $3.00

ON THE IMPROVEMENT OF THE UNDERSTANDING, Benedict Spinoza. Also contains Ethics, Correspondence, all in excellent R. Elwes translation. Basic works on entry to philosophy, pantheism, exchange of ideas with great contemporaries. 402pp. 5⅜ x 8½. 20250-X Pa. $4.50

THE TRAGIC SENSE OF LIFE, Miguel de Unamuno. Acknowledged masterpiece of existential literature, one of most important books of 20th century. Introduction by Madariaga. 367pp. 5⅜ x 8½.
20257-7 Pa. $4.50

THE GUIDE FOR THE PERPLEXED, Moses Maimonides. Great classic of medieval Judaism attempts to reconcile revealed religion (Pentateuch, commentaries) with Aristotelian philosophy. Important historically, still relevant in problems. Unabridged Friedlander translation. Total of 473pp. 5⅜ x 8½. 20351-4 Pa. $6.00

THE I CHING (THE BOOK OF CHANGES), translated by James Legge. Complete translation of basic text plus appendices by Confucius, and Chinese commentary of most penetrating divination manual ever prepared. Indispensable to study of early Oriental civilizations, to modern inquiring reader. 448pp. 5⅜ x 8½. 21062-6 Pa. $5.00

THE EGYPTIAN BOOK OF THE DEAD, E. A. Wallis Budge. Complete reproduction of Ani's papyrus, finest ever found. Full hieroglyphic text, interlinear transliteration, word for word translation, smooth translation. Basic work, for Egyptology, for modern study of psychic matters. Total of 533pp. 6½ x 9¼. (Available in U.S. only) 21866-X Pa. $5.95

THE GODS OF THE EGYPTIANS, E. A. Wallis Budge. Never excelled for richness, fullness: all gods, goddesses, demons, mythical figures of Ancient Egypt; their legends, rites, incarnations, variations, powers, etc. Many hieroglyphic texts cited. Over 225 illustrations, plus 6 color plates. Total of 988pp. 6⅛ x 9¼. (Available in U.S. only)
22055-9, 22056-7 Pa., Two-vol. set $16.00

THE STANDARD BOOK OF QUILT MAKING AND COLLECTING, Marguerite Ickis. Full information, full-sized patterns for making 46 traditional quilts, also 150 other patterns. Quilted cloths, lame, satin quilts, etc. 483 illustrations. 273pp. 6⅞ x 9⅝. 20582-7 Pa. $4.95

CORAL GARDENS AND THEIR MAGIC, Bronsilaw Malinowski. Classic study of the methods of tilling the soil and of agricultural rites in the Trobriand Islands of Melanesia. Author is one of the most important figures in the field of modern social anthropology. 143 illustrations. Indexes. Total of 911pp. of text. 5⅝ x 8¼. (Available in U.S. only)
23597-1 Pa. $12.95

THE PHILOSOPHY OF HISTORY, Georg W. Hegel. Great classic of Western thought develops concept that history is not chance but a rational process, the evolution of freedom. 457pp. 5⅜ x 8½. 20112-0 Pa. $4.50

LANGUAGE, TRUTH AND LOGIC, Alfred J. Ayer. Famous, clear introduction to Vienna, Cambridge schools of Logical Positivism. Role of philosophy, elimination of metaphysics, nature of analysis, etc. 160pp. 5⅜ x 8½. (Available in U.S. only) 20010-8 Pa. $2.00

A PREFACE TO LOGIC, Morris R. Cohen. Great City College teacher in renowned, easily followed exposition of formal logic, probability, values, logic and world order and similar topics; no previous background needed. 209pp. 5⅜ x 8½. 23517-3 Pa. $3.50

REASON AND NATURE, Morris R. Cohen. Brilliant analysis of reason and its multitudinous ramifications by charismatic teacher. Interdisciplinary, synthesizing work widely praised when it first appeared in 1931. Second (1953) edition. Indexes. 496pp. 5⅜ x 8½. 23633-1 Pa. $6.50

AN ESSAY CONCERNING HUMAN UNDERSTANDING, John Locke. The only complete edition of enormously important classic, with authoritative editorial material by A. C. Fraser. Total of 1176pp. 5⅜ x 8½. 20530-4, 20531-2 Pa., Two-vol. set $16.00

HANDBOOK OF MATHEMATICAL FUNCTIONS WITH FORMULAS, GRAPHS, AND MATHEMATICAL TABLES, edited by Milton Abramowitz and Irene A. Stegun. Vast compendium: 29 sets of tables, some to as high as 20 places. 1,046pp. 8 x 10½. 61272-4 Pa. $14.95

MATHEMATICS FOR THE PHYSICAL SCIENCES, Herbert S. Wilf. Highly acclaimed work offers clear presentations of vector spaces and matrices, orthogonal functions, roots of polynomial equations, conformal mapping, calculus of variations, etc. Knowledge of theory of functions of real and complex variables is assumed. Exercises and solutions. Index. 284pp. 5⅝ x 8¼. 63635-6 Pa. $5.00

THE PRINCIPLE OF RELATIVITY, Albert Einstein et al. Eleven most important original papers on special and general theories. Seven by Einstein, two by Lorentz, one each by Minkowski and Weyl. All translated, unabridged. 216pp. 5⅜ x 8½. 60081-5 Pa. $3.50

THERMODYNAMICS, Enrico Fermi. A classic of modern science. Clear, organized treatment of systems, first and second laws, entropy, thermodynamic potentials, gaseous reactions, dilute solutions, entropy constant. No math beyond calculus required. Problems. 160pp. 5⅜ x 8½. 60361-X Pa. $3.00

ELEMENTARY MECHANICS OF FLUIDS, Hunter Rouse. Classic undergraduate text widely considered to be far better than many later books. Ranges from fluid velocity and acceleration to role of compressibility in fluid motion. Numerous examples, questions, problems. 224 illustrations. 376pp. 5⅝ x 8¼. 63699-2 Pa. $5.00

HOUSEHOLD STORIES BY THE BROTHERS GRIMM. All the great Grimm stories: "Rumpelstiltskin," "Snow White," "Hansel and Gretel," etc., with 114 illustrations by Walter Crane. 269pp. 5⅜ x 8½.
21080-4 Pa. $3.50

SLEEPING BEAUTY, illustrated by Arthur Rackham. Perhaps the fullest, most delightful version ever, told by C. S. Evans. Rackham's best work. 49 illustrations. 110pp. 7⅞ x 10¾.
22756-1 Pa. $2.50

AMERICAN FAIRY TALES, L. Frank Baum. Young cowboy lassoes Father Time; dummy in Mr. Floman's department store window comes to life; and 10 other fairy tales. 41 illustrations by N. P. Hall, Harry Kennedy, Ike Morgan, and Ralph Gardner. 209pp. 5⅜ x 8½.
23643-9 Pa. $3.00

THE WONDERFUL WIZARD OF OZ, L. Frank Baum. Facsimile in full color of America's finest children's classic. Introduction by Martin Gardner. 143 illustrations by W. W. Denslow. 267pp. 5⅜ x 8½.
20691-2 Pa. $3.50

THE TALE OF PETER RABBIT, Beatrix Potter. The inimitable Peter's terrifying adventure in Mr. McGregor's garden, with all 27 wonderful, full-color Potter illustrations. 55pp. 4¼ x 5½. (Available in U.S. only)
22827-4 Pa. $1.25

THE STORY OF KING ARTHUR AND HIS KNIGHTS, Howard Pyle. Finest children's version of life of King Arthur. 48 illustrations by Pyle. 131pp. 6⅛ x 9¼.
21445-1 Pa. $4.95

CARUSO'S CARICATURES, Enrico Caruso. Great tenor's remarkable caricatures of self, fellow musicians, composers, others. Toscanini, Puccini, Farrar, etc. Impish, cutting, insightful. 473 illustrations. Preface by M. Sisca. 217pp. 8⅜ x 11¼.
23528-9 Pa. $6.95

PERSONAL NARRATIVE OF A PILGRIMAGE TO ALMADINAH AND MECCAH, Richard Burton. Great travel classic by remarkably colorful personality. Burton, disguised as a Moroccan, visited sacred shrines of Islam, narrowly escaping death. Wonderful observations of Islamic life, customs, personalities. 47 illustrations. Total of 959pp. 5⅜ x 8½.
21217-3, 21218-1 Pa., Two-vol. set $12.00

INCIDENTS OF TRAVEL IN YUCATAN, John L. Stephens. Classic (1843) exploration of jungles of Yucatan, looking for evidences of Maya civilization. Travel adventures, Mexican and Indian culture, etc. Total of 669pp. 5⅜ x 8½.
20926-1, 20927-X Pa., Two-vol. set $7.90

AMERICAN LITERARY AUTOGRAPHS FROM WASHINGTON IRVING TO HENRY JAMES, Herbert Cahoon, et al. Letters, poems, manuscripts of Hawthorne, Thoreau, Twain, Alcott, Whitman, 67 other prominent American authors. Reproductions, full transcripts and commentary. Plus checklist of all American Literary Autographs in The Pierpont Morgan Library. Printed on exceptionally high-quality paper. 136 illustrations. 212pp. 9⅛ x 12¼.
23548-3 Pa. $12.50

A MAYA GRAMMAR, Alfred M. Tozzer. Practical, useful English-language grammar by the Harvard anthropologist who was one of the three greatest American scholars in the area of Maya culture. Phonetics, grammatical processes, syntax, more. 301pp. 5⅜ x 8½.   23465-7 Pa. $4.00

THE JOURNAL OF HENRY D. THOREAU, edited by Bradford Torrey, F. H. Allen. Complete reprinting of 14 volumes, 1837-61, over two million words; the sourcebooks for *Walden*, etc. Definitive. All original sketches, plus 75 photographs. Introduction by Walter Harding. Total of 1804pp. 8½ x 12¼.   20312-3, 20313-1 Clothbd., Two-vol. set $70.00

CLASSIC GHOST STORIES, Charles Dickens and others. 18 wonderful stories you've wanted to reread: "The Monkey's Paw," "The House and the Brain," "The Upper Berth," "The Signalman," "Dracula's Guest," "The Tapestried Chamber," etc. Dickens, Scott, Mary Shelley, Stoker, etc. 330pp. 5⅜ x 8½.   20735-8 Pa. $4.50

SEVEN SCIENCE FICTION NOVELS, H. G. Wells. Full novels. *First Men in the Moon, Island of Dr. Moreau, War of the Worlds, Food of the Gods, Invisible Man, Time Machine, In the Days of the Comet*. A basic science-fiction library. 1015pp. 5⅜ x 8½. (Available in U.S. only)   20264-X Clothbd. $8.95

ARMADALE, Wilkie Collins. Third great mystery novel by the author of *The Woman in White* and *The Moonstone*. Ingeniously plotted narrative shows an exceptional command of character, incident and mood. Original magazine version with 40 illustrations. 597pp. 5⅜ x 8½.   23429-0 Pa. $6.00

MASTERS OF MYSTERY, H. Douglas Thomson. The first book in English (1931) devoted to history and aesthetics of detective story. Poe, Doyle, LeFanu, Dickens, many others, up to 1930. New introduction and notes by E. F. Bleiler. 288pp. 5⅜ x 8½. (Available in U.S. only)   23606-4 Pa. $4.00

FLATLAND, E. A. Abbott. Science-fiction classic explores life of 2-D being in 3-D world. Read also as introduction to thought about hyperspace. Introduction by Banesh Hoffmann. 16 illustrations. 103pp. 5⅜ x 8½.   20001-9 Pa. $2.00

THREE SUPERNATURAL NOVELS OF THE VICTORIAN PERIOD, edited, with an introduction, by E. F. Bleiler. Reprinted complete and unabridged, three great classics of the supernatural: *The Haunted Hotel* by Wilkie Collins, *The Haunted House at Latchford* by Mrs. J. H. Riddell, and *The Lost Stradivarius* by J. Meade Falkner. 325pp. 5⅜ x 8½.   22571-2 Pa. $4.00

AYESHA: THE RETURN OF "SHE," H. Rider Haggard. Virtuoso sequel featuring the great mythic creation, Ayesha, in an adventure that is fully as good as the first book, *She*. Original magazine version, with 47 original illustrations by Maurice Greiffenhagen. 189pp. 6½ x 9¼.   23649-8 Pa. $3.50

THE DEPRESSION YEARS AS PHOTOGRAPHED BY ARTHUR ROTH-STEIN, Arthur Rothstein. First collection devoted entirely to the work of outstanding 1930s photographer: famous dust storm photo, ragged children, unemployed, etc. 120 photographs. Captions. 119pp. 9¼ x 10¾.
23590-4 Pa. $5.00

CAMERA WORK: A PICTORIAL GUIDE, Alfred Stieglitz. All 559 illustrations and plates from the most important periodical in the history of art photography, *Camera Work* (1903-17). Presented four to a page, reduced in size but still clear, in strict chronological order, with complete captions. Three indexes. Glossary. Bibliography. 176pp. 8⅜ x 11¼.
23591-2 Pa. $6.95

ALVIN LANGDON COBURN, PHOTOGRAPHER, Alvin L. Coburn. Revealing autobiography by one of greatest photographers of 20th century gives insider's version of Photo-Secession, plus comments on his own work. 77 photographs by Coburn. Edited by Helmut and Alison Gernsheim. 160pp. 8⅛ x 11.
23685-4 Pa. $6.00

NEW YORK IN THE FORTIES, Andreas Feininger. 162 brilliant photographs by the well-known photographer, formerly with *Life* magazine, show commuters, shoppers, Times Square at night, Harlem nightclub, Lower East Side, etc. Introduction and full captions by John von Hartz. 181pp. 9¼ x 10¾.
23585-8 Pa. $6.95

GREAT NEWS PHOTOS AND THE STORIES BEHIND THEM, John Faber. Dramatic volume of 140 great news photos, 1855 through 1976, and revealing stories behind them, with both historical and technical information. Hindenburg disaster, shooting of Oswald, nomination of Jimmy Carter, etc. 160pp. 8¼ x 11.
23667-6 Pa. $5.00

THE ART OF THE CINEMATOGRAPHER, Leonard Maltin. Survey of American cinematography history and anecdotal interviews with 5 masters—Arthur Miller, Hal Mohr, Hal Rosson, Lucien Ballard, and Conrad Hall. Very large selection of behind-the-scenes production photos. 105 photographs. Filmographies. Index. Originally *Behind the Camera.* 144pp. 8¼ x 11.
23686-2 Pa. $5.00

DESIGNS FOR THE THREE-CORNERED HAT (LE TRICORNE), Pablo Picasso. 32 fabulously rare drawings—including 31 color illustrations of costumes and accessories—for 1919 production of famous ballet. Edited by Parmenia Migel, who has written new introduction. 48pp. 9⅜ x 12¼. (Available in U.S. only)
23709-5 Pa. $5.00

NOTES OF A FILM DIRECTOR, Sergei Eisenstein. Greatest Russian filmmaker explains montage, making of *Alexander Nevsky,* aesthetics; comments on self, associates, great rivals (Chaplin), similar material. 78 illustrations. 240pp. 5⅜ x 8½.
22392-2 Pa. $4.50

HOLLYWOOD GLAMOUR PORTRAITS, edited by John Kobal. 145 photos capture the stars from 1926-49, the high point in portrait photography. Gable, Harlow, Bogart, Bacall, Hedy Lamarr, Marlene Dietrich, Robert Montgomery, Marlon Brando, Veronica Lake; 94 stars in all. Full background on photographers, technical aspects, much more. Total of 160pp. 8⅜ x 11¼. 23352-9 Pa. $6.00

THE NEW YORK STAGE: FAMOUS PRODUCTIONS IN PHOTO-GRAPHS, edited by Stanley Appelbaum. 148 photographs from Museum of City of New York show 142 plays, 1883-1939. *Peter Pan, The Front Page, Dead End, Our Town,* O'Neill, hundreds of actors and actresses, etc. Full indexes. 154pp. 9½ x 10. 23241-7 Pa. $6.00

DIALOGUES CONCERNING TWO NEW SCIENCES, Galileo Galilei. Encompassing 30 years of experiment and thought, these dialogues deal with geometric demonstrations of fracture of solid bodies, cohesion, leverage, speed of light and sound, pendulums, falling bodies, accelerated motion, etc. 300pp. 5⅜ x 8½. 60099-8 Pa. $4.00

THE GREAT OPERA STARS IN HISTORIC PHOTOGRAPHS, edited by James Camner. 343 portraits from the 1850s to the 1940s: Tamburini, Mario, Caliapin, Jeritza, Melchior, Melba, Patti, Pinza, Schipa, Caruso, Farrar, Steber, Gobbi, and many more—270 performers in all. Index. 199pp. 8⅜ x 11¼. 23575-0 Pa. $7.50

J. S. BACH, Albert Schweitzer. Great full-length study of Bach, life, background to music, music, by foremost modern scholar. Ernest Newman translation. 650 musical examples. Total of 928pp. 5⅜ x 8½. (Available in U.S. only) 21631-4, 21632-2 Pa., Two-vol. set $11.00

COMPLETE PIANO SONATAS, Ludwig van Beethoven. All sonatas in the fine Schenker edition, with fingering, analytical material. One of best modern editions. Total of 615pp. 9 x 12. (Available in U.S. only) 23134-8, 23135-6 Pa., Two-vol. set $15.50

KEYBOARD MUSIC, J. S. Bach. Bach-Gesellschaft edition. For harpsichord, piano, other keyboard instruments. English Suites, French Suites, Six Partitas, Goldberg Variations, Two-Part Inventions, Three-Part Sinfonias. 312pp. 8⅛ x 11. (Available in U.S. only) 22360-4 Pa. $6.95

FOUR SYMPHONIES IN FULL SCORE, Franz Schubert. Schubert's four most popular symphonies: No. 4 in C Minor ("Tragic"); No. 5 in B-flat Major; No. 8 in B Minor ("Unfinished"); No. 9 in C Major ("Great"). Breitkopf & Hartel edition. Study score. 261pp. 9⅜ x 12¼. 23681-1 Pa. $6.50

THE AUTHENTIC GILBERT & SULLIVAN SONGBOOK, W. S. Gilbert, A. S. Sullivan. Largest selection available; 92 songs, uncut, original keys, in piano rendering approved by Sullivan. Favorites and lesser-known fine numbers. Edited with plot synopses by James Spero. 3 illustrations. 399pp. 9 x 12. 23482-7 Pa. $9.95

THE COMPLETE WOODCUTS OF ALBRECHT DURER, edited by Dr. W. Kurth. 346 in all: "Old Testament," "St. Jerome," "Passion," "Life of Virgin," Apocalypse," many others. Introduction by Campbell Dodgson. 285pp. 8½ x 12¼.   21097-9 Pa. $7.50

DRAWINGS OF ALBRECHT DURER, edited by Heinrich Wolfflin. 81 plates show development from youth to full style. Many favorites; many new. Introduction by Alfred Werner. 96pp. 8⅛ x 11.   22352-3 Pa. $5.00

THE HUMAN FIGURE, Albrecht Dürer. Experiments in various techniques—stereometric, progressive proportional, and others. Also life studies that rank among finest ever done. Complete reprinting of *Dresden Sketchbook*. 170 plates. 355pp. 8⅜ x 11¼.   21042-1 Pa. $7.95

OF THE JUST SHAPING OF LETTERS, Albrecht Dürer. Renaissance artist explains design of Roman majuscules by geometry, also Gothic lower and capitals. Grolier Club edition. 43pp. 7⅞ x 10¾   21306-4 Pa. $3.00

TEN BOOKS ON ARCHITECTURE, Vitruvius. The most important book ever written on architecture. Early Roman aesthetics, technology, classical orders, site selection, all other aspects. Stands behind everything since. Morgan translation. 331pp. 5⅜ x 8½.   20645-9 Pa. $4.50

THE FOUR BOOKS OF ARCHITECTURE, Andrea Palladio. 16th-century classic responsible for Palladian movement and style. Covers classical architectural remains, Renaissance revivals, classical orders, etc. 1738 Ware English edition. Introduction by A. Placzek. 216 plates. 110pp. of text. 9½ x 12¾.   21308-0 Pa. $10.00

HORIZONS, Norman Bel Geddes. Great industrialist stage designer, "father of streamlining," on application of aesthetics to transportation, amusement, architecture, etc. 1932 prophetic account; function, theory, specific projects. 222 illustrations. 312pp. 7⅞ x 10¾.   23514-9 Pa. $6.95

FRANK LLOYD WRIGHT'S FALLINGWATER, Donald Hoffmann. Full, illustrated story of conception and building of Wright's masterwork at Bear Run, Pa. 100 photographs of site, construction, and details of completed structure. 112pp. 9¼ x 10.   23671-4 Pa. $5.50

THE ELEMENTS OF DRAWING, John Ruskin. Timeless classic by great Viltorian; starts with basic ideas, works through more difficult. Many practical exercises. 48 illustrations. Introduction by Lawrence Campbell. 228pp. 5⅜ x 8½.   22730-8 Pa. $3.75

GIST OF ART, John Sloan. Greatest modern American teacher, Art Students League, offers innumerable hints, instructions, guided comments to help you in painting. Not a formal course. 46 illustrations. Introduction by Helen Sloan. 200pp. 5⅜ x 8½.   23435-5 Pa. $4.00

THE AMERICAN SENATOR, Anthony Trollope. Little known, long unavailable Trollope novel on a grand scale. Here are humorous comment on American vs. English culture, and stunning portrayal of a heroine/villainess. Superb evocation of Victorian village life. 561pp. 5⅜ x 8½.
23801-6 Pa. $6.00

WAS IT MURDER? James Hilton. The author of *Lost Horizon* and *Goodbye, Mr. Chips* wrote one detective novel (under a pen-name) which was quickly forgotten and virtually lost, even at the height of Hilton's fame. This edition brings it back—a finely crafted public school puzzle resplendent with Hilton's stylish atmosphere. A thoroughly English thriller by the creator of Shangri-la. 252pp. 5⅜ x 8. (Available in U.S. only)
23774-5 Pa. $3.00

CENTRAL PARK: A PHOTOGRAPHIC GUIDE, Victor Laredo and Henry Hope Reed. 121 superb photographs show dramatic views of Central Park: Bethesda Fountain, Cleopatra's Needle, Sheep Meadow, the Blockhouse, plus people engaged in many park activities: ice skating, bike riding, etc. Captions by former Curator of Central Park, Henry Hope Reed, provide historical view, changes, etc. Also photos of N.Y. landmarks on park's periphery. 96pp. 8½ x 11.
23750-8 Pa. $4.50

NANTUCKET IN THE NINETEENTH CENTURY, Clay Lancaster. 180 rare photographs, stereographs, maps, drawings and floor plans recreate unique American island society. Authentic scenes of shipwreck, lighthouses, streets, homes are arranged in geographic sequence to provide walking-tour guide to old Nantucket existing today. Introduction, captions. 160pp. 8⅞ x 11¾.
23747-8 Pa. $6.95

STONE AND MAN: A PHOTOGRAPHIC EXPLORATION, Andreas Feininger. 106 photographs by *Life* photographer Feininger portray man's deep passion for stone through the ages. Stonehenge-like megaliths, fortified towns, sculpted marble and crumbling tenements show textures, beauties, fascination. 128pp. 9¼ x 10¾.
23756-7 Pa. $5.95

CIRCLES, A MATHEMATICAL VIEW, D. Pedoe. Fundamental aspects of college geometry, non-Euclidean geometry, and other branches of mathematics: representing circle by point. Poincare model, isoperimetric property, etc. Stimulating recreational reading. 66 figures. 96pp. 5⅝ x 8¼.
63698-4 Pa. $2.75

THE DISCOVERY OF NEPTUNE, Morton Grosser. Dramatic scientific history of the investigations leading up to the actual discovery of the eighth planet of our solar system. Lucid, well-researched book by well-known historian of science. 172pp. 5⅜ x 8½.
23726-5 Pa. $3.50

THE DEVIL'S DICTIONARY. Ambrose Bierce. Barbed, bitter, brilliant witticisms in the form of a dictionary. Best, most ferocious satire America has produced. 145pp. 5⅜ x 8½.
20487-1 Pa. $2.25

"OSCAR" OF THE WALDORF'S COOKBOOK, Oscar Tschirky. Famous American chef reveals 3455 recipes that made Waldorf great; cream of French, German, American cooking, in all categories. Full instructions, easy home use. 1896 edition. 907pp. 6⅝ x 9⅜.   20790-0 Clothbd. $15.00

COOKING WITH BEER, Carole Fahy. Beer has as superb an effect on food as wine, and at fraction of cost. Over 250 recipes for appetizers, soups, main dishes, desserts, breads, etc. Index. 144pp. 5⅜ x 8½. (Available in U.S. only)   23661-7 Pa. $2.50

STEWS AND RAGOUTS, Kay Shaw Nelson. This international cookbook offers wide range of 108 recipes perfect for everyday, special occasions, meals-in-themselves, main dishes. Economical, nutritious, easy-to-prepare: goulash, Irish stew, boeuf bourguignon, etc. Index. 134pp. 5⅜ x 8½.
23662-5 Pa. $2.50

DELICIOUS MAIN COURSE DISHES, Marian Tracy. Main courses are the most important part of any meal. These 200 nutritious, economical recipes from around the world make every meal a delight. "I . . . have found it so useful in my own household,"—*N.Y. Times.* Index. 219pp. 5⅜ x 8½.   23664-1 Pa. $3.00

FIVE ACRES AND INDEPENDENCE, Maurice G. Kains. Great back-to-the-land classic explains basics of self-sufficient farming: economics, plants, crops, animals, orchards, soils, land selection, host of other necessary things. Do not confuse with skimpy faddist literature; Kains was one of America's greatest agriculturalists. 95 illustrations. 397pp. 5⅜ x 8½.
20974-1 Pa.$3.95

A PRACTICAL GUIDE FOR THE BEGINNING FARMER, Herbert Jacobs. Basic, extremely useful first book for anyone thinking about moving to the country and starting a farm. Simpler than Kains, with greater emphasis on country living in general. 246pp. 5⅜ x 8½.
23675-7 Pa. $3.50

PAPERMAKING, Dard Hunter. Definitive book on the subject by the foremost authority in the field. Chapters dealing with every aspect of history of craft in every part of the world. Over 320 illustrations. 2nd, revised and enlarged (1947) edition. 672pp. 5⅜ x 8½.   23619-6 Pa. $7.95

THE ART DECO STYLE, edited by Theodore Menten. Furniture, jewelry, metalwork, ceramics, fabrics, lighting fixtures, interior decors, exteriors, graphics from pure French sources. Best sampling around. Over 400 photographs. 183pp. 8⅜ x 11¼.   22824-X Pa. $6.00

ACKERMANN'S COSTUME PLATES, Rudolph Ackermann. Selection of 96 plates from the *Repository of Arts,* best published source of costume for English fashion during the early 19th century. 12 plates also in color. Captions, glossary and introduction by editor Stella Blum. Total of 120pp. 8⅜ x 11¼.   23690-0 Pa. $4.50

SECOND PIATIGORSKY CUP, edited by Isaac Kashdan. One of the greatest tournament books ever produced in the English language. All 90 games of the 1966 tournament, annotated by players, most annotated by both players. Features Petrosian, Spassky, Fischer, Larsen, six others. 228pp. 5⅜ x 8½.   23572-6 Pa. $3.50

ENCYCLOPEDIA OF CARD TRICKS, revised and edited by Jean Hugard. How to perform over 600 card tricks, devised by the world's greatest magicians: impromptus, spelling tricks, key cards, using special packs, much, much more. Additional chapter on card technique. 66 illustrations. 402pp. 5⅜ x 8½. (Available in U.S. only)   21252-1 Pa. $4.95

MAGIC: STAGE ILLUSIONS, SPECIAL EFFECTS AND TRICK PHOTOGRAPHY, Albert A. Hopkins, Henry R. Evans. One of the great classics; fullest, most authorative explanation of vanishing lady, levitations, scores of other great stage effects. Also small magic, automata, stunts. 446 illustrations. 556pp. 5⅜ x 8½.   23344-8 Pa. $6.95

THE SECRETS OF HOUDINI, J. C. Cannell. Classic study of Houdini's incredible magic, exposing closely-kept professional secrets and revealing, in general terms, the whole art of stage magic. 67 illustrations. 279pp. 5⅜ x 8½.   22913-0 Pa. $4.00

HOFFMANN'S MODERN MAGIC, Professor Hoffmann. One of the best, and best-known, magicians' manuals of the past century. Hundreds of tricks from card tricks and simple sleight of hand to elaborate illusions involving construction of complicated machinery. 332 illustrations. 563pp. 5⅜ x 8½.   23623-4 Pa. $6.00

MADAME PRUNIER'S FISH COOKERY BOOK, Mme. S. B. Prunier. More than 1000 recipes from world famous Prunier's of Paris and London, specially adapted here for American kitchen. Grilled tournedos with anchovy butter, Lobster a la Bordelaise, Prunier's prized desserts, more. Glossary. 340pp. 5⅜ x 8½. (Available in U.S. only)   22679-4 Pa. $3.00

FRENCH COUNTRY COOKING FOR AMERICANS, Louis Diat. 500 easy-to-make, authentic provincial recipes compiled by former head chef at New York's Fitz-Carlton Hotel: onion soup, lamb stew, potato pie, more. 309pp. 5⅜ x 8½.   23665-X Pa. $3.95

SAUCES, FRENCH AND FAMOUS, Louis Diat. Complete book gives over 200 specific recipes: bechamel, Bordelaise, hollandaise, Cumberland, apricot, etc. Author was one of this century's finest chefs, originator of vichyssoise and many other dishes. Index. 156pp. 5⅜ x 8.   23663-3 Pa. $2.75

TOLL HOUSE TRIED AND TRUE RECIPES, Ruth Graves Wakefield. Authentic recipes from the famous Mass. restaurant: popovers, veal and ham loaf, Toll House baked beans, chocolate cake crumb pudding, much more. Many helpful hints. Nearly 700 recipes. Index. 376pp. 5⅜ x 8½.   23560-2 Pa. $4.50

YUCATAN BEFORE AND AFTER THE CONQUEST, Diego de Landa. First English translation of basic book in Maya studies, the only significant account of Yucatan written in the early post-Conquest era. Translated by distinguished Maya scholar William Gates. Appendices, introduction, 4 maps and over 120 illustrations added by translator. 162pp. 5⅜ x 8½.
23622-6 Pa. $3.00

THE MALAY ARCHIPELAGO, Alfred R. Wallace. Spirited travel account by one of founders of modern biology. Touches on zoology, botany, ethnography, geography, and geology. 62 illustrations, maps. 515pp. 5⅜ x 8½.
20187-2 Pa. $6.95

THE DISCOVERY OF THE TOMB OF TUTANKHAMEN, Howard Carter, A. C. Mace. Accompany Carter in the thrill of discovery, as ruined passage suddenly reveals unique, untouched, fabulously rich tomb. Fascinating account, with 106 illustrations. New introduction by J. M. White. Total of 382pp. 5⅜ x 8½. (Available in U.S. only)   23500-9 Pa. $4.00

THE WORLD'S GREATEST SPEECHES, edited by Lewis Copeland and Lawrence W. Lamm. Vast collection of 278 speeches from Greeks up to present. Powerful and effective models; unique look at history. Revised to 1970. Indices. 842pp. 5⅜ x 8½.   20468-5 Pa. $8.95

THE 100 GREATEST ADVERTISEMENTS, Julian Watkins. The priceless ingredient; His master's voice; 99 44/100% pure; over 100 others. How they were written, their impact, etc. Remarkable record. 130 illustrations. 233pp. 7⅞ x 10 3/5.   20540-1 Pa. $5.95

CRUICKSHANK PRINTS FOR HAND COLORING, George Cruickshank. 18 illustrations, one side of a page, on fine-quality paper suitable for watercolors. Caricatures of people in society (c. 1820) full of trenchant wit. Very large format. 32pp. 11 x 16.   23684-6 Pa. $5.00

THIRTY-TWO COLOR POSTCARDS OF TWENTIETH-CENTURY AMERICAN ART, Whitney Museum of American Art. Reproduced in full color in postcard form are 31 art works and one shot of the museum. Calder, Hopper, Rauschenberg, others. Detachable. 16pp. 8¼ x 11.
23629-3 Pa. $3.00

MUSIC OF THE SPHERES: THE MATERIAL UNIVERSE FROM ATOM TO QUASAR SIMPLY EXPLAINED, Guy Murchie. Planets, stars, geology, atoms, radiation, relativity, quantum theory, light, antimatter, similar topics. 319 figures. 664pp. 5⅜ x 8½.
21809-0, 21810-4 Pa., Two-vol. set $11.00

EINSTEIN'S THEORY OF RELATIVITY, Max Born. Finest semi-technical account; covers Einstein, Lorentz, Minkowski, and others, with much detail, much explanation of ideas and math not readily available elsewhere on this level. For student, non-specialist. 376pp. 5⅜ x 8½.
60769-0 Pa. $4.50

AMERICAN ANTIQUE FURNITURE, Edgar G. Miller, Jr. The basic coverage of all American furniture before 1840: chapters per item chronologically cover all types of furniture, with more than 2100 photos. Total of 1106pp. 7⅞ x 10¾.   21599-7, 21600-4 Pa., Two-vol. set $17.90

ILLUSTRATED GUIDE TO SHAKER FURNITURE, Robert Meader. Director, Shaker Museum, Old Chatham, presents up-to-date coverage of all furniture and appurtenances, with much on local styles not available elsewhere. 235 photos. 146pp. 9 x 12.   22819-3 Pa. $6.00

ORIENTAL RUGS, ANTIQUE AND MODERN, Walter A. Hawley. Persia, Turkey, Caucasus, Central Asia, China, other traditions. Best general survey of all aspects: styles and periods, manufacture, uses, symbols and their interpretation, and identification. 96 illustrations, 11 in color. 320pp. 6⅛ x 9¼.   22366-3 Pa. $6.95

CHINESE POTTERY AND PORCELAIN, R. L. Hobson. Detailed descriptions and analyses by former Keeper of the Department of Oriental Antiquities and Ethnography at the British Museum. Covers hundreds of pieces from primitive times to 1915. Still the standard text for most periods. 136 plates, 40 in full color. Total of 750pp. 5⅜ x 8½.

23253-0 Pa. $10.00

THE WARES OF THE MING DYNASTY, R. L. Hobson. Foremost scholar examines and illustrates many varieties of Ming (1368-1644). Famous blue and white, polychrome, lesser-known styles and shapes. 117 illustrations, 9 full color, of outstanding pieces. Total of 263pp. 6⅛ x 9¼. (Available in U.S. only)   23652-8 Pa. $6.00